BATTLE HAREM

BOOK ONE

ISAAC HOOKE

BOOKS BY ISAAC HOOKE

Military Science Fiction

Battle Harem

Battle Harem 1

Battle Harem 2

Battle Harem 3

AI Reborn Trilogy

Refurbished

Reloaded

Rebooted

ATLAS Trilogy
(published by 47North)

ATLAS

ATLAS 2

ATLAS 3

Alien War Trilogy

and more nukes were dropped. Needless to say, the aftereffects weren't all that great on the environment.

While humanity had used their tech to clear the clouds of nuclear winter, the entire eastern hemisphere remained uninhabitable to this day. Rumors said there were still bioweapons living out there in the uninhabited zones, *mutated* bioweapons, but no one ever went there except the military anyways.

No one cared to.

Though Jason probably would be, shortly. At least, a version of him might be.

He stared at the sign above the door.

AI Worx - Put Your Mind To Work.

With a sigh, he entered.

An android was seated behind the reception desk. She was nearly identical to a human being, except for the eyes. They always had that odd, glassy quality to them. She also showed up as an android on the digital HUD that was projected over his vision, courtesy of his augmented reality glasses—part of the ID feature that ran whenever he focused on anyone. Of course, she was also way too beautiful to be human, but then again, given the advances in plastic surgery and rejuvenetics, anyone could make themselves appear as young and beautiful as they wanted—if they had the creds.

"Hello, welcome to AI Worx, how can I help you today?" the android said.

"I'm here to sell a copy of my mind," Jason said.

She smiled widely. "I see. Have a seat, someone will be with you shortly."

He'd only just sat down when another android

BOOKS BY ISAAC HOOKE

Military Science Fiction

Battle Harem

Battle Harem 1

Battle Harem 2

Battle Harem 3

AI Reborn Trilogy

Refurbished

Reloaded

Rebooted

ATLAS Trilogy
(published by 47North)

ATLAS

ATLAS 2

ATLAS 3

Alien War Trilogy

Hoplite

Zeus

Titan

Argonauts

Bug Hunt

You Are Prey

Alien Empress

Quantum Predation

Robot Dust Bunnies

City of Phants

Rade's Fury

Mechs vs. Dinosaurs

A Captain's Crucible

Flagship

Test of Mettle

Cradle of War

Planet Killer

Worlds at War

Space Opera

A Cold Day in Mosul

Terminal Phase

J ason was a little short on creds. Everyone was, given that half the world had been burned away by a gamma ray burst from a faraway star, part of an attack by an invading alien race known as the Banthar. The people of Earth had repelled those aliens fifty years ago with the help of a few brave individuals known as Mind Refurbs—essentially human minds uploaded into the bodies of state of the art war machines.

Jason was one of the lucky ones who happened to live in the western hemisphere. Africa, Europe, the Middle East, Russia, the Far East, Australia… all lost. Those continents were covered in pockets of radiation from the nuclear bombs humanity had detonated in an attempted to eradicate the aliens and their creations. See, after the Banthar mothership was destroyed, pockets of bioweapons remained roaming the surface below. Hunter killer teams were sent to destroy them, and more nukes were dropped. Needless to say, the aftereffects weren't all that great on the environment.

While humanity had used their tech to clear the clouds of nuclear winter, the entire eastern hemisphere remained uninhabitable to this day. Rumors said there were still bioweapons living out there in the uninhabited zones, *mutated* bioweapons, but no one ever went there except the military anyways.

No one cared to.

Though Jason probably would be, shortly. At least, a version of him might be.

He stared at the sign above the door.

AI Worx - Put Your Mind To Work.

With a sigh, he entered.

An android was seated behind the reception desk. She was nearly identical to a human being, except for the eyes. They always had that odd, glassy quality to them. She also showed up as an android on the digital HUD that was projected over his vision, courtesy of his augmented reality glasses—part of the ID feature that ran whenever he focused on anyone. Of course, she was also way too beautiful to be human, but then again, given the advances in plastic surgery and rejuvenetics, anyone could make themselves appear as young and beautiful as they wanted—if they had the creds.

"Hello, welcome to AI Worx, how can I help you today?" the android said.

"I'm here to sell a copy of my mind," Jason said.

She smiled widely. "I see. Have a seat, someone will be with you shortly."

He'd only just sat down when another android

entered from a back hallway. She was just as easy on the eyes as the last one.

"Hello, Jason," the woman smiled brightly, and held out a hand.

He shook it.

"I'm Nancy," she continued. "I'm here to guide you through the scanning process. This way, please."

Jason got up and followed her into the back room. The pristine white walls had a clinical feel to them.

"I feel like I'm visiting the dentist or something," he commented.

Nancy smiled. "Yes, a lot of our customers tell us that. Did you know we also offer in-home scanning? If you ever desire a change in contract terms, or want a new scan done for any reason, we can come directly to your home."

"Oh, I didn't know that," Jason said. Actually he did, but he didn't want beautiful androids coming to his apartment. His neighbors would think he had ordered a call girl or something.

Nancy led him inside a small room that had a large, swivel-mounted optical instrument similar to the kind one might find in an optometrist's office.

"Okay, I take it back, now it feels like I'm visiting the eye doctor."

"We get that a lot, too," Nancy said. She pointed at the chair in front of the optical instrument. "Have a seat."

Jason sat down.

"So before we take the scan, I'd like you to review the digital document I'm sending," Nancy told him.

Jason nodded. He received a document request on his HUD, and accepted. His viewer launched immediately, taking up the center of his vision.

"Basically, the document says that you waive all rights to the Mind Refurb we are going to create," Nancy said. "Including all ownership, and right of termination. Once you sign the document, and accept the credits, the scan is ours in perpetuity. Do you understand?"

"Yeah," Jason said. He was trying to read the document, but it was full of legalese, and he found himself looking up every second word on the cloud, via his augmented reality glasses. He ended up skimming it.

"I see you've reached the end," Nancy said. There must have been a hidden pixel in the bottom of the document, one that linked out to somewhere on the cloud, notifying her. "Now comes the licensing phase. You can choose to license up to one hundred active copies of your mind, with the pay scale rising commensurately for each level. If—"

"I'm only licensing one copy," Jason said. He wasn't comfortable having more than one version of himself out there, at least at the moment. If his financial situation further tanked, he'd think about it. Right now, one licensed copy would give him all the money he needed for the next little while.

"You'll receive one hundred thousand micro credits for licensing only one active copy," Nancy said.

"That's fine," Jason said. He noticed how she had used the *micro* credit delimiter, to make it sound like he was getting a lot. In reality, he was getting a hundred *credits*.

Nancy nodded. "One it is. But keep in mind, even though you are licensing only one *active* copy of your mind, you are also allowing us to make a single backup copy, which we will keep if we ever have the need to restore your active copy for whatever reason. We have the right to create unlimited backups: every time a new backup copy is made, any previous backups will be destroyed, as per the terms of the contract."

"Sounds good," Jason said. He paused. "I don't suppose you're going to tell me what my Mind Refurb is going to be doing?"

"Unfortunately, there is no way to tell," Nancy said. "As you know, Mind Refurbs are integrated throughout the fabric of society. Some run corporations. Others, buses. Some Mind Refurbs we never use at all, and simply keep locked away in the archives. It varies you see, depending on the suitability of the mind to the task. There are many factors involved. I can see what your various aptitudes are after a quick scan, but there's no guarantee you'll be assigned to any of them. There's also the privacy issue."

Jason nodded. "You're not a Mind Refurb, are you?" Refurbs could be installed into specially modified androids, like Nancy—in fact, that's what most wealthy people did when they died these days. They could even transfer their entire wealth to the android, ensuring a comfortable inheritance. Given that, it was doubtful any Mind Refurb would end up working in a place like this. Still, he had to ask.

Nancy actually laughed at that. "No. I'm an ordinary AI core. I was never human. Nor would I want to be."

Jason pursed his lips. "Why not?"

She smiled patiently. "Memories of my previous human frailty, of aging, of the general struggle of the human condition? I could do without all that."

"Fair enough," Jason said. "Then what about the military? Will I be put into a war machine?"

Nancy shrugged subtly. "If your mind proves compatible with the different operational programs run by the military, then yes, it's possible your Mind Refurb will end up in the body of an advanced military machine."

"I'll be going to the uninhabited zones, won't I?" Jason pressed.

"I must reiterate: it isn't you," Nancy said. "But a copy of you."

"But it's a copy that will have my complete memories, and personality," Jason said. "It will think it's me."

"That is true," Nancy admitted.

"So will my copy be going to the uninhabited zones?" Jason said. "Drafted by the military to explore the radioactive wastelands for alien bioweapons?"

"As I told you, I have no way of knowing that," Nancy said. "But there is a chance, yes. So if you're worried about that, I'd suggest you don't sign the contract."

"No," Jason said. "I'll sign. I was just curious as to what mischief my other self would get up to." He glanced at the digital signature area. He checked off that he was allowing only one active copy of his mind to exist at any given time, and then he signed it.

"Very good," Nancy said.

He dismissed the document as Nancy swiveled the optical instrument in front of his face. It looked like a phoropter, like the kind optometrists used to test sight. A thick half mask made of steel, it had adjustable lenses drilled through the metal where his eyes were located.

Nancy pressed the device forward until the arch between the two lenses was sitting on the bridge of his nose.

"There will be a few bright flashes," Nancy said. "Do your best not to blink."

The flashes came; Jason blinked involuntarily of course, but he tried to keep his eyes open between flashes. Soon his vision was marred with afterimages.

"There, it's done," Nancy said. Her eyes defocused as she checked the data on her own augmented reality display, one that was built into her brain. "Everything seems good. I'll go ahead and deposit the one hundred thousand micro credits into your account."

He slid his augmented reality glasses back on. He noticed a notification flashing in the lower right of his HUD. He enlarged it.

You've got money!

He tried to access his bank account: the biometric features of his augmented reality glasses scanned his eyeballs to confirm he was the account owner. A moment later he was looking at his bank transactions. There, at the top: one hundred credits.

"I got it," Jason said.

"Of course," Nancy said. "That's it. I'll escort you to the door."

"Okay," Jason said.

He followed Nancy out of the room, through the hall, and to the lobby.

"Thank you for choosing AI Worx," Nancy told him. "You've put your mind in good hands."

"Yeah," Jason said. "Sure."

He stepped through the front door, feeling for all the world like he'd just sold his soul.

J ason blinked.

He stared at a sky painted a sickly yellow.

He sat up. Around him, a barren yellow landscape filled the view from horizon to horizon. The surface was rocky, with no sign of any green. There were a few rock buttresses scattered at different points along that terrain, but otherwise, no real landmarks. There were no skyscrapers. No skylanes separating delivery drones from passenger vehicles. No paved streets. No pedestrians.

No civilization.

He lifted a hand toward his face, and was greeted with a forearm made of rivets and metal. His wrist and finger joints were servomotors, while metallic shafts formed the actual hand and digits.

Have I fallen asleep in virtual reality again?

He reached toward his face to rip off the AI glasses, and was relieved when he felt the familiar frame-like shape of the glasses. But when he tugged, the pair didn't come off. He explored more with his fingers, and realized the frame was thicker than the usual pair of AI glasses, more like a visor.

And it was attached firmly to his head.

The hell?

Well, he had a HUD—he could see different status indicators on the right and left of his display. So he must be wearing his augmented reality glasses.

That was the only explanation.

Unless…

He looked down, and was greeted by a pair of metallic legs. They were thick, barrel-like. Like his hands, they were formed of a series of servomotors and shafts. His waist was little different.

It can't be.

Jason focused on those different HUD status indicators more intently. He realized he'd never seen anything like them before.

On the left there was a Team Status column, currently empty, and a Damage Readout display.

He focused on the Damage Readout, and a representation of his body filled the center of his vision. It appeared humanoid, and yet wasn't entirely human: it was far too blocky for that. Instead, it looked more like an Innukshuk, the rock slabs the Inuit piled into manlike shapes to mark trade routes and hunting grounds.

And how the hell did I know that?

Below the Damage Readout, was another status indicator: *Drone Repair Unit status: 100%.*

He hovered his eyes over that, and a small tooltip appeared.

Drone Repair Unit status indicates the health of your personal fleet of repair drones, which can make spot repairs after battles.

Uh, okay.

His eyes caught on a model number displayed beneath the representation of his body.

Vulture Mech, Bipedal Variant 22A. Firmware version: 1.0.4b.

He dismissed the Damage Readout and lay back down.

I'm a copy. A Mind Refurb. And I've been injected into a mech. Like in some kind of twisted anime.

He could feel the grit of the surface pressing into his upper body and the back of his arms, no doubt thanks to tactile sensors embedded in his metal skin. But he hardly noticed it. He didn't care. He gazed unblinkingly upward.

His mind kept cycling through a mix of powerful emotions. Regret, for what he once was. Anger, for what the military had done to him. Sadness, for losing all his friends and family. Confusion, as to why he'd been dumped out here with no guidance whatsoever.

He wasn't sure how long he simply lay there, staring dejectedly at the yellow sky. Maybe a few minutes. Maybe an hour.

Well, no point in wallowing in self-pity. What's done is done. At least I'm alive.

He finally sat up again, and this time scrambled entirely to his feet. He felt clumsy, as if this body wasn't his own—which it wasn't. He lost his balance and fell halfway, then forced himself to try again. This time he managed it, and stood to his full height. He realized he must have stood at least ten meters tall. In fact, an altimeter overlaying his vision reported that his sight was currently positioned nine point eight three meters above the surface.

The military had installed his consciousness into a mech and then abandoned him in the middle of nowhere. Was he supposed to figure out his mission on his own? Was this some kind of test? Or training? He somehow doubted that the army would dump a trillion credit machine in the middle of nowhere and expect it to fend for itself. Something definitely didn't smell right about the whole situation.

He rotated in place, surveying the landscape around him. There was a large, egg-shaped pod nearby. Its surface was completely white. He started walking toward it—the loud humming of his legs, and thudding that came when he planted his feet, was distracting, but he did his best to ignore them both. When he reached the pod, he found several fabrics lying beside it, connected by carbon fiber threads: it looked like one large, deflated parachute, and five smaller ones.

He searched the pod, but couldn't find anything of interest. The insides were padded with gel-like white cushions, and that was it.

He glanced at the barren wasteland around him once more. He noticed a small notch on the upper half of his HUD, and when he focused on it, the notch folded down, revealing a rear view video feed, no doubt sourced from an aft-facing camera.

Well, well, well, I have eyes on the back of my head.

He tried to smile, or frown, or make any expression, but the tactile feedback from his face told him none of his expressions were taking.

He studied the right hand HUD indicators. In the upper area was a battery display. It currently read 100%.

When he focused on it, instead of a tooltip, a larger battery profile appeared. It reported his solar panels as fully operational. His battery stores were also completely full. According to the different tooltips, his battery would drain faster when he operated during the night or other low sunlight conditions, only to be replenished again in the sun.

Well, at least I don't have to worry about running out of power. As long as the sun keeps shining.

Below the battery indicator was a section titled: Combat Abilities and Weapons.

He pulled that up. Yes! His right arm was equipped with two weapons that were buried within his forearm, above the wrist. The first was some kind of energy weapon, the second a laser beam. Both of those drew power from his battery to fire. His left arm had a rocket launcher—currently he had no rockets—and some kind of railgun. That gun fired pellets on a magnetic accelerator; the ammo could be replenished by shoving large chunks of rock into a processing panel in his upper bicep.

He also had a countermeasure system, called a Battle Cloak, that would send out a series of small seekers to intercept any rockets fired his way. Unfortunately, he currently had no seekers in his inventory, rendering it useless.

He activated the energy weapon mount; a panel opened in his thick, right forearm, and a large weapon turret emerged. A crosshairs appeared over his vision. He aimed at one of the distant rock buttresses, and when he focused on it, the view zoomed in.

Nice.

He aligned the crosshairs with the center of the rock, and thought of firing. Didn't work. He squeezed his fist.

That did it.

A bright bolt emerged from his arm, and traveled rapidly across the rocky plains. When it struck the rock, it incinerated a large blast crater around the impact site, and also sent out a shockwave that fragmented the surrounding minerals, releasing shrapnel in all directions.

Very, very nice.

He tried his laser next, and created dark bore holes in the rubble. While the impact sites were smaller, the damage was more concentrated, and the beam traveled the distance instantly, whereas a fast enemy could dodge the slower energy bolt.

He did some more investigating of his HUD, getting a feel for the system, and found an "Engage Virtual Reality Interface" option. That sounded interesting.

He tried it, and immediately the landscape fell away, replaced by... nothingness. He was surrounded by white in all directions.

He glanced down at himself. He was human again. Or at least, his avatar was. He was completely naked.

He imagined some clothes, and in an instant, a casual jeans and T-shirt combination materialized, covering his body. He imagined a mirror in front of himself, and then saw his familiar features. When he smiled, he could feel the muscles of his face moving, and his reflection mimicked him.

Well, at least I have a face *here.*

He imagined a city street around him, and skyscrapers. He even imagined pedestrians, and they too appeared, bustling back and forth, oblivious to his presence. So oblivious, in fact, that one of them shouldered right into him, hard.

"Hey, watch it!" Jason shouted at the man.

But the individual kept moving. Jason had to smile at that.

Why am I talking to him? He's not human. None of them are. Generated by some sub-process of my main AI core.

He created a cafe patio around him, jutting from the skyscraper to his left, and railed it off from the pavement. He sat down at one of the tables and materialized a few waitresses and other patrons, and then ordered a drink.

He wasn't sure it would work, but apparently the VR subroutine built into his AI core had enough smarts to deal with the situation he'd visualized, because the waitress returned a moment later with a tall glass of beer.

He took a sip.

It tasted real.

Well, at least they got the VR right.

He knew where he'd be spending the majority of his time.

He logged out of the VR environment, and appeared right back in the real world, exactly where he'd left off. His body had remained standing in place. He glanced at his power cell. It had crept back up to 95%, despite his VR usage.

He checked his surroundings, and proceeded toward the ruined buttress. An overhead map appeared in the upper right of his display. His dot was green, and fixed at the center, while the terrain scrolled past. He found that he could rotate the map so it appeared as an isometric perspective, and he left it that way, because it seemed more immediate to him.

He reached the collapsed rock tower and then knelt beside it. He had felt a bit exposed walking his ten-meter mech across those barren plains, but now that he had cover, the feeling lifted.

Who am I kidding? Any military satellites overhead would have spotted me already.

Then again, the profile of his ten-meter tall mech would have readily stood out while he was lying unconscious on the plains earlier. A military retrieval team was probably on the way. The fact that one hadn't arrived already told him he couldn't have been unconscious for very long.

He wasn't sure yet if he would go willingly. And this was as good a place as any to defend from.

He ripped a chunk of rock from the rubble and shoved it into the processing panel of his upper bicep.

He tried firing the railgun in his left arm, aiming out at another nearby rock tower. Surprisingly, the internal processor had already created a bunch of tiny rounds, and the slugs released in streams of light that reminded him of a Gatling gun. The distant rock chipped away, with large chunks breaking off.

Well, at least he wasn't defenseless.

He ceased firing, but left the railgun deployed in his left arm, and the laser turret his right. He scanned the sky, and the far horizons.

An hour passed.

He explored his HUD user interface in between searching the different horizons, getting a feel for his system. There was supposed to be some sort of Containment Code wrapped around his mind, ensuring he didn't do things he had no clearance for, or use UI—user interface—elements he didn't have access to, but everything was unlocked. He'd also heard Mind Refurbs were supposed to have no emotions, yet he had them all —as evidenced by his earlier meltdown when he'd first awakened. There was a UI option that allowed him to vary the intensity of the different emotions as he wished, or to turn all of them completely on or off.

From what he knew about Mind Refurbs, there was also supposed to be something called an Accomp, or accompanying AI, embedded in his system. Essentially it was a partition of his mind, or AI core, providing him backup processing power that was capable of monitoring his external surroundings, making targeting calculations, and so forth, but it seemed he didn't have one. There were different monitors he could set, however, on the external cameras, to issue a warning if motion was detected, for example. That would be useful if he ever needed to be dragged out of VR in a hurry.

He also found a communications interface, and he sent out a general broadcast. No answer came. He also had the option to send a distress signal, but he wasn't quite sure he wanted to do that yet.

He was free, at the moment. Though how long that would last, he didn't know.

Another hour went by. He spent it reviewing the digital manual that came with his mech in its entirety— its location was linked on his HUD. While reading it, he found out a few interesting tidbits. Apparently, when he first turned on, he was supposed to get a latitude and longitude beamed down to him from satellites in orbit, and failing that, from either the fallback GPS or GLONASS satellites, and finally the cloud, but he couldn't connect to any of those at the moment, so he couldn't verify his location. He had no Internet, and no idea where he was.

He continued reading, and came upon the section describing the "Teaching AIs." Here was a set of programs that could teach him how to do virtually anything, by overlaying the instructions over his vision in realtime while he performed the task.

He pulled up the interface, and chose: "How to Program Your VR Environment."

A small digital avatar appeared on his HUD: it was a cartoonish man with gray hair spouting all over the place, and big round glasses. He looked like a mad scientist.

"Hello!" the avatar said. "I'm Janson your VR guide! Today I'm going to teach you the basics of setting up your VR environment! First and foremost, all you need to do is imagine—"

Jason pulled up his VR environment and followed along, creating the tutorial environment. Then he dismissed everything to the default white backdrop, planning to customize it later. He continued reading the digital manual.

One of his favorite discoveries while reading it was the ability to adjust his time sense. That's right. His internal processor had a clock speed expressed in tera-hertz, or trillions of cycles per second. A scheduler allocated those cycles among the different background processes that needed to run, including those involved in consciousness. By varying the cycles per second devoted to consciousness, he could alter his perceived time sense. There were a thousand different settings, ranging from the slowest—where the world completely froze around him, and not even his own speed-enhanced servomotors could keep up—to the fastest—where time passed in a blur. The latter would have been handy in his past life during long distance drives across the country.

There were a few intermediary presets. One, called Bullet Time, was located part ways between zero and normal time; in Bullet Time, his body could move at close to normal speed, thanks to a power boost to his servomotors, while time around him slowed right down, allowing him to zip between opponents who weren't capable of robot speeds. It would be useless against mechs and combat robots of course, but it worked wonders on most organic forms of life. Great for dodging missiles and other projectiles, even shrapnel. But it also used up a lot more juice, battery-wise.

He experimented with that mode for a little bit: he picked up a small boulder, held it to shoulder height and released it. He switched to Bullet Time as it dropped, then tested how far he could run away and back again while still being able to catch the boulder before it hit the ground. He was surprised at how fast he could move for his size, but it was still slightly disappointing, since he could only move away a few paces, which seemed a lot less than what he had imagined, based on what the manual had told him. In the fine print, he noticed that the Bullet Time section was meant mostly for smaller robots, which could move a lot faster than the larger mechs.

Now they tell me.

Also apparently when Bullet Time was active, the drain on his power cell increased, especially if he amped up the output of his servomotors at the same time.

As a speed test, Jason activated Bullet Time, and fired his energy weapon out across the plains. He increased his servomotor throughput and tried to run alongside the energy bolt. While it had slowed down significantly, he couldn't catch up, and had only made it halfway to the buttress before the bolt struck. The impact caused shards of rock to explode from the impact site in slow motion.

He reverted to ordinary time and glanced at his battery level in the upper right. Down to 90%. That was a bit more drain on the battery than he would have liked. Then again, he had increased his servomotor output to the max. The power levels actually went up a percent as he watched. He glanced skyward, toward the molten sun.

Gotta love solar power.

A third hour passed, and still no retrieval team showed up.

This definitely had to be a training exercise. Because the only other option wasn't an option: the military didn't know he was out there. For that to be the case, all of the satellites in orbit would've had to have been destroyed.

But that was only possible if there had been another alien invasion.

Jason refused to believe it.

He scrambled to his feet. "Enough of this sitting around shit. It's time to take my destiny in my own hands."

But he had only just risen to his feet and started walking away from the rubble, when an alarm sounded.

His Damage Readout was flashing, and a miniature silhouette of his mech overlaid the lower left of his vision; the right leg was highlighted.

Glancing down, he saw that bore holes were appearing in the armor there.

He was being struck by laser fire.

3

J ason dove behind the cover of the rubble. He glanced at his overhead map, and saw the red dot that had appeared to the east, behind a rock buttress fifteen hundred meters from him. That was where his internal sensors had calculated the source of the laser blasts, based both on the impact locations, and camera data.

He accessed that camera data, so that it appeared in a window in the center of his vision. He rewound the feed until the rock buttress in question was in view, and then paused it and zoomed in.

He saw another mech crouched behind it. This one was humanoid like his own, though it had a slightly bigger mid-section, and a flatter head—to make room for the rocket launchers on each shoulder. Those launchers were currently empty, as far as he could tell. Thankfully.

There was a laser turret in its right arm, aimed at

his position. And in its left arm, something else... it looked like a sword of some kind. He didn't think he'd want to get hit by the thing.

A quick ID told him the mech was some sort of Shadow Hawk variant. Coming in at slightly taller than him, at twelve meters.

Jason pulled up the communications interface on his UI. The Shadow Hawk was available as a recipient. He highlighted it, and hit connect.

The mech accepted his request, and the line went green.

"Uh, hello," Jason said. "Uh, why are you firing at me?"

No answer.

"This is some sort of training exercise, I think," Jason said. "They're trying to see how we handle abnormal situations. So, uh, maybe stop firing and we can talk?"

Still no answer.

He then wondered if the mech was part of some retrieval team. But if so, why wasn't it answering his hails?

Jason decided now would be a good time to issue a distress call. He pulled up the interface, and hit engage.

"All right, well, you leave me no choice but to defend myself," Jason said. "I won't hesitate to use deadly force if I have to."

In return, the line only fed him static.

All right then. I guess we're going to fight.

He lifted his energy cannon over the top of the rubble. It had a built-in scope, and he was able to switch his viewpoint to that of the weapon, so he didn't have to expose his head.

He zoomed in on the buttress. The Shadow Hawk wasn't there anymore.

A proximity alarm sounded.

His rear view feed was still active at the top of his HUD, and motion drew his eyes to the video feed.

The mech was directly behind him.

How?

Its left hand was drawn back, preparing to impale him with the sword that jutted from its forearm. Lightning bolts sparked up and down the weapon.

Jason switched to Bullet Time and rolled out of the way before it could strike.

But the Shadow Hawk likewise reverted to Bullet Time, and came at him. They were evenly matched, when it came to speed. Jason dodged two quick blows from that electrical sword, blows that would have seemed a blur to any outside watchers.

The Shadow Hawk pointed the laser turret in its other arm at his chest area. Jason rotated his body to the side, while at the same time thrusting his arm outward and throwing off the aim.

Then he swung his railgun toward the Shadow Hawk's chest, and squeezed.

Slugs began to drill into the Shadow Hawk's chest, but after the third impact, the mech vanished entirely, leaving behind a puff of red smoke.

What—

His proximity alarm sounded again. According to

the overhead map, the mech was coming down from directly above.

Jason dove to the side, and that electrical sword smashed into the ground behind him, penetrating right up to the hilt embedded in the Shadow Hawk's forearm.

Cuts through rock like hot butter.

He rolled to his feet and deployed the energy weapon in his right forearm, then he fired both his left and right weapons at the same time. He targeted the sword with his railgun, and the laser turret with his energy weapon.

The Shadow Hawk withdrew the sword to protect it from the slugs, and tried to rotate its body away to avoid the energy bolt. It partially succeeded, but the bolt still struck the tip of the laser, searing it off.

That the mech hadn't teleported right away told him it had a cooldown interval.

He adjusted his aim, targeting the center of mass, and unleashed everything he had.

But then the mech vanished a third time. He glanced around, searching for the Shadow Hawk. There was no sign of it.

A teleporter? He didn't even know the military had tech like that. Then again, he'd heard their scientists and been experimenting with alien technology captured from the last invasion…

He decided to dive behind the rubble again, just in case he hadn't destroyed that laser turret. He slid his energy cannon over the lip of the rubble, and began searching for signs of the Shadow Hawk.

And then, just like that, the mech was on top of him.

Jason spun around, wrestling with the Shadow Hawk. It had flung both of his arms wide, and he wasn't able to draw them inward to get a bead on the mech with his weapons—the machine was stronger than he was.

The Shadow Hawk head-butted him, three times. He felt nothing, but his Damage Readout told him his head area was suffering severe denting. If this kept up, he'd lose his front cameras.

Jason rolled his head to the side when the next head butt came in. Then he swung his arms inward in a move he'd learned from MMA grappling videos, and broke the lock the Shadow Hawk had on him. He was still operating in Bullet Time—he had to, to counter the mech's own accelerated speed—and managed to flip himself on top of the unit. Then he rammed his energy gun into its face.

He expected the mech to teleport away, but it remained present. That told him that teleporting cost a lot of power. The Shadow Hawk was likely running under ten percent, and would have to recharge for a while before it could teleport again.

"That's about enough," Jason said. "You're going to tell me who the hell you are, and why you're attacking me."

"I'm War Bitch," a woman's voice came over the comm. A small speaker symbol appeared next to the Shadow Hawk's name on his HUD, indicating the mech was the source.

"War Bitch?" Jason pressed.

"That's right, asshole," the woman said. "I'm War

Bitch to you." She tried to head butt him, but he pulled back.

"Geez," Jason said. "No need to get all touchy feely on me. So why are you attacking me?"

"What do you think?" War Bitch said.

"Well, if you've given yourself the name War Bitch, I guess that explains a lot," Jason said.

War Bitch didn't answer.

"Look, I think we're on some shared survival trial of some kind," Jason said. "It's probably in our best interests to team up."

"War Bitch teams up with no one," she said.

"There's also a chance this isn't a test at all," Jason said. "It's possible that the military is no longer in control of this region. That the spy satellites have been shot down. And that aliens are invading."

There was quiet on the comm for a moment, and then War Bitch burst out in raucous laughter. "Aliens? You think aliens are invading? You're a moron. But if this is a survival trial, I'm going to win. I'm going to show the Brass that I deserve to be team leader."

"By trashing another one of their eight trillion credit machines?" Jason said. "I don't think they'll be too happy."

"Then if they didn't want us to fight, why haven't they intervened?" War Bitch said.

"Refer to my last comment about aliens invading," Jason said.

War Bitch chuckled again. "You're so dense. This is obviously a virtual reality environment."

"It's not VR," Jason said. "I've already checked.

This is the real world. Haven't you experimented with your unit yet? There's an option to launch a VR simulation."

"Well yeah, but that's simply another VR environment nested inside of this one," War Bitch said.

"Let me guess, the next thing you're going to tell me is, you don't think you're a Mind Refurb either," Jason said.

"Oh, I'm a Mind Refurb all right," War Bitch said. "Just not the kind that wants to make friends with my competitors."

And with that, she vanished.

Jason realized she'd been stalling the whole time. And now they'd have to fight all over again.

His proximity alert sounded behind him. He narrowly dodged to the side as the mech's sword plowed into the rock behind him. Evidently she'd withdrawn the weapon in time to save it from his railgun.

"Stay still!" War Bitch said.

Jason leaped onto her back as she withdrew the sword, and wrapped the crook of his elbow around her neck, and hauled her to the ground in a chokehold.

"You sure know how to treat a woman!" War Bitch said indignantly.

"Only when she's trying to kill me!" Jason said.

She elbowed him hard in the rib cage, but he absorbed the blow. Then the sword came sliding under her arm, and slid just underneath his rib cage area, the sword digging a glancing blow into the metal there. It was on course to penetrate his upper arm, so he released her.

She swiveled her foot around in a sweep kick as he backed away, and she tripped him. But he thrust out a hand, grabbing onto a boulder behind him, and steadied himself.

War Bitch came in, sword swinging. Jason dodged left, then right. He was sorely tempted to try intercepting that sword with one of his forearms, but was worried the wicked looking blade would sever the limb. He recalled how easily it penetrated rock, after all.

"I'm not… trying… to kill you," she said between swings. "Only cut off… your head."

That latter statement cued him, and he ducked as her sword came in. Then he wrapped his arms around the hilt portion of her sword, and leaped upward. He aimed his energy cannon down at her body, and fired at the shoulder joint at point blank range. He ripped her arm right off as he leaped away.

"Ugh!" War Bitch said. "Now you're going to pay."

Jason held the dismembered arm toward her, and waved the sword menacingly. "Stay back!" He noted that the electrical bolts traveling up and down the blade had ceased, now that the weapon was disconnected from its power source.

He tossed the arm aside, and pointed both his railgun and energy weapon at her.

She raised her remaining arm into the air. "I surrender."

"Good," Jason said. "I don't want to hurt you."

"So you say," War Bitch told him. "You only, uh, ripped my arm off. That's not hurting me or anything."

She lowered her remaining arm, aiming at him. The

laser turret folded away, replaced by what looked like a launcher of some kind. A formidable looking steel tip protruded from it.

"I didn't want to have to do this, but you leave me no choice," War Bitch said.

"Wha—"

Before he could answer, the steel tip erupted from the launcher, and rammed him in the chest. It was a harpoon, connected by a steel chain to the launching unit.

War Bitch dashed past him, scooping up her severed arm, and then turned around and set off at a run.

"Stop!" Jason said, but he was dragged to the ground almost immediately as the chain grew taut.

He tried to get up, but couldn't. The different rocks embedded in the sand crunched into his armor. An alarm appeared on his HUD, and the chest area of his mech highlighted repeatedly on his Damage Readout to indicate the different dents that were appearing.

He aimed his energy cannon upward at the chain and fired. But just as he squeezed the trigger, he hit another rock, and it threw off his aim. He lifted the weapon to try again, but then the chain went slack, dropping to the sand.

The harpoon end dug itself out of his chest piece, and retracted.

"Thank you," Jason said, scrambling to his feet. He aimed his two weapons at her. "Don't do that again."

But she wasn't looking at him. Her gaze was directed behind him.

He felt it then. A strange rumbling. Turning around,

he saw dust on the horizon. It was sourced from a stampede of some sort of incoming quadrupeds.

He zoomed in.

These were unlike any quadrupeds he'd ever seen before.

Alien bioweapons.

4

J ason stared at the incoming creatures.

They looked a little like wolves covered in greenish fur, except their heads had been replaced by what could best be described as that of a T-Rex. He decided to mentally refer to them as Rex Wolves. From their lips dripped an acidic saliva that dissolved the ground underneath them.

Each of them was about the size of a small house.

"Uh," War Bitch said. "They look friendly. Doggy?"

"I don't think they want to be friends," Jason said.

"Where the hell did those come from?" War Bitch said.

"They're mutants from the uninhabitable zone," Jason said.

"Well, at least you didn't blame aliens this time," War Bitch said.

"They were originally made by aliens, yes," Jason

said. "Who knows, these ones could very well be the byproducts of a new invasion."

"If only you could see me roll my eyes right now," War Bitch said.

"You know, that's not something I miss about the human experience," Jason said.

"What, rolling your eyes?" she asked.

"No, seeing a chick named War Bitch rolling her eyes," Jason replied.

"Har," War Bitch said. "You know, it looks like they're coming straight for us."

"That's because they are," Jason said. "Hurry, this way!" He took off at a run to the east.

"Why should I follow you?" War Bitch shouted to his back.

"Fine, stay there then!" Jason said over his shoulder. "After all, this is all VR, right? According to you…"

He raced toward one of the intact rock buttresses. It towered about forty-five meters above the ground.

Suddenly the Shadow Hawk appeared on top. "Ha! Beat you to it. Look who's following who now."

Jason took a running leap, making use of the instructions he'd read in the manual to amp up his servomotors beforehand, and he launched well into the air. He grabbed onto the buttress about thirty meters up. His first handhold broke away, but the second held. He climbed, hand over hand, toward the top.

When he reached the uppermost edge, War Bitch slammed her sword down on him, forcing him to let go.

"My buttress!" she said. "Find your own!"

Jason crashed to the ground thirty meters below. He

scrambled to his feet. There was no time to find another tower: the incoming creatures were almost upon him.

He backed against the rock, and aimed his weapons toward the Rex Wolves. He fired his railgun, drilling into the creatures. He repeatedly unleashed bolts from his energy weapon at the same time, striking Wolves in the heads and bodies, causing either body part to explode in a pleasant rain of gore.

But the creatures kept coming.

He kept firing, switching exclusively to the energy cannon, and forming barricades of dead bodies. Some of the Rex Wolves behind the fallen tripped over the bodies, and he took them down as they slid across the ground.

But more Wolves always came.

He wouldn't be able to keep this up for much longer; he glanced at his ever-diminishing power supply: he'd have to pause to recharge his batteries soon.

So far War Bitch hadn't contributed. He'd destroyed her only ranged weapon, after all; well, the only one he knew of: the laser turret. And her harpoon wouldn't be much help against these things.

Finally Jason had to stop firing: his battery levels had fallen far too low. He couldn't fire his energy weapon, or his laser. And he'd used up all of his railgun ammunition.

The Rex Wolves closed, surrounding Jason. Their acid saliva dripped onto the rocky ground, sending up fumes of green smoke as the minerals below melted, promising destruction when those jaws enveloped him.

The beasts formed a half circle in front of him and

slowly sealed the noose. They snarled at any in behind that tried to shove past them: this was their kill. Other creatures among them, meanwhile, leaped at the sides of the buttress behind him, snapping at the top, trying to get War Bitch.

One of the Rex Wolves abruptly lashed out toward him. Jason still had enough power left for Bullet Time, so he activated it, and dodged out of the way. He slammed his fist into the creature's big eye, causing the ball to explode.

The Rex Wolf howled in pain, withdrawing, just as another snapped at him.

Jason ran toward it, and ducked underneath those jaws. He straightened his fingers and held them together, stabbing upward as he continued underneath the creature. His fingers met resistance, but he continued to shove upward, until he penetrated the skin to the hard muscle tissue underneath. He ran all the way to the rear of the animal, slitting open its entire underside. He hadn't penetrated through to the organs underneath the transversal muscle tissue, but he'd definitely injured the creature, and it was losing a lot of blood.

It howled just as badly as the other Rex Wolf, and quickly ran away.

He shut off Bullet Time, because his power bar was beginning to flash ominously. Without warning one of the creatures bit down on him. His body protruded from either side of its mouth as his HUD reported an immense pressure on his chest assembly. The acid was etching through the surrounding metal, further weakening his structure. If he didn't break free soon, he was gone.

A blur of motion drew his gaze upward. War Bitch had leaped off the buttress. She held her severed arm in hand, with the sword still extended from the forearm. It struck the Rex Wolf that had him, cutting off its head.

Jason fell to the ground and broke free.

Another beast snapped at her, but she teleported away before it grabbed her. The Rex Wolf shrieked, and then toppled forward with green blood oozing from its maw: War Bitch was on top of it, her sword penetrating its neck.

She withdrew the arm and, ducking, swung at another creature that dove at her. The sword ripped through its neck.

She continued to fight with her severed arm, the sword at its tip soon becoming steeped in green blood. Even though the weapon wasn't electrified, it readily took down any Rex Wolf that came at her.

Jason grabbed one of the severed limbs she'd cut off, and used it as a cudgel to strike at the other Rex Wolves that came at him. The wicked crescent moon talons at its tip readily sliced into those wolves he targeted. Those he didn't kill usually backed away to nurse their injuries, while the dead began to form a big pile in front of them. So big, in fact, that the wolves began coming at them from the sides, and then from the top of the buttress.

Finally, the attack ceased.

Jason shoved his way through the dead bodies, toppling them. There were several living Rex Wolves beyond it, nursing their wounds. Some weren't wounded at all though, and Jason had the impression they hadn't attacked. They backed away when they saw him: many of them lowered their heads. One thing that stood out immediately regarding these surviving beasts: they were all smaller than the others.

"What are they doing?" War Bitch asked.

"Not sure," Jason replied. He began wiping the blood off his body using the fur of one of the nearby corpses—he didn't want to block his solar panels. His power cell indicator was still flashing.

War Bitch meanwhile waved her severed arm and sword, and shouted: "Get! Get!"

The nearest wolves ran away for a bit, but then stopped, and ducked their heads, coming back.

"What's wrong with them?" War Bitch said.

One of the Rex Wolves broke away from the others. It kept its head down, and its mouth closed so that it wouldn't drip acid.

"I don't know," Jason said. He finished wiping the blood off his body, and stepped into the sun. He was relieved when his power indicator began to climb. "Maybe they're confusing us for alpha members of the pack?"

"How could they possibly confuse us for alpha members of the pack?" War Bitch said.

"Well, look at how small their eyes are, relative to the rest of their bodies," Jason said. "My guess is they utilize their senses of smell and hearing to navigate more than anything else. With the former taking precedence, at least in a social context. We're smeared in the blood of their brethren. Or you are, anyway. You smell like them."

"I smell like their insides, more like," War Bitch said.

"Maybe," Jason said.

"What about you?" War Bitch said. "You just wiped off all that blood onto one of them, transferring its scent to your hull."

"Yeah, but they were acting this way before that," Jason said. "Either way, we've killed all their alphas. And for some reason, that's caused them to bond with us."

"I don't think so," War Bitch said. "I used to run a kennel when I was a human. And I know dogs. Look at how small all of these beasts are, at least compared to the others. They were born only recently. Probably in the last few days. And they've bonded with us as their mothers, now that we've killed off their real family."

"Oh, wonderful," Jason said. "Just what I need, a bunch of baby Rex Wolves following me around, thinking I'm their mommy."

"Rex Wolves?" War Bitch said.

"That's what I've taken to calling them," Jason said.

"Not sure I like it," War Bitch said. "But whatever. I'm going to try mimicking their sounds." Via her external speakers, she played back a recording of a shriek one of the beasts had made earlier.

The Rex Wolves lowered their reptilian ears and crouched slightly in alarm.

"Nicely done, scare them won't you?" Jason said.

"Hmm…" War Bitch said. "How about…" She

emitted a gentle low that sounded a cross between a puppy and a dinosaur.

The Rex Wolves perked up slightly.

"What was that?" Jason asked.

"Exactly what it sounded like," War Bitch said. "I took one of their earlier howls and merged it with the low of a real puppy."

She approached the closest creature, holding out one arm. It let her come right up to it, and she petted it underneath the chin. Its lip curled back slightly in pleasure.

"It's going to need milk," Jason said.

War Bitch backed away, and gestured toward the pile of bodies.

"Come," War Bitch told the creature. She walked away toward the dead bodies, and waited patiently. "Come!"

The animal didn't obey.

"I don't think it's going to listen to you," Jason said. "Not yet."

Jason approached one of the dead Rex Wolves, and examined its underbelly. Nope, that was a male. He went to the next. It was female, but didn't have what he was looking for. Finally, on the third, he found a pair of swollen udders. And there were no injuries on its body. Well, save for its lack of a head. But if he arranged the body a certain way, perhaps he could mask the smell of blood from the hindquarters.

He dragged the body by the legs to War Bitch, and set the udders down next to the Rex Wolf. It backed away slightly, but then came forward curiously, sniffing.

Because of the way Jason had dragged the body in, the head was positioned well away from the living beast.

The young Rex Wolf promptly wrapped its lips around the udder, and began to suckle.

"There we go!" War Bitch said excitedly. "That's a good boy!"

That opened the floodgates; the other Rex Wolves came forward, one at a time, and began to suckle the teat. There weren't enough nipples for them all, and one Rex Wolf, the runt of the family, didn't get one. It tried to force one of the other wolves away, but it snarled at the runt, who promptly backed away.

"Aw, poor little guy." War Bitch went to that one and wrapped her arms around it. Though it was a "runt," it was still about half as big as her mech. "I'm going to call him Runt."

When one of the Rex Wolves had had its fill, War Bitch guided the Runt to the body.

"There's not going to be any milk left," Jason said.

"Maybe, maybe not," War Bitch said. The little guy tried to suckle, but seemed dissatisfied, and gave up after a short while.

"Told you," Jason said.

War Bitch carried the runt to another Rex Wolf in the pack, one that also had a swollen rump, and shoved its face into the teat. Runt began to suckle.

"Of course, this brings up the question, how are we going to feed them going forward?" War Bitch said.

"First she attacks me, and now she wants to raise alien creatures with me," Jason said.

"Technically, they're not aliens, since they were

created from Earth-based DNA," War Bitch said. "Otherwise they wouldn't be able to survive in our atmosphere."

"All right, alien bioweapons then," Jason said. "If you want to get technical. Look, I don't have any desire to raise these things as pets."

"Fine, I'll do it," War Bitch said. "It's the least we can do, since we killed their parents."

"Their parents attacked us, in case you forgot," Jason said.

"I haven't forgotten," War Bitch said. "It was simply a case of mistaken identity."

"Mistaken identity?"

"Yes," War Bitch said. "The pack mistook us for prey. They won't make that mistake again."

"They certainly won't," Jason said, examining the bodies. He returned his attention to War Bitch. "So you've agreed to team up with me, then, it sounds like?"

"I suppose so, for now," War Bitch said. "It's fairly obvious you're in need of my help. Though I'm still kinda pissed that you cut off my arm."

"You don't have any working repair drones?" Jason asked.

"No," War Bitch said. "When I woke up, my inventory of the drones was completely empty."

"Let me help you with that, then," Jason said. He nodded toward her arm.

He activated his repair drone subsystem, and a panel slid open in his lower leg. The drones began to buzz outside.

One of the Rex Wolves came running at Jason. No,

not at him, but for a drone: it snatched it right out of the air and chomped it into a ruined pile of metal.

"Hey!" Jason said.

"I could have told you that would happen," War Bitch said.

Jason promptly recalled them, and sealed his leg panel as a couple of the excited Rex Wolves gathered around.

"We'll have to go somewhere private," War Bitch said. She wrapped her arms around Jason, and the world winked.

He was standing on top of the nearby rock buttress, and overlooking the plains below.

The small creatures were looking around in confusion.

"Hey doggies!" War Bitch shouted over her speakers.

The Rex Wolves turned toward the buttress, and began jumping up and down happily when they saw her again. Even Runt, who had finished his meal. They tried to scale the rock tower, but it was too high for them.

Good.

Jason once more activated his drone subsystem, and allocated three of them to repairing War Bitch's severed limb.

"You'll have to hold it in place until they get the joins fixed," Jason said.

"Yup, I read the manual, too," War Bitch said. She pressed her severed arm into the shoulder socket.

Meanwhile, the drones swerved around the joint,

issuing repairs, melting the raw materials of her arm that were too damaged for repair, and reusing them to 3D print brand new pieces.

Jason had the rest of his drones work on repairing his own injuries. He had a lot of dents from the little joyride War Bitch had taken him on. Not to mention the bite and acid marks when one of the Rex Wolves had scooped him up.

He punched the rock underneath a few times until it was broken down enough that he could pick up a handful. He did that, and shoved it into the ammo-processing chamber of his left bicep.

While the drones worked to repair the two units, War Bitch looked up at him. "Tara."

"What?" Jason said.

"My name is Tara," she said.

"Jason," he told her. "What happened to War Bitch?"

"Just a name I came up with when I thought we were being judged by the Brass," Tara said.

"The Brass..." Jason said. "That's the second time you've mentioned that word. You come from an army background?"

"I do," she said. "I'm a private first class. Or I was, when I got my scan done. Feels like yesterday. Wait, it *was* yesterday, as far as I'm concerned."

"Feels like only a few hours since my own scan," Jason said.

"You just woke up?" Tara asked.

"Some hours ago," Jason said. "Why, how long have you been awake for?"

"Five days now," Tara said. She cocked her expressionless head slightly. "You know, this is actually a really bad form of communication. We're going to have to rig avatars in our HUDs at some point, so we can at least read each other's facial expressions. Until then, how about we reconvene in VR?"

"Sure, why not," Jason said.

5

J ason received the VR invite a few seconds later, and he accepted. He put his body on standby mode, setting a background process to wake him should the cameras detect any motion in the distance. He was able to mark the young Rex Wolves as friendlies, so that they wouldn't trigger an awake event.

In moments he found himself standing on the beach-side patio of a beautiful mansion. There were no other houses on the stretches of beach on either side of him, so that meant he was on a ranch or estate of some kind. A horse and rider were approaching in the distance at a gallop. The rider was a woman dressed in a diaphanous white dress. Her long dark hair streamed out behind her. She was extremely fit, with a flat belly much tighter than his own.

Wait a second, I can make my belly as flat and muscular as I want.

He did just that, reducing his body fat slider closer to

zero. Before he could make any other changes, his eyes were drawn back to the incoming rider: he could see the slight outline of her breasts underneath the translucent fabric as they bobbed up and down with each gallop, and he increased his time sense to enjoy the view.

When she arrived, she pulled the horse up short, and Jason restored his time sense to normal.

She looped one leg over the horse, and leaped down. Jason's eyes were drawn to her pubic area, but disappointingly she was wearing panties underneath the translucent fabric, denying him a view. But the fact that she wasn't wearing a bra made him extremely happy.

"That was quite the entrance," Jason said, forcing himself to look at her face. It was difficult.

Tara gave him an unimpressed look, then shoved passed him into the house proper. Jason followed her.

He couldn't help but stare at her hourglass figure as he followed her inside.

He knew she was doing this on purpose, dressing provocatively to get some sort of reaction out of him, but he promised himself he wouldn't give her the pleasure of doing so.

"So this is your little slice of paradise, is it?" Jason said. He swept his gaze across the high-end furniture around him, but none of it could hold his attention for long, and he found himself staring at that tight little butt again.

Tara reached the kitchen counter and spun around.

Jason immediately lifted his eyes to her face, trying to pretend they'd stayed at that level the whole time.

"A drink?" Tara said.

Jason shook his head. "Don't drink," he lied. He didn't want to encourage her, after all. At least that was what he told himself. But that spectacular figure of hers, and—

This is silly. None of this is real. We're machines...

Tara shrugged. "Too bad for you." She materialized a glass of wine in her hand—it contained a sparkling white—and she leaned back against the counter to take a sip. The counter top and the bar stools in front of it were fashioned out of bamboo, as if they were meant to convey an island atmosphere.

She gestured toward her surroundings. "I modeled this place after my childhood home. I grew up on a ranch in Honolulu. It wasn't so close to the beach, but hey, the wonders of VR."

"Nice," Jason said. "I've only just begun experimenting with my VR."

"I look forward to seeing what you've done with yours," Tara said.

"Hey, you're assuming I'll invite you," Jason said.

Tara shrugged. "I don't really care if you do." She glanced down at his body, then back up to his face. There was no desire in her eyes; mostly, it seemed, curiosity. "Have you altered your avatar at all?"

"No," he told her. "This is exactly what I look like in real life."

"I thought as much," Tara said. She smirked slightly, then took another drink.

"What's that supposed to mean?" Jason said.

"Nothing," she said. Her sea blue eyes sparkled mischievously.

"What about you?" Jason said. "Did you change your avatar?"

"Of course," Tara said. "I'm much more beautiful in real life."

Jason frowned. "I see."

"Do you?" she said. She dropped the glass, but before it hit the ground, it vanished. She walked toward him, swaying her hips provocatively, and extended her arms, so that for a moment he thought she was going to wrap them around his neck in an embrace. He simply stared at her, entranced.

But then she yawned, and he realized she was stretching. She lowered her arms and walked right past him, seating herself on one of the couches overlooking the patio and the beach beyond.

"Have a seat," Tara said.

Jason approached, and was about to sit down beside her, when she pointed at the couch that was situated at a perpendicular angle to that one.

"Not here," Tara said. "There."

"Someone's not pushy or anything," Jason said. But he obeyed, sitting on the other couch.

Tara stretched out, so that she was lying down on her chosen couch. "I want to lounge."

"It's your VR environment..." Jason said.

She glanced at him. "So how about you? I was in the army when I scanned, and what were you?"

"A nobody," Jason said. "Just someone trying to make ends meet."

"You didn't have access to Basic Pay?" Tara said.

"No," Jason said, gazing out at the beach outside. He watched the waves lap against shore. "I lived in too nice of a place. Inherited it from my parents, you see, before they decided to join the Mars colony."

"I don't know what anyone ever sees in Mars," Tara said.

"Neither do I," Jason said. "Believe me." He returned his gaze to her face. She definitely had modified her avatar to look better. No one looked this good in real life. "So what did you do as a private first class in the army?"

"The usual," Tara said. "Remote operation of autonomous drones. I lived aboard a ship that operated in the Pacific Theater. We sent our drones into the uninhabited areas of China, always on the lookout for any surviving bioweapons. I worked on that post for only a year, and I only ever encountered one herd of the creatures. They were nothing like my new doggies, of course. I relayed the coordinates to the bombers, who came in and dropped a few clusters, wiping them out."

"Only a single herd?" Jason said.

"That's right," Tara said.

"We've only been here a few hours, well, days for you, and already we've encountered a pack of bioweapons," Jason said. "I think you just weren't in one of the hot spots."

"Probably not," Tara admitted. "My particular team was restricted to operating along the coast."

"There you go," Jason said. "So you were just a drone babysitter, huh?"

"That's right," Tara said. "All army personnel are, these days. Even infantry. Because I'm sure you know, autonomous drones and combat robots aren't allowed to fire unless human operators are behind the controls. By law."

"You'd think that law would have changed since the alien invasion," Jason said. "But nope. And that reminds me, did you notice we have no lock downs on our minds? No Rules of Engagement. Full access to our emotions. I did some reading up on Mind Refurbs before getting my scan done. I thought there was supposed to be something called Containment Code that would prevent us from disobeying orders. Or from feeling emotions."

"There is," Tara said. "But for some reason, the army didn't apply that code to us before installing us into these war machines. That's why I thought this was all some kind of grand experiment. Now I'm not sure what to believe." She tapped her luscious lips. "So what do you think is going on? Truly."

"I already told you," Jason said. "If it's not a survival trial, it has to be an alien invasion. Either that, or someone sabotaged the satellites."

"I still think we could be operating entirely in VR," Tara said. "Because if it was a survival trial, the military wouldn't be risking our units like this. But if it's not, sabotage sounds like the more likely option to me. The question is, who would sabotage all the military surveillance satellites that pass over the uninhabited zones, and why?"

"Don't know," Jason said. "Could be part of some

virus meant to target all satellites. There are a bunch of rogue hacking groups out there, motivated by money and political agendas. It could be anyone."

Tara materialized another wine glass, this one filled with a red. Incredible, Jason could smell its subtle aroma from here. She's really amped up the potency of the drink in her VR.

"I've been heading west," Tara said. "Based on my calculations, there should be a city nearby. It was once known as Brussels."

"Brussels?" Jason said.

"That's right," Tara said. "It was part of Europe, before the invasion."

"How do you know where we are?" Jason asked her.

"I've been making a map of the area," Tara said. "Crossing dried out riverbeds, and burned up forests. I even came across a small town. Its signs were still intact. With all that data, I've been able to get a fairly good idea of where we are."

"Why do you want to go to Brussels?" Jason said. "It'll be empty."

"Yes," Tara said. "But at least we can set up a defensible base of operations. Unless you're happy staying out in the open, taking shelter on top of a rock buttress for the rest of your life."

"That's a good point," Jason said. "But it does make me wonder how long I was lying on those plains before I woke up."

"Probably not long at all," Tara said. "You haven't seen what comes out at night." She shuddered.

"What?" Jason asked.

"Roving bands of bioweapons," Tara replied. "Creatures from your worst nightmares. They'll hunt anything that moves. Even if they can't eat you, they'll devour you, and shit out your undigested parts."

"Well, either I got lucky, and these roving bands overlooked me," Jason said. "Or you're right, and I wasn't lying there long at all."

"How much dust was on your hull when you woke?" Tara asked.

"Not much," Jason replied. "In fact, I don't think any dust had settled on me at all."

"There you go," Tara said.

"How about you?" Jason asked.

"I wasn't covered in dust either," Tara replied. "So neither of us were out there very long at all. But getting back to the topic of the city… who knows? There might even be a working Internet we can connect to. They still had a lot of fiber optic lines in the area fifty years ago. We can find out what's going on in the world, maybe shed some light on our predicament." She took another sip, and Jason found himself staring at her throat longingly. His eyes drifted inevitably to her breasts; she caught him, and he quickly averted his gaze, feeling his cheeks grow hot.

"You know," Tara said, "if you weren't a machine, I'd probably…"

"Yes?" Jason met her gaze.

She smirked suddenly, and sat up. She drew her legs to her chest, hiding her breasts. "I probably wouldn't be talking to you right now."

"I see how it is," Jason said.

Tara shrugged. "We are what we are."

"Well, I think we've dallied here long enough," Jason said. "It's time to head west, to Brussels, wouldn't you say? Set ourselves up a base of operations?"

Her eyes twinkled. "And so it is. We also have some new pets to feed."

"Oh, I'm looking forward to that," Jason said, unable to hide the sarcasm from his voice.

Somehow he doubted there would be any feeding going on, considering they had no idea where they were going to find any food.

6

When Jason lifted the shroud of VR and returned to that bleak partition of reality known as the real world, he discovered only four of the Rex Wolf pups had remained behind, including Runt. The others had run off.

"Guess the parent-child bond wasn't as strong as we thought," Jason said, trying to keep the mockery in his tone down to a minimum. In truth, he'd been hoping all the creatures would run off.

"I'm going to name the big one Bruiser," Tara said from beside him. "The one that follows it around, Lackey."

"Lackey? That's a terrible name for a dog," Jason said.

She ignored him. "And the other guy, the one with the hair all over the place, Shaggy."

He glanced at her. It was hard to imagine that big, faceless war machine could harbor such a beautiful woman within its AI core. A woman who was currently taking in a bunch of acid-dripping bioweapons as pets.

Then again, he himself was a deadly killing machine. Also without a face.

"We still don't have a way to feed them," Jason said.

"We'll find a way," Tara said.

"Unless we can convince them to go cannibal on their brethren down there…"

"You're disgusting," Tara told him.

The drones finished repairing Tara, and he ordered them to 3D print more of themselves so that she could replenish her stock. First he had to pulverize more of the rock underneath them. Thankfully it was high in metals, so the drones had a ready supply of printing material.

His own drones finished repairs to his hull, and he ordered them to help the others with the 3D printing work.

When Tara had a complete drone repair swarm, Jason recalled his own. They returned to the storage compartment in his leg and the panel sealed.

As the rest entered her leg compartment, she turned toward him. "Thanks, by the way. You're all right. For a machine."

"Sure thing," Jason said.

Tara leaped down. "Runt. Runt!"

The little one came running to her. But so did the other three. She proceeded to tell them their names repeatedly, in the same way owners did with their dogs.

Jason didn't pay much attention. He had leaped

down behind her, and was already starting out to the west.

She can catch up.

She knew where he was going after all.

He'd updated his map location based on the coordinates Tara had fed him. They only had about two hundred kilometers to Brussels.

In a few moments, she was at his side, with the Rex Wolves behind her. Their footfalls left imprints in the dusty surface, and made resounding thuds with each step.

"You like my war dogs?" Tara said.

His noise canceler muted the external thudding from their tread, so he could actually hear her.

"Not as much as their owner," Jason said.

"Really?" Tara asked.

"Uh, considering you're actually human, yeah" Jason said.

"I'm not human," Tara said. "Neither are you."

"That's not entirely true," Jason said. "Sure, my mind is trapped in a mech, but inside I'm human. Through and through."

"If you say so," Tara said.

"Seriously," Jason said. "What defines the human condition? Is it truly our exterior world? Or our rich inner world?"

Tara didn't answer for a few moments, and jogged quietly at his side. "When I awoke, I spent my first two days completely in VR. I couldn't face what I'd become. I set up my inner world all cozy and hoped to just forget about what happened to me. But on the second day, as I stared out across the virtual beach, something clicked inside of me. I realized that the inner world wasn't real. I realized that I wasn't going to give up. That I would fight. And so I became War Bitch, and ever since then, I haven't gone back to VR. Well, not until earlier, when we convened our little meeting."

"All right," Jason said. "But that's not even the inner world I was talking about. Because VR is just another manifestation of an exterior world. Sure, it might not be the 'real' one, but it's still just a world. The inner world I'm talking about extends beyond VR, beyond the real world. It exists independently of either. It holds our moral compass, our imagination, our hopes and dreams. That world is what makes us human, not VR, not this."

He and Tara were able to sustain a running velocity of forty kilometers per hour. They had a faster top speed of course, but going faster than forty was recommended, at least by the manual, only for short spurts: it was harder on the servomotors, not to mention the power cells. At forty kilometers per hour, when running in the sunlight, they were also able to keep their battery levels relatively constant. It dropped slowly, about one percent every ten minutes, or six percent an hour.

So at forty kilometers per hour, that meant they'd reach Brussels in five hours, with only a thirty percent decrease in battery power.

The big dogs were a different story, however. At first they were able to keep pace, but as the two and a half hour mark neared, the beasts showed signs of flagging.

Jason decided to call a halt.

He turned toward Tara. "Are they hungry?"

"You were never a pet owner, were you?" Tara asked.

"No," he admitted.

Tara regarded the animals, those big wolves with the heads of T-Rexes. "I'd say they're more tired than hungry. Which is a bit strange, considering their size. Creatures like these probably need to eat their body weight in meat at least once every few days. I'm going to run a detailed scan."

She held out a hand, and a beam of light erupted from her open palm. She ran it over the greenish fur of one of the creatures. Those photons would penetrate the atoms composing the fur, bounce off different identifying molecules inside it, and then return to the collector for analysis. It was completely safe to the subjects in question, of course.

"Interesting," Tara said. "This fur isn't composed of dead hair follicles, like you'd find in a human being. It's actually alive. And more like the leaves of a coniferous tree than anything else."

"What are you saying?" Jason asked.

"Chlorophyll," Tara said. "The greenish color is chlorophyll. These creatures are self-sustaining, at least to a degree. They still need to eat, but they can last for long bouts without any food… they can probably survive a week or longer between meals. Likely they hadn't even needed the mother's milk we gave them, or if they had, their requirement for drinking it lasted only a short period after birth."

"So the aliens spliced chlorophyll into their genes fifty years ago," Jason said.

Tara nodded. "A gene that carried down through the generations, showing up in all of their mutations since then."

While Jason waited for the dogs to recover, he surveyed his surroundings. The same bleak, slightly rocky terrain dominated. There were no buttresses here, but there were outcrops.

He and Tara had been following along what had once been the banks of a river, judging from the wide trench carved into the ground beside them.

"What's wrong?" Tara said, noticing his outward gaze.

"Nothing," Jason said. "Only... well, aren't there supposed to be little European towns dotting the countryside on the way to the bigger cities? A few farms and associated farmhouses? Maybe a winery? Instead, all we have is that same bleak, rock-sand terrain, just a constant around us. The alien micro machines and their bioweapons sure did a bang up job of transforming the landscape during the invasion."

"Sure," Tara said. "And the nukes and cluster bombs that the different military powers dropped in the region since then have finished the job."

"Sounds like you're not proud of your humanity," Jason said.

"Sometimes I'm not," Tara muttered.

"We're not to blame for what our forefathers did," Jason said. "You know that."

"That's true," Tara said. "But still, I'm glad I'm not completely human, not anymore."

"Yeah, you're only a war machine designed to inflict destruction, even better…" Jason said.

She didn't reply.

"Well, anyway, all of this makes me wonder how much of Brussels will even be standing," Jason said.

"Guess we'll find out," Tara said. She stood. "Looks like the dogs are rested. Even Runt is chomping at the bit."

Jason glanced at the Rex Wolves: they were rough-housing each other. Well, except for Runt, who was running in circles, chasing his own tail.

"Maybe chlorophyll DNA was a bad idea on the part of the aliens," Jason said. "It's like they're kids on a candy rush."

"Did you have kids?" Tara said.

"No," Jason replied.

"Then how would you know?" Tara took off at a run, and the four dogs followed. He shook his head, and released a burst of speed to catch up.

After only a couple of minutes on the run, the four Rex Wolves broke off, racing away to the north.

"Runt!" Tara said. "Bruiser! Lackey! Shaggy! Come back!"

"Let them go," Jason said.

"No." Tara swerved to the north.

With a sigh that carried over the comm, Jason followed.

In the distance, he spotted a herd of bright green… porcupines seemed the best term. They sat in place, lounging in the sun, obviously equipped with the same chlorophyll DNA as the Rex Wolves, though perhaps in greater abundance, given the needle-like spines that enveloped them.

The herd remained stationary only an instant after he sighted them: the giant green porcupines had become aware of the incoming Rex Wolves, and they got up as one, taking off at a run.

Bruiser began to bark loudly, and the four dogs picked up the pursuit, with Bruiser on point because of his speed, and Runt on drag.

There were two laggards among the porcupine herd, and the Rex Wolves homed in on them.

"Are you sure these dogs of yours were born in the last week?" Jason said while pursuing. "They behave nothing like puppies."

"They're not dogs, in case you haven't noticed," Tara said. "But you're right, I can't be sure."

"So maybe they haven't bonded you as a mother after all," Jason said.

"Maybe not," Tara agreed. "But they're willing to accept me as their master, and that's good enough."

The porcupine creatures were about the same size as the Rex Wolves; Jason lifted his right arm, and deployed his energy weapon, figuring he'd do the dogs a favor.

Tara reached across from where her mech was running beside him, and gently lowered his arm. "Let them subdue the prey on their own. They need to learn."

Jason lowered his energy weapon, and folded it away.

Bruiser leaped at the porcupine that was lagging the

most, and wrapped his salivating jaws around its thick body, pulling the creature to the ground. The porcupine struggled in place, but then Lackey came in and bit off the head. That ended its struggling.

Shaggy tackled the next lagging porcupine, clamping his jaws around the neck. The porcupine struggled for several moments, its life force slowly bleeding away.

Runt meanwhile hovered around Shaggy, yipping his moral support. The rest of the herd continued running away.

"If they have chlorophyll needles on their skin, why do they need blood?" Jason said as he watched the creature die.

"Obviously they have a cardiovascular system," Tara said.

"So essentially they're super evolved plants," Jason said.

"That's one way of looking at them," she agreed.

Eventually the animal that Shaggy had pinned to the ground ceased moving, and then the Rex Wolf released him. Shaggy oozed that acidic saliva onto the meat first to soften it up, and then dug in.

Bruiser and Lackey were already dining on the porcupine they'd taken down. The sharp needles dug into their faces and necks, but the animals didn't seem to notice or care. Apparently their gullets were resilient enough to handle the needles as well, because they swallowed entire sections of skin and muscle whole.

"Guess they were ready to move off of milk," Tara commented.

Runt hovered near Shaggy. The little guy was whining, but Shaggy ignored him, except for the occasional snap when Runt tried to get too close to the kill.

Finally Shaggy tore off a big chunk that was free of needles, and tossed it to Runt, who yipped happily and dug in. Runt growled at the meat, striking it with his paws as he dug in, as if he was mad at it.

"I love them," Tara said dreamily.

"You would." Jason walked away, not really in the mood to see peaceful creatures disemboweled and eaten. Still, it was the circle of life, he supposed.

A circle he was no longer part of.

I can never die.

He wasn't sure whether that was good or bad.

Actually, not true. I can die. If something out here gets to my AI core, I'm gone.

While he could no longer die of natural causes, he'd always have to be on the defense, especially in a land like this, where *unnatural* causes were the primary source of death.

When the animals had had their fill, Jason and Tara headed west once more. Before leaving, Tara scooped up some meat, and shoved it into her storage compartment.

"What are you doing?" Jason asked.

"Need this to properly train the dogs," Tara replied.

7

As they got closer to the city, the small party did eventually begin to pass the husks of farmhouses and the farms they were built upon. Oftentimes the walls were smashed in, the barns collapsed, no doubt thanks to the roving bands of bioweapons. Those farms gave way to villages whose buildings were made of plaster walls and tile roofs. Again, they were often husks, and there was no metal of any kind.

During the invasion, the alien micro machines had relied upon metal to reproduce, so things like antennae and window frames were completely stripped away in those regions where the machines had passed, but since most of the buildings were made of plaster and concrete, they survived. The micro machines had sometimes derived metal from the terrain, extracting iron ore from exposed rocks for example, but they had preferred the already processed metals found in human constructions, hence the complete plundering of anything metallic. And given what he saw around him, the aliens had certainly done a thorough job of ransacking the place.

There were a lot of abandoned rubber tires though, no doubt thanks to the vehicles that had once existed here. There was also a road, but it was hard to discern, given all the dust that had blown over it. Potholes marred its surface, and blast craters had carved away huge chunks of it.

The buildings became denser as the party moved west. They all seemed so small to him, almost like doghouses, thanks to his size. That was one of the problems with being a mech: your sense of proportions got all messed up.

There were lots of places for bioweapons to hide around them. Jason didn't want to spend time looking for those creatures, however—that wasn't his mandate. Occasionally the dogs ran off to pursue some scent or other, but they always promptly returned. One time, when the Rex Wolves came back the pack ran right past Jason and Tara, evidently afraid of whatever it was they'd encountered. Jason kept an eye to the north, wondering what the hell they'd stirred up, but thankfully nothing ever came that way.

Jason was the first to spot the city proper up ahead. He zoomed in while he ran, gazing over the rooftops of the intervening villages, and switching control of his feet over to autonomous sensors.

Like in the countryside, surprisingly many of the buildings were intact.

"Do you see it?" Tara said.

"Yes," Jason told her. "You think there are any humans hiding inside?"

"No," Tara said. "The residents would have been ground up by the machines and fed to the alien bioweapons, along with all other animals on the continent. And if any managed to survive the passage of the machines, the roaming packs of mutated bioweapons would have long ago finished them off. That, or the radiation."

"And now those mutants only feed on each other," Jason said.

"That's what it seems like," Tara said. "Those that don't live off the sun, anyway."

He reverted his zoom level, and continued toward the city.

In about ten minutes he had reached the outskirts, according to the map. The buildings here looked no different than those of the outlying villages—they were either one or two stories tall, sometimes three. The road was almost completely intact, and didn't have blast craters. But it still had a ton of potholes—that's what happened when the local government didn't maintain the roads for fifty years.

Jason halted, as did Tara. The dogs obediently did the same.

Jason glanced at Bruiser. The bioweapon was sitting on its hind legs, and its mouth was open, its tongue drooping as it panted.

"I wonder if these Rex Wolves would make good scouts?" Jason said.

"The kids aren't trained," Tara said. "But why don't

you send ahead one of your repair drones? Attach a camera to it, and we're good to go."

"Except I don't have a spare camera," Jason said. "You?"

"No, but the repair drones can print anything we have aboard our mechs..." Tara said. "Servomotors. Cameras..."

"Good point," Jason said. He checked the library of Teaching AIs, and found one that dealt with programing drones.

Gotta love having your mind stored inside an AI core.

"I'll be right back," Jason said. "Keep the kids occupied, will you?"

"I love how I've got you calling them kids now," Tara said.

Jason frowned. Or at least he would have, if he had lips.

He traveled into the street, passing between the two story apartment buildings. It was somewhat cramped: because of his size, it was almost like traveling through a corridor. The roofs beside him were covered in red brick tiles.

When he was far enough away from the dogs so that the drones wouldn't attract their attention, he pulled himself onto a single story building and sat down, letting his long legs dangle over the edge.

He activated the appropriate Teaching AI and the mad scientist avatar appeared. Jason opened up his drone repair panel, and, following along with the avatar's instructions, he installed the necessary blueprints into the flash memory of three drones. Any more than that, and they'd just get in each other's ways.

Then the drones got to work. He instructed them to take apart one of their own to use as materials for the camera and support equipment, since he had a lot of drones to spare.

In a few moments the machines had taken apart and melted down one of their own, and then used the raw material to begin printing up the camera, along with the necessary transmitter and receiver. When it was done, he installed the appropriate gear in his mech and the drone he had chosen to act as scout, and allowed the remaining drones to finish the connections.

In his local database, he had a selection of prepro-grammed scout firmwares to choose from. He reviewed the different documented features of each, and chose the one that seemed most suited to the job, titled Explorer. He flashed that program into the scout's ROM, and then activated the drone using the remote interface.

He was pleased when the camera feed appeared in the upper right of his vision. Via the remote interface, he had complete control over the scout—he could assume direct control and fly it personally if he wanted to, but he could also dispatch different commands with the help of his map, sort of like in a real time strategy game. He selected the Explorer on his map, and with his mind drew a quick spiral path out from his current position, and instructed the drone to follow it before returning.

As the scout buzzed into the air, he minimized the

video window, and placed it in the upper right of his display. He set the Explorer to alert him if any motion was detected.

He recalled his remaining drones to his leg compartment and sealed the panel.

"All right, we're good," Jason said.

Tara and the dogs joined him, and they continued into the city. They passed a chain grocery store. The front doors and windows were smashed in.

"You think there's any food for the dogs in there?" Tara asked.

"Doubt it," Jason said. "With their keen noses, they would have already been dashing inside if so. Anything of value would have been raided by the bioweapons years ago. Especially considering that the micro machines would have digested any cans, leaving behind the food."

"Oh well," Tara said.

Jason glanced at the sky. "It'll be night soon. We'll have to find a place to hole up before these Nightmares of yours begin roving the streets."

"I'm not sure if they'll actually come inside the city," Tara said. "But then again, I don't see why they wouldn't. There are lots of places for mutants to hide here. This is probably their prime hunting ground."

Jason halted, exasperated. "So you tell me this *now*, after we've already come all this way?"

"Don't get me wrong, I still think we'll be the safest here," Tara said. "They roam the countryside, too."

"I think I would have preferred a cave somewhere," Jason said.

"Sorry, big guy," Tara said. "All caves are already taken. Trust me, I've tried. Where do you think the Nightmares make their homes?"

"Oh," Jason said. "Okay."

The drone continued passing over the city, but didn't catch sight of anything that was moving. Of course, it probably helped that the buzz from the Explorer would have alerted any bioweapons on the ground well before passing overhead.

"Are you reading any available Internet hotspots?" Tara asked.

"No," Jason said. "If there are any landlines here, like you said, we'll have to visit a data center to find them."

"Too bad any routers we'd need to access them will have been dissolved by the micro machines," Tara said.

"We'll just print more, if we have to," Jason said.

"Oh yeah," Tara said. "I keep forgetting about the drones..."

"For a woman with a machine memory, you're awfully forgetful," Jason said.

"Hey, cut me some slack, I'm still getting used to being a machine," Tara said.

Jason paused at an intersection. "Okay, turn north here."

"Why?"

"Well, according to the map, there's a warehouse that way," Jason told her.

He thought it a little odd that the map data would be so accurate, containing detailed descriptions of all the buildings in the city, pre invasion. Then again, maybe it wasn't odd. The detailed data only reinforced the fact that the military had intended him to be on some sort of mission in the region, and they had wanted him to be prepared for it, whatever that mission might be.

"The warehouse is big enough to fit our mechs," Jason continued. "It'll be almost like a tent for us. There's enough room for the dogs, too."

"I kind of liked it better when you called them kids," Tara said.

"That was a mistake," Jason said. "Anyway, it should be as good a base of operations as any."

A few blocks later they reached the warehouse. The garage doors were gone—apparently they'd been made of metal. But the rest of the concrete structure remained intact.

There was more room in the street here so that Jason was able to lower himself to the ground easily enough. A good thing, because he had to low-crawl to fit through the garage entrance, but once he had pulled himself inside he was able to stand to his full height.

There were smashed wooden crates lining the floor. Metal racks had probably formed aisles across the warehouse in its heyday, but the micro machines would have eaten those away a long time ago.

"Well, looks cosy-ish," Tara said.

Bruiser, Lackey, Shaggy and Runt promptly chose spots for themselves amid the crushed wood, which they treated as bedding.

"The kids agree," Tara said.

"Sure," Jason said. He plunked himself down next

to the far wall, propping his back against the concrete so that he could gaze at the entrance. He recalled the Explorer, and set it to guard the front entrance. By then, evening had arrived, and the sky was slowly darkening. The inside of the warehouse was growing dim to match.

Tara sat down beside him. She slid her metal legs over his.

"Um, that's a bit within my personal space," Jason said.

"What?" Tara whined. "I need a footrest before I can fall asleep."

Jason forcefully shoved her off him. "I'm not that footrest."

"Hmph," Tara said. "I'm going to sleep. Care to visit my VR for a quick drink first?"

"I don't drink, remember?" Jason said.

"You're such a liar," Tara said.

"Believe what you want," Jason said.

"Have a coffee then," Tara said.

"I don't drink coffee," Jason said.

"A juice?" she pressed. "A water?" When Jason didn't answer, she sighed. "Good night."

"'Night," Jason told her.

Her head lowered slightly. That was the only external sign she'd gone offline.

According to the manual, the AI cores had a sleep mode that allowed critical systems to remain operational, while the consciousness subroutine switched to idle mode. Sleep mode provided the lowest draw on their batteries, and thus at night, when there was no sun to recharge them, it was the preferred mode of operation.

The manual also encouraged the use of that mode because the human mind was accustomed to hours of complete downtime, to allow memories to set, and whatnot. While Jason's AI core offloaded such tasks to background processes, and didn't technically need downtime per se, studies had shown that Mind Refurbs who slept regularly were generally happier and more content than their non-sleeping counterparts. Again, at least according to the manual.

With those thoughts on his mind, he activated his external monitoring systems, linking one of them to the Explorer, and initiated sleep mode.

8

J ason reactivated. The warehouse was completely dark around him, which meant he had been awakened early.

He switched to LIDAR, and white wireframes popped into existence, highlighting the walls and other objects around him.

There were no currently active proximity alerts, so he reviewed his logs.

The alert had been triggered by the Explorer, but the scout had inexplicably canceled it. There was no reason left in the logs. He studied the video feed, which had switched to night vision mode—the street and surrounding buildings were represented in different shades of green. He rewound the feed to the point where the alert had sounded, and saw a flash in the distance, above the rooftops.

Odd.

Jason tried to get up, but he was pinned.

Suppressing a sudden panic, he looked down and exhaled in relief.

While he was under, Tara had sneaked her feet back over his, using his thighs as a footrest.

He sighed, and picked her feet off him, setting them down on the floor beside him. She didn't wake up. Or maybe she had, but was pretending she hadn't.

Well, if she *was* still asleep, her motion sensors would promptly wake her when his next actions registered.

Jason hauled his heavy mech body upright and walked toward the entrance. He tried to plant his feet as quietly as possible, but it was difficult when you weighed as much as he did, and your feet were cast out of a metal and polycarbonate composite. If his motions didn't wake Tara, his footfalls would. The Rex Wolves were already stirring, in fact.

As he approached the far side of the warehouse, he noted that his sleep had been refreshingly deep, and free of dreams. He wondered if sleep was always like that, for a Mind Refurb.

He approached one of the open garage entrances, and crouched down to peer outside. He surveyed the wireframe representation of the street and surrounding buildings his LIDAR returned, which overlaid the dark shadows visible beneath the night sky. Everything seemed normal out there.

He heard a thudding behind him, and a moment later Tara crouched down beside him to peer through another garage exit.

"What is it?" Tara said.

"The Explorer picked up some flashes in the distance," Jason said. "I'm not seeing any sign of them now."

He waited for a few moments, and his gaze drifted to the stars overhead. The moon was out, shining in a dull crescent.

"I wondered if the stars and moon still existed," he said softly over the comm.

"Why wouldn't they?" Tara asked.

"I don't know," Jason said. "We don't know how long it's been before we were awakened, after all. Could be a few weeks. Could be hundreds of years. Maybe thousands."

"That's true," Tara said. "We've been talking like the invasion happened fifty years ago. Could have been a thousand."

"Or it could be fifty," Jason said. "That's the thing. We don't know."

"Well, I could have told you that the stars and moon still existed," Tara said. "But you never asked."

"I know," Jason said.

"I could tell you a lot of things…" Tara said.

Jason turned toward her, but saw only the outline of her faceless head on the LIDAR.

"Come to my VR tonight," Tara said.

"Why?" Jason said.

"I just want to talk," Tara said. "Face to face, with another human. Not these simulacrums I've generated to keep me company."

"I didn't know you had any…" Jason said.

"Oh, of course I do," Tara said. "I spent the whole

first day perfecting them. Sexy hunks, at my beck and call, ready to obey my every command. I kept them deactivated when you visited my VR."

"Maybe I should look into creating my own," Jason said. "The female versions, I mean," he quickly appended.

"Why, when you have all the female company you need at the moment?" Tara said.

"You're going to be at my beck and call, ready to obey my every command?" Jason said.

"Well, no, but—" Tara began.

"There you go," Jason finished for her.

He surveyed the area outside one last time, and was just about to turn around and go back to his bed of broken crates, when he spotted a flash above one of the rooftops.

"There it is again," Jason said.

"I saw it," Tara told him.

Jason sent his Explorer forward to scout, but since he had a better zoom level on his mech, plus LIDAR, whereas the scout only had night vision, he also scrambled outside, crawling through the opening, and then stood to his full height.

Tara joined him. He only had to take two steps, and he was next to the single story building across from the warehouse. He gazed into the distance, activating night vision mode to abet his LIDAR.

There was a region of raised land outside the city to the east. A valley of sorts that was devoid of buildings—none of the outlying towns and villages extended there. He wasn't sure if that valley had been present before the invasion, or if it was something the nukes had dug up, but it didn't really matter what created it.

"Do you see them?" Tara said.

"Who?" Jason said.

"There's a mech out there, staving off some Nightmares," Tara said.

Jason checked the Explorer's feed, but got nothing.

He returned his attention to his local cameras, and then he spotted... something. He zoomed in.

"I don't see the mech, but I see these Nightmares of yours," Jason said.

In the dim light from the moon, at first he thought the Nightmares were essentially jellyfish... he saw several bulbous shapes hovering in the air, with tentacles trailing down to the surface. But as he studied the creatures longer, he realized those tentacled bulbs were attached by thin stalks to the body of a bigger creature behind it. That creature was about twice the size of his own mech, and it stood on four, tree-like legs. It was from those legs that the stalks emerged.

He spotted smaller shapes caught up in those tentacles, and realized they fanned out all around the body; there were smaller mutants caught up in the web formed by those tentacles. Jason was reminded of a baleen whale straining plankton from the ocean, but in this case the prey were slightly larger than plankton, just as the predator was slightly larger than a whale.

A massive head bent down from the upper body to chew away one of the mutants that had been caught. That head was at the top of a wormlike neck, and there didn't appear to be any other features on the head, at least not as recorded by the LIDAR, except for a large toothy maw, which promptly swallowed the mutant it had torn from the tentacles.

He counted three of the Nightmares in total. At their feet, a herd of quadrupeds were howling away as they leaped at those legs in full assault; they didn't look like the Rex Wolves, but more like some kind of giraffes with octopus heads. Octoraffes.

"Why are they fighting?" Jason said. "Don't they know they're going to lose?" He watched Octoraffes get snagged by those tentacles surrounding the legs left and right. Some were able to break free, but most were not.

"The Nightmares have a nose for ferreting out mutants," Tara said. "I'm guessing the smaller creatures have a nest in the mountains, and these are the males assigned to protect the herd. The females and their litters will be deeper in the valley."

"Great," Jason said. "You know, since we're harboring a few mutants ourselves, eventually we'll attract their attention."

"Maybe," Tara said. "But that's why you've got the big guns, hey?"

A flash came from underneath the legs, and then a moment later the LIDAR silhouette of a mech emerged on the other side of the Nightmare. That mech was fending off the quadrupeds, while at the same time dodging the head of a Nightmare that kept striking down at it, trying to snatch it up.

The flash came again, and this time the mech flew skyward, toward the elevated torso at the top of those legs.

"Whoa, jumpjets," Jason said. "Nice."

"It's one of ours, I think," Tara said.

He ran an ID against the thermal profile of the mech, and the model number returned as Highlander.

"Looks that way," he told her.

"Should we help it out?" Tara said.

"Probably," Jason said. "Though if the pilot is anything like you were when first we met, our offer of help might not be taken kindly." He switched to an open band. "Unidentified mech, do you need assistance?"

No answer.

The Highlander had landed on the torso of the nightmare, behind the neck. The head was twisting back to strike the mech, but then a swarm of small shapes darted down from the sky, enveloping the head.

A loud bellow echoed across the plains.

Meanwhile, another Nightmare swept its head across the torso, hitting the Highlander, which was sent tumbling toward the ground. It released a jumpjet burst at the last moment to cushion its fall.

The surrounding mutants leaped on the mech.

"Well, guess we're going in," Jason said after a moment.

Bruiser growled beside him.

"Uh, maybe the kids should stay home," Jason said.

"Why?" Tara said. "I'm raising them to be war dogs. Come on Bruiser!"

She leaped over the building in the direction of the valley. The Rex Wolves followed her, barking eagerly.

Jason sighed, then pulled himself over the building and pursued. With the help of his map, he chose a path through the city that was interrupted only by single story buildings, allowing him to easily surmount any that got in his way.

In a few minutes he was leaving the city behind, for the rocky plains, and the valley.

He pulled ahead of Tara and the dogs, and as he neared the fighting, Octoraffes broke away from their doomed assault on the Nightmares to intercept his party. Now that he was closer, he had a better idea of their size: their bodies were a little smaller than that of his Vulture mech, but their necks allowed those octopus heads to reach right up to his own.

The two Octoraffes in the lead swerved directly toward him.

"Oh no you don't," Jason said. He swiveled the railgun and energy weapons into his arms. Then he lined up the crosshairs and opened fire, mowing down those Octoraffes.

He cleared the remaining mutants that blocked his path to the closest Nightmare, and then began hammering at the big creature's legs. His weapon caused big craters to form in the legs, and blood and gore gushed everywhere. But the Nightmare remained on its feet.

Meanwhile, Tara teleported to the torso of the huge beast, and stabbed her glowing sword into the base of its neck.

"Hey, no fair," Jason said. "Stealing my kills."

"They take more than that to kill!" Tara said.

As if to prove her point, the stricken Nightmare flicked its head around, and scooped her up in its jaws.

It crunched down, but she'd managed to orient her sword toward its palate, and the blade stabbed right through the upper part of its mouth, emerging on the surface.

The creature howled in pain, and flung her to the side; she went tumbling away, and her blade slid out.

She fired her grappling hook as she plunged toward the ground, and it impacted underneath the jaw. She drew the connecting chain inward, reeling herself in toward the neck. When she reached it, she struck once again.

Jason continued firing at those legs; the tentacled jellyfish sections had tightened together, drawing the Octoraffes they'd snagged all along their feet to act as shields. He simply raised his aim, and began taking chunks out of the creature's underside.

But then another of the Nightmares came at him, and its head impacted his torso, sending him hurling away. He struck the ground hard several meters away, and slid quite a ways before coming to a halt. He had a large dent in his chest assembly, as reported by his Damage Report screen.

"I got this one!" Tara said. "You help the Highlander!"

Jason scrambled upright. Octoraffes kept coming in at the three Nightmares, keeping them occupied. Tara seemed to have everything under control, at least with the current Nightmare she fought.

So he focused his attention on the Highlander's last known position. It wasn't there. He checked his over-head map: the Explorer was still traveling overhead, and it fed the positions of all friendlies and tangos directly to his overhead map. The Explorer had marked off the Highlander's latest position: he cast his glance that way, about two hundred meters into the valley, away from the main fighting, where another cluster of Octoraffes had gathered.

Well, gathered was perhaps too mild of a word. More like swarmed. If the Highlander was still there, then it was buried underneath at least twenty of the Octoraffes that were trying to get a piece of it. He couldn't see the actual mech, not with all those bioweapons piled on top of it.

The Rex Wolves were fighting along the periphery of that horde; they knew they wouldn't be able to take on the Nightmares, so they focused on what they could handle, instead.

As he watched, Bruiser tore into the neck of an Octoraffe, and pinned it to the ground. Lackey watched his back, and kept the other mutants at bay.

The pinned creature tried to wrap the tentacles from its head around the dog, but Bruiser ignored the suction cups that wrapped around his fur, and simply kept up the pressure. In moments, those tentacles flopped to the ground. Bruiser released him, and with Lackey at his side, picked out another foe.

Shaggy meanwhile bit into an Octoraffe that was bothering Runt, and scared it away. Then another Octoraffe plowed into them both, and all three wrestled on the ground.

For a moment Jason found himself rooting for the Octoraffes. He didn't really want the burden of protecting these mutants from the uninhabitable zone. He would have enough trouble taking care of himself as it was, he was sure. He hated taking care of animals, or dependents. It was why he'd never had any pets.

No, that's cruel thinking on my part. Besides, there's no litter to clean. And I could use the company. Tara's going to raise them, anyway.

Those thoughts passed through his head as he switched to Bullet Time and fired in turn at the different Octoraffes that had enveloped the Highlander's position. He used only his energy weapon, wanting to conserve his railgun ammunition. He kept an eye on his power levels, which were draining significantly, especially without the sun to recharge.

Before he could finish, a swarm of what could best be described as insects slammed into the Octoraffes, ripping several of them away. Those that remained had the flesh ripped from the upper halves of their bodies, revealing muscle and sometimes bone underneath.

The Highlander abruptly smashed through the weakened creatures.

Jason caught a glimpse of its body: the upper half was very much like his own, with a blocky head, arms, and torso, but the lower half was radically different: in place of legs, the hips were connected to a steel carapace, from which emerged eight jointed appendages. It was like a Centaur of sorts, except instead of a combination of a man and a horse, it was a man and a spider. Jumpjet nozzles poked out from everywhere underneath the carapace, which no doubt served as a massive fuel repository for all the propellant required for the mech to take flight.

And then the swarm of insects surrounded the mech, crawling all over the surface, forming a protective, spherical shell that enwrapped the midsection.

Jason realized those weren't insects, but micro machines.

More alien tech we've stolen for ourselves.

Two more Octoraffes attempted to leap onto the Highlander, but the micro machines lashed out, forming living spears that impaled each one. The spears retracted, breaking apart to return to their shell around the mech, and the mutants meanwhile dropped dead.

"I don't need your help," a female voice intoned over external speakers.

Here we go again…

"All right," Jason said, using his own speakers. He raised his hands. "You won't get it."

But then the huge head of a Nightmare bashed into the Highlander from the side, and the mech was sent flying from view.

The itsy bitsy spider…

His proximity alert sounded, and he narrowly dove to the side as one of those giant legs came down on him. The Nightmare's foot slammed into the ground, and several tentacles wrapped around him, hoisting him into the air. He tried to break free, but he was held fast.

Shit.

The other nearby Octoraffes scattered, along with the Rex Wolves. They knew a losing fight when they saw one.

That's loyalty for you.

"Hey Tara, baby, I could use some help here," Jason transmitted.

"Don't call me baby," Tara replied.

A loud shriek pierced the air, and beside him, one of the Nightmares hit the ground with a stentorian crash. He realized that the shriek hadn't come from that particular Nightmare, but the one that held him prisoner. The huge beast that had fallen wouldn't be shrieking ever again: Tara had managed to completely slice off its head.

The head of his captor came in on Jason, obviously intending to pluck him from the snare and into its mouth.

"Oh no you don't." Jason's railgun arm had enough mobility for him to aim it directly at that open maw, and he fired.

The head snapped backward, and issued a thunderous moan that was so loud his noise cancelers kicked in to stifle it.

He tried to lift the railgun higher for another shot, but the tentacles tightened around him, and he couldn't move the arm at all.

His right arm was little better: he could shift the aim of his energy weapon a little bit to the left and right, and that was it.

To the right...

The Nightmare's hind foot was behind him, and on his right. He just needed to line up the crosshairs...

He shifted his energy weapon as far to the right as he could, but wasn't able to get a bead. His machine memory told him that according to the manual, the muzzle had a free-floating mode that allowed him to adjust the aim a further ninety degrees independently of the direction of the weapon itself.

Nice.

He swiveled the muzzle another few degrees to the right, lining it up with the Nightmare's leg. Most of the snagged mutants were situated in the outer section to act as a shield, leaving the inner flanks exposed.

He unleashed several shots. He altered the aim each time, slowly directing the muzzle upward, so that it was like he was ripping a long, lengthwise wound up into the leg.

The entire limb split open, and the Nightmare roared in outrage.

And then collapsed to one side.

He was drawn upward as those legs swung outward, and then bounced as the upper body hit the ground, transmitting the force to the legs. He was bounced again when the legs hit the ground, and then he settled in place.

"Thanks for the distraction," Tara said, her Shadow Hawk running alongside. She promptly cut through the neck.

He glanced at the Nightmare. "You really like cutting off the heads of these things, don't you?"

"It's the fastest way to kill them," Tara said. "Besides, the neck was already partially severed, thanks to our Highlander friend."

"Yeah, that might be a misclassification," Jason said. "She should be called a Spider."

"Check your database," Tara said. "Highlanders look like Spiders."

"Oh." Jason turned toward the last Nightmare.

It was currently occupied by the Highlander, which had jetted onto its broad back. Micro machines had formed a large blade, and were attempting to saw through the neck while the head repeatedly flung backward, trying to knock the Highlander off. But the spider mech was agile, and either dodged to the side with its legs, or its jumpjets.

"Let's help her out," Tara said. She wrapped an arm around Jason.

"Wha—"

Before he could get the word out, Tara had fired her grappling hook. It struck the upper body near the dorsal section, and she reeled it in, drawing Jason and herself upward.

When they smashed into the flank, Tara released him, and Jason began to fall. He promptly punched his hand into the flesh of the beast, but it wasn't good enough to break the surface. It was like punching into elephant skin; but he was a machine, and not even the thickest skin in the world could stop him. He switched to Bullet Time, amped up the power output of his arm servomotors, and tried again.

This time his fist penetrated. He slammed his arms into the surface, pulling himself upward. When he was high enough, he used the holes he created as footholds.

In that manner he scaled the flank, and pulled himself onto the upper surface. Tara was already there.

He switched to normal time, and hurried to the forward section of the Nightmare's back.

Tara stabbed her blade into the neck next to the wounds created by the micro machines. Jason meanwhile fired his energy weapon beside that, and together, the three mechs finished severing the head in under two seconds. The Nightmare didn't even have time to bring its head in for another sweeping pass of its back before the neck fell away entirely.

As the creature began to fall sideways like a chopped-down tree, the Highlander jetted away, and the micro machine swarm followed her, wrapping around her body.

Tara meanwhile teleported to the ground.

That left Jason alone to ride out the crash.

"Uh, thanks for the lift?" Jason said.

He leaped away at the last moment before impact, and felt the shockwave along the ground. He stumbled forward, lost his balance, and ended up rolling into the rocky dirt.

He clambered to his feet, but the Highlander was already running out of the valley, and toward the city. Jason could see why: now that the Nightmares were handled, the whole herd of Octoraffes was coming out.

Bruiser, Lackey, Shaggy, and Runt were at the forefront of the herd; necks tucked in, ears held back, tails streaming out behind them, as they fled at their top speeds.

"Time to go!" Tara said.

9

J ason amped up his servos and leaped over a single story building in his path like a track and field athlete would leap a hurdle.

Up ahead, Tara led the way in her Shadow Hawk, while beyond her was the eight-legged Highlander. That mech moved from building to building with ease—it used its jumpjets whenever a distance was too far, or a wall too high.

Behind him, the Rex Wolves were hot on his heels, followed by the Octoraffes, which were quickly flowing into the city like a river that had burst its banks. The creatures leaped over the single story homes just as easily as Jason and the dogs.

"You'd think they'd thank us for saving them from the Nightmares, and for providing them with a month's supply of quality meat," Tara said. "But noooo, they have to get greedy."

"Maybe they can't help it," Jason said. "Maybe they chase anything that moves."

"Go ahead and stop moving then if you want to test your theory," Tara said.

"That's all right," Jason said.

He occasionally held his energy weapon over his shoulder as he ran, and squeezed the trigger. He switched the weapon to "smart targeting" mode, and the muzzle rotated to fire at the designated mutants. He'd marked the four Rex Wolves as friendlies, so the animals remained untouched. Even so, he tried to point his weapon away from the dogs, and he kept an eye on his overhead to confirm that the green dots of the big animals remained following behind him.

"We have to get her!" Tara said, swerving left to follow the Highlander.

"Why?" Jason said. "We should be heading to the tallest buildings. Find a defensible position."

"Well, that's what she's doing for one," Tara said. "But I want her, because we need to know what she knows. Maybe she can tell us what's going on in the world!"

"I somehow doubt that," Jason said. "She's probably just as in the dark as we are."

He heard a yelp behind him, and a glance at his rear view feed told him Runt had gone down. Shaggy had stopped to intercept the Octoraffe that had grabbed Runt. In seconds more would be on them.

Jason paused, and spun about to bring his energy cannon fully to bear. He jumped onto the rooftop of a nearby dwelling to get a better view, but unfortunately the roof couldn't take his weight, and he crashed inside.

Ah well.

He opened fire at the mutants that were racing toward Shaggy and Runt; he was doing his best to keep the creatures at bay.

Meanwhile Shaggy finished biting away the Octoraffe that had pinned his brother, and the two resumed their flight; Jason shot the Octoraffe as it got up to pursue, and exploded its tentacled head.

Bruiser and Lackey passed him, and he waited for Shaggy and Runt to reach him before he continued the flight. He kept firing at the incoming mutants the whole time.

The Explorer mirrored his movements from above, keeping track of the enemy. They were slowly closing. They would have already overwhelmed his position if he hadn't been firing.

A dark smear abruptly swept across the night, passing over the pursuing creatures. Several of them howled, others were knocked into the air.

It was the micro machines.

Jason ran faster. He didn't want those machines to mistake him for an enemy.

He scooped up Shaggy in one arm, and Runt the other.

Up ahead, Tara had done the same with Bruiser and Lackey.

Past her, the Highlander had fired its jumpjets to land halfway up a tall skyscraper in the downtown core: the mech was using its eight legs to climb the rest of the way, with the tips latching onto the concrete, or using the adjacent empty window frames for support. All metal in that building would have been stripped away, no doubt making it dangerously unstable. Then again, it had been standing since the invasion, so it should be able to hold the Highlander's added weight. And the weight of Tara and Jason.

Tara reached the edge of an adjacent building, which was taller, and teleported to the rooftop with her two charges.

"Whoa, what's the range on your teleporter?" Jason transmitted.

"The top of this building is at the very limit at the moment," Tara responded. "I can go a little farther when I'm not carrying dogs with me."

She materialized in front of him, and held out her arms. Jason tossed her Shaggy and Runt as he rushed toward her.

She grabbed them out of the air and disappeared once more—according to the map, she was back on the rooftop.

"What about me?" Jason said as he continued toward her building.

"Not enough power," Tara transmitted. "You're on your own, sorry Hun."

"Ah, shit."

Jason amped up his servos and took a running leap at the building. He slammed into the surface several stories up, causing pieces of concrete to break away and plunge down to the street. He began climbing. There were open windows on either side of the edge he'd landed on, and he used them for purchase, making good progress.

Unfortunately, those same open windows provided the Octoraffes with the perfect hand and footholds. They flowed onto the four faces of the building and began to pursue. He saw it all on the overhead map, which was continually updated by the Explorer.

He paused every few meters to fire at the climbers within his line of sight. Usually he could take out two or three with one shot: the stricken Octoraffe would release the building, and then plunge into the others below, ripping some of them off before bouncing away.

In that way, he continued climbing the southeast corner, keeping the south and east faces clear.

"You might want to watch the northwest corner," he transmitted to Tara.

"On it," Tara said.

He glanced at the overhead map, and saw her move to the northwestern corner. The red dots climbing the building on the two adjacent faces began to drop away. She had a laser in her right arm, and apparently was putting it to good use.

The Highlander was also doing a good job of keeping the Octoraffes at bay on the other building: she'd reached the rooftop, and had her micro machines swirling constantly around the upper half, hamstringing the mutants so that they released the walls, plunging to their deaths.

Jason finally reached the top, and maintained his position on the southeast corner, which gave him a good line of sight on the creatures below. He had to quit using his energy cannon, however, since the power drain was too great, and switched instead to his laser, and used it sparingly. He interspersed his shots with slugs from his railgun; when he exhausted its ammo, he slammed his fist several times into a section of the rooftop, crushing it, and slid the chunks of concrete into the ammo-processing compartment in his left bicep.

Meanwhile, the Rex Wolves watched snarling from the edges. They were ready to swat at any mutants that got too close.

All that added weight was beginning to take a toll on the old building. Concrete clumps began to break away underneath the Octoraffes, from the windows they used for purchase. The damage began to accelerate, particularly on the western face, until that entire side began to slide, forming an avalanche of debris that crushed the mutants on that flank.

The building tipped to the west.

"Hang on!" Jason said.

"Get the kids!" Tara said.

Jason wrapped his arms around Runt and Shaggy, while Tara scooped up Bruiser and Lackey.

The building was tipping directly toward the one harboring the Highlander. Because their building was taller than the other skyscraper, the rooftop edge would land only a few stories below its top level.

Jason retreated to the farthest edge with Tara, and as the building came in to impact, he took a running leap up off of it, and arced toward the other rooftop.

He landed, and used Bullet Time to safely release

the two dogs, and land with the least possible damage to his body. He restored to normal time and stood up.

Tara had landed beside him. She'd also released her Rex Wolves, so that all four stood between their mechs, and the Highlander.

The latter turned toward them.

From the side of the building, a large swarm of micro machines swooped upward into the air, and stabbed down like a big knife toward the dogs.

"No!" Tara dashed forward, positioning herself in front of the dogs. "Don't! They're with us!"

That knife formed of micro machines halted at the last possible moment, its sharp tip hovering over Tara's chest assembly, right where her AI core was located.

Tara swept her sparking sword out in front of her, slicing the big knife in half, and causing the constituent micro machines to scatter. Then she spun on the mech. Beside her, Bruiser and Lackey were growling wildly at the Highlander.

"Don't fight us!" Tara said. "We have to work together if we want to win this."

Jason came forward. "She's right," he said in the most authoritative voice he could muster. "If we don't team up, those creatures will overwhelm us."

The Highlander said nothing, but then turned her attention to the edges of the rooftop. Because of the unintended distraction Jason and Tara had provided, some of the Octoraffes had reached the top, and were beginning to clamber onto the roof.

Jason's power levels were so low now that he didn't dare fire either his laser or his energy weapon. Instead, he simply bashed in the heads of any creatures that clambered onto his section of roof, and that seemed to work well enough.

Tara was doing the same on her side, joined by the Rex Wolves. The Highlander meanwhile handled the rest of the Octoraffes.

In another five or so minutes, the mutated bioweapons finally gave up. They retreated from the base of the building, and flowed across the streets toward their distant valley.

Jason watched them go. "Well that was fun."

The micro machines gathered on the rooftop, and then swarmed around the Highlander's torso, forming a sphere around it and above the carapace.

"Now, you're going to answer some questions," Tara said to the Highlander via her external speakers.

But the mech turned to go.

"Hey!" Tara said. "I'm talking to you."

The Highlander ignored her, and crawled to the building edge on her eight legs.

"Fine, we'll do this the hard way," Tara said.

She pointed her right arm at the Highlander and released the harpoon.

A convex half circle flashed into existence a meter in front of the Highlander, and the harpoon bounced off harmlessly. The mech had activated an energy shield.

The Highlander cocked its head, then glanced askance at Tara.

"Uh, I think you made her mad..." Jason told Tara.

All of a sudden those micro machines swarmed outward off of the body. Jason's power levels were too low to use Bullet Time, so before he could react, hundreds of them had wrapped his torso, binding his arms to his sides. He attempted to break free, but the micro machines had knit themselves together quite well, and he couldn't budge. They also fastened his feet together, so he could do little more than hop in place.

Tara fared little better, and the Rex Wolves were similarly bound up, though they were hogtied, with three of their four limbs secured.

"I told you to leave me alone," the Highlander said in that haughty female voice. "But you wouldn't listen. You wouldn't take no for an answer."

10

J ason could do nothing as the mech paced imperiously in front of her prisoners.

"The question is, what do I do with you now?" the Highlander said. "If I free you from these binds, do you swear to leave me alone? Or will you force me to destroy you?"

"We'll leave you alone," Jason said quickly.

"Hm," the Highlander said. "I'm not sure I believe you. That was a little quick."

"We just want a few answers," Tara said.

"Answers…" the Highlander said.

"What are you doing here?" Jason said. "What are any of us doing here?"

"You mean you don't know?" the Highlander said.

"No," Jason said. "The last we remember, we just had brain scans taken, then we woke up here. No training. No mission introduction. No nothing."

"You're lying," the Highlander said. "You were sent to hunt me. Admit it."

"He's telling the truth," Tara said. "We have no idea why we're here. And no idea who you are."

The Highlander's head angled back and forth, as if the virtual pilot was shaking her head. "I can't tell if you're lying or not. I'm going to have to bring you into VR. I need to see your faces."

"We can transmit our faces," Tara said. "There's an avatar transmission mode, I think…"

"No," the Highlander said. "It has to be in VR. Mine. I want complete control. If you agree to this, I'll consider letting you go."

Jason received a message.

The Highlander unit has requested full access to your VR interface. Do you accept? (Y/N)

That meant he would be completely in her power, and would have no control of his avatar whatsoever. He glanced at Tara, but she didn't return his gaze. He looked at his HUD. Her indicator had turned yellow, meaning she was in sleep mode. Or in VR.

He took a gulp, and accepted the request.

JASON WAS CLAD IN A LOINCLOTH. He was on his knees, being dragged across a tiled floor by two strongmen. They wore a loincloth like Jason, but the difference was they had thick sandals to protect their feet.

Jason flinched every time his knees struck a gap between tiles, as it sent pain coursing up into his body.

He tried to bring up his HUD to dial down his pain settings, but it wouldn't come up.

Yup, I'm in her complete control.

He was being carried underneath a colonnade of some kind. To his left resided a sandstone wall, carved with hieroglyphics. To his right, a small pond resided at the center of a courtyard. There were flamingos wading in the water. Several cats lounged on the turf beside the pond. Beyond it, he could see an immense ancient city, replete with amphitheaters, parliament buildings, and residences. There were three pyramids in the distance.

"Great," Jason said. "We've got ourselves an Ancient Egypt aficionado."

The strongmen ignored him.

Ahead of him, he spotted two more strongmen carrying another prisoner between them. It was Tara. She was dressed just as skimpily as he was, with a loincloth wrapped around her hips, and a thin tube of dark fabric wrapped around her breasts.

The strongmen carried the two prisoners toward each other. There was an intersection up ahead, which seemed to be their destination.

"What trouble have you gotten us into now?" Tara said as they reached the intersection.

"*Me?*" Jason said. "This wasn't my fault!"

The strongmen turned into the intersection and carried them into the hallway beyond.

"I thought you weren't going to accept," Tara said. "You were supposed to break free while I distracted her in here."

"*Now* you tell me," Jason said. "Wait a second.

That's not even a plan. She would have stayed in the real world until I accepted, too."

Tara shrugged, though it was little more than a jerk, thanks to her captors.

The hallway opened up into a throne room of sorts. It was partially open to the outdoors, with a vaulted roof overhead, supported by pillars on all sides, sort of like a big gazebo.

A carpet filled with intricate designs led to a small dais, reached by steps. A woman lay there on a chaise lounge, reclining on various pillows, her back propped against the ivory-veneered backrest, an arm draped over the intricately carved wooden armrest, and her legs stretched across the daybed portion. Her other arm rested on a bent knee in a posture that Jason thought was meant to exude not only relaxation, but sensuality.

She was dressed in a fringed bikini, with thin tassels of black thread hanging from both the top and bottom portions. The faint outline of abdominal muscles rippled across her flat belly with each breath. She wore a mask, also fringed, that hung down over the bridge of her nose to conceal most of her face, revealing only her forehead and her eyes, which were painted with kohl to look catlike.

A nearby servant in a loincloth waved a large frond up and down, cooling her. The tassels of her mask shivered beneath the induced breeze.

"You gotta be kidding me," Jason said.

Beside the lounging woman, a shirtless man in knee-high boots stepped forward. He wore an ancient Egyptian headdress, striped blue and gold; the voluminous cloth hung liberally from either side of his face, giving him the appearance of a hooded cobra. A painful-looking whip hung from his hips.

"Bow before Cleopatra!" the man said.

The strongmen released Jason and Tara, who were still on their knees.

"Cleopatra?" Jason said, unable to keep the smile from his lips.

"Bow!" the man said.

The strongmen forced Jason and Tara forward so that they were completely prostrate.

He held that pose for a few seconds. A glance at Tara told him that she was just as uncomfortable.

He glanced up, toward this "Cleopatra."

"Uh," Jason said.

"You may rise," Cleopatra said. "But remain on your knees."

Jason did so, as did Tara beside him.

Cleopatra sat upright, then stood.

She took the steps on the dais down to him, then she ran a hand across his chest.

"That'll be five credits," Jason said.

She snorted, and withdrew her hand. "Cute." She stepped back a pace. "So you say you didn't come here to kill me?"

"No, of course not," Jason said. "Why would I do that?"

"Then what are you doing here?" Cleopatra asked. The tassels hanging underneath her mask blew out slightly as she spoke.

"Like we said already, we have no idea," Jason said.

"We had our scans done, then woke up in the uninhabited zone. I've only been active for a day now."

"And who's she?" she nodded toward Tara.

"Just some random chick I picked up," Jason said.

"Thanks…" Tara said.

Jason shrugged. "It's true." He kept his gaze on Cleopatra. "She only woke up a few days ago. We're just trying to stay alive at the moment."

"And what about those…" She curled her nose. "*Dogs*. How did you acquire them?"

"Just some pets we befriended along the way," Tara said.

Cleopatra glanced at Tara, and her eyes narrowed in suspicion. "One does not simply *befriend* the bioweapons in this place."

"Well, we did just that," Jason said. "I guess it helps that we killed the rest of their pack."

"You killed their pack," Cleopatra said, sounding doubtful. "And they became your friends."

"Yeah I know, it's messed up," Jason said. "But I guess they figured, they didn't have a family anymore, and we treated them nice enough, so they might as well go with us."

Cleopatra retreated to her dais, and sat back down. "I've been monitoring your cardiopulmonary subroutines. Your heartbeat and respiration. Your sweat levels. All of these are simulated down to the gland level. I've made sure that you couldn't turn off these subroutines, nor your emotions. I've also been watching your faces for micro expressions, and similarly insured that you couldn't disable these tells. I see no signs that you're lying."

"All right then," Jason said. He tried to stand, but the strongman beside him forced him back down.

She took off her mask, revealing an exquisitely carved jaw, high cheekbones, and unblemished skin. Combined with that toned body, she was about as perfect as a woman could get.

She looked at him expectantly.

"I'm Sophie," she said. "This is how I look in real life. My avatar is completely unmodified."

"All right, great, you're beautiful," Jason said. "Can we go now?"

She frowned. She gave Tara a confused look, one that quickly turned into a scowl.

When she returned her attention to him, she'd managed to smooth out her features again.

"I want to join you," Sophie said. "I, too, awakened only a week ago. I've been struggling for answers. The two of you are the closest I've come to these answers. The closest to human companionship..." She waved a hand at the servants around her. "These simulacrums look great on the outside, but they have very little depth." She glanced toward the man in the Egyptian headdress behind her. "Jeeves, tell me the meaning of life?"

"To pulverize your enemies, turn their offspring into slaves, and add their women to your harem!" the man said.

"See what I mean?" Sophie told Jason. She glanced

at the man. "It should be, add their men to my harem. *Men*."

"Men," Jeeves corrected.

"Who names their Egyptian servant Jeeves?" Tara said.

Sophie shrugged. "He's essentially a glorified butler. I called him Jeeves when I first materialized him, back when I was still constructing my VR. Did you know there's a complete world builder in the toolset? You can find it under the modifications tab."

Jason had noticed that tab, but he hadn't had much time to play around with it yet.

"Anyway," Sophie continued. "I had created a traditional butler dressed in a suit, serving me in my palatial home. I was the Queen of England then, circa twenty-first century. But I soon grew bored. And I always loved cats, so I figured, what cultures in history loved cats as much as I do? And then I realized it…!"

"So we have our princess figure," Tara said. "Let me guess, you were a secretary of some kind in real life."

"Hardly," Sophie said. "There are no more jobs for secretaries, you know that. Most people do their business remotely these days, and the few secretaries left are androids. No, I was a model of course."

She said the later snootily, raising her chin slightly.

"And we're supposed to be impressed?" Jason said. "Because you put on clothes designed by other people, and got paid a few credits to let people take pictures of you?"

"Well, I wasn't really that kind of model…" Sophie said.

"Oh?"

"Yes, I was a social media model," Sophie said. "You know, I get paid for making holographic videos starring *moi*, and sponsored products. Great supplement to my allowance."

"Ah," Jason said. "That's not really a model at all then. Sounds really bad, actually."

Sophie's face darkened. "Yeah okay, maybe. But I could have been a great model. I mean look at me." She indicated her body. "And then I had to go and throw it all away by scanning my mind for a few quick bucks."

"Wait, you said allowance a few seconds ago," Jason said. "You mean from your parents. How old are you?"

"Twenty-five," Sophie said.

"And you're still getting an *allowance?*" Jason said. "Shouldn't you be eligible for Basic Pay or something?"

She shook her head. "My parents are rich. I'm not eligible."

"Well that would explain the PES," Tara said.

"PES?" Sophie said.

"Yeah," Tara told her. "Princess Entitlement Syndrome."

"I don't have PES!" Sophie said.

"Of course you don't," Tara said. "That's because I made it up. But you've certainly got a princess level of entitlement going for you."

Sophie regarded her coolly. "You know you're in my complete power here, right? I can do whatever I want. Torture you, even. And you'd feel every ounce of pain."

"Go ahead…" Tara dared.

"Okay then," Jason said, standing. This time when

one of the strongmen tried to force him down, Jason sidestepped and tripped the man. The other strongman took a step toward him, but Sophie raised a hand and the big man stopped.

"Our mech bodies are still waiting out in the real word, in case you forgot…" Jason said.

Sophie shrugged. "What's the hurry? I have monitors running in the background. I'll be alerted if anything moves out there, or you two try to get away."

"You can join us," Jason said.

Sophie's face lit up. Then she clapped her hands. The VR background turned completely white, and all the simulated characters vanished.

"Thank you," Sophie said.

Jason was relieved when his VR HUD appeared. He logged out as fast as he could, before she could change her mind.

He appeared in the real world once more, where he was still bound on the rooftop by micro machines in the dark of night. The city seemed quiet around them. The Rex Wolves lowed miserably beside him now and then.

The micro machines abruptly released him and the others, swarming back to the Highlander mech, wrapping around its torso and rear carapace, forming a rippling sphere.

He glanced at Tara, and she was free, too. As usual, he was amazed at how different they all looked as compared to their avatars. It was a bit jarring. But that's what happened when you put human minds into deadly killing machines, he supposed.

The Rex Wolves had also been released, and the four of them tensed, unsure what was going to happen.

Jason patted Shaggy on the head. "It's okay, boy. She's with us, now."

Tara similarly calmed Bruiser and Lackey.

"By the way, there's something I've been wondering…" Jason told Sophie. "Why didn't you use your energy shield earlier than you did?"

"I did use it, but the mutants wore it down," Sophie said. "When the shield recharged, I used it again."

"Your battery levels must be just as low as our own by now," Jason said.

"Not as low, I think," Sophie said. "I don't have laser or energy weapons to worry about." She indicated her micro machines.

"Good point." Jason wondered where those machines got their power in turn, but that was a question for another time.

The building shook slightly.

"Okay, we can't stay here," Jason said. "Not after the other building kind of smashed into this one." He glanced at the Highlander. "You've been here a bit longer than we have. You have a base of some kind in the city, I assume?"

"No," Sophie said. "I only just arrived in the area. I don't usually travel at night—too many roving bands of mutant bioweapons—but the city was close, so I thought I'd make a run for it. That was a mistake, as you saw. Then again, it was also good, because I met you."

"And me," Tara said.

"That was implied," Sophie said.

"So no base," Jason said. "Well, we have a warehouse we found, but I'd rather not hit the street at the moment. Both of you have hinted that the mutants prefer hunting at this hour, and I've had my fill of fighting. I need to recharge my batteries. Literally."

The rooftop shook again slightly.

Jason glanced at his overhead map, and his Explorer confirmed that there were no more tangos in the immediate area, at least none that were out in the open. He picked out a building, and ran a quick calculation using the trigonometric functions built into his AI core.

"There's a building just to the north," Jason said. "Four stories tall. It's an apartment building of some kind. I'm highlighting it on the map, if you feel so inclined to accept my shared data." He flicked the "share map data" icon toward their names on his HUD, and they promptly accepted. "Should be out of the path of these two buildings when they fall. It can easily hold all of us. Tara, can you teleport us down there one by one?"

"Battery's too low at the moment," Tara said.

"Sophie, do you have enough fuel to carry us down individually?" Jason said.

"No," Sophie said. "Only enough for myself."

"All right, we'll meet you there," Jason said. "Guess we'll have to hit the street after all, but only for a few moments." He glanced at Runt and Shaggy. "Come on, dogs, this way." Jason leaped off the eastern side of the rooftop, and fell the few stories to the building that had collapsed onto it. He was a little worried that the exterior would break away, or that the building would shift, but it held him. The slope was thirty-five degrees, allowing him to easily hurry down near the edge. He had to take care not to step into any of the window frames.

He glanced in his rear view display and confirmed that Tara and the dogs were racing along behind him, similarly balanced close to the edge and avoiding the open windows. Those dogs sure had great night vision.

Meanwhile, the characteristic glow of Sophie's jumpjets filled the air as she arced down toward the target building.

Jason reached the streets and leaped off the sloped building, landing with a loud thud. He hurried to the north, and another thud followed by four soft padding sounds told him that Tara and the Rex Wolves had landed.

He thought the collapse of those two towers was imminent, because of the shaking he'd felt, but the two buildings remained standing while he hurried across the street.

He reached the apartment building, and waited for Tara and the Rex Wolves. He was still covered in Octoraffe blood, so he walked over to Runt. "Hey boy." The animal panted happily in his direction.

Jason began smearing his body against the animal's fur.

"What are you doing?" Tara asked.

"Wiping off the blood," Jason said.

"On his fur?" Tara said. "Stop that!"

Jason ignored her. "I need to clear up my solar panels."

"Yeah, but what about his fur!" Tara said. "It has chlorophyll! The blood will block it!"

Jason stepped back. Runt was already licking the spots where Jason had rubbed him. "He's licking it off."

Tara dragged Runt away, so Jason went to Bruiser next and hoisted the animal up to give a big hug. He moved the big Wolf in a rubbing motion, and the animal growled at him.

He set Bruiser down and then rubbed his back against the animal, but it backed away indignantly.

"Jason!" Tara said, moving in front of Bruiser protectively.

"All right all right, I'm done," Jason said.

He pulled himself onto a single story building beside it, then hauled himself onto the apartment building proper—it required jumping up and grabbing onto the rooftop edge, and then hauling himself over.

Sophie was waiting for him. Jason turned around, and gave Tara a hand, then similarly helped the dogs up —they leaped into his arms one by one; even Runt was able to reach him. When that was done, he recalled the Explorer, because the scout's power cells would deplete soon, and needed to be charged in daylight. He set it down on the edge of the rooftop.

With Tara's help, he coaxed the different wolves to assume guard positions on each of the four corners, and he did the same along with the other two mechs. The party would have formed quite a sight to any onlookers, he was sure.

Down the street, *still* the two buildings remained standing.

"You two might as well sleep," Jason said. "I'll keep watch tonight."

"Wake me for second watch," Tara said.

"No," Jason said. "I'll watch all night."

"You're not going to sleep?" Tara asked.

"Nope," Jason said. "I'm a machine. I don't have to sleep."

"In the manual, it says—"

"I know what it says," Jason said. "I'll forgo sleep tonight."

"You'll drain your batteries…" Sophie said.

"I have just enough to last until morning if I keep very still," Jason said. "Now sleep, both of you."

The two of them deployed their repair swarms, and then remained motionless as the small drones worked.

He glanced at his HUD, and saw their indicators turn yellow, indicating that their consciousness subroutines were idling.

He gazed out into the dark. He wasn't sure how much use he would be if an attack came, given his current energy levels. He probably didn't need to keep watch either, given the scout, and the monitoring subroutines he had set up that would alert him to any motion in the streets.

But he wanted to exist fully in the moment tonight. He felt a weariness that sleep wouldn't eliminate. Besides, he wanted to *think*.

He deployed his repair drones, and the units repaired the damage to his hull that had occurred during the last fight. They finished up with plenty of energy to spare; when they returned to the storage compartment and connected to the charge ports, he tapped into their batteries to replenish his own. His power level went up by five percent. It wasn't much, but it would help if there was an attack of any kind. In the morning, while he recharged, the drones would, too.

So he sat there for the rest of that night, pondering the predicament he was in, and wondering what he was going to do about it. He decided that they'd have to shore up the warehouse, and make it more defensible. Or they could set up shop in the city's subway system maybe, and convert that into an underground base. Yes, that seemed the better strategy, given their current situation. He could pulverize the concrete walls from nearby buildings, print up Jersey barriers and other fortifications, and place them strategically underground. There might even be iron ore underneath those subway tunnels.

He planned out everything, and made detailed notes to share with the girls in the morning.

During that time, he occasionally paused to gaze out at the city using his night vision. He often focused on the "n" shape formed by the skyscraper and the tower that had smashed into it, and wondered when the pair would fall. Near morning, both buildings finally collapsed.

When the sun finally rose, he had a good idea of what he and the girls needed to do in the short term.

Girls. He had to laugh at that. He glanced at their outlines in the dark, and could see the silhouettes of their wicked weapons. These "girls" could give a small army a run for the money.

By then, most of the blood that had remained on his hull after rubbing himself against the dogs had dried and peeled off. So as the rays of sunlight hit his hull, his power levels began to increase.

All is good again in the world.

11

W hen the girls awakened, Jason told them
his plans.

"We're going to stay in this city," Jason said. "And
hole up in the subway system, at least until a retrieval
team comes for us."

"What then?" Sophie said. It was still hard to get
used to hearing that sensual voice coming from the
spider mech. No different than Tara's voice from the
other war machine, he supposed. "Are we to give up our
freedom, and let the military take us back?"

"I haven't decided yet," Jason said. "If anything,
once we build a secure Base of Operations, at least we
give ourselves the option of successfully fighting back."

"Unless they decide to nuke us," Tara said.

"That's why we're going to turn the subway system
into an impenetrable bunker," Jason said.

"First of all, our mechs are too big to fit in the

subway system," Sophie said. "Second of all, ever heard of bunker busters?"

"We're obviously going to have to 3D print a few drills," Jason said. "To enlarge the subway. And second of all, we'll have to reinforce it against bunker buster attacks."

"It's not going to be easy," Sophie said.

"No," Jason said. "I did some quick sketches. Here, take a look."

He hit the transmit button on his HUD.

"These are pretty basic," Sophie said. "I guess I was expecting architectural diagrams."

"We've got a whole database of human knowledge in our AI cores," Jason said. "I read through a basic course in architecture last night, which helped me make that sketch. Once I get charged up, I plan to switch to Bullet Time and do some extensive reading. Feel free to help me out."

"I think our first order of business should be to look for an Internet connection," Tara said. "So we can find out what's going on."

"Sure," Jason said. "But we're going to need a base of some kind if we plan to stay here. That warehouse we stayed in last night has too many vulnerabilities. And staying on top of this apartment won't cut it either. You saw how easily those mutants were able to scale the walls of a tower ten times as tall. We need something with a choke point. The subway system will give it to us. I thought, given your military background, you'd understand that."

"You were in the military?" Sophie asked Tara. Her voice sounded mocking.

"Yeah," Tara said. "What's it to you."

"Oh, nothing," Sophie said. "You got to play with boys and their toys. I'm almost a bit jealous."

"You might want to adjust your sarcasm settings," Tara said. "You got them dialed way up."

"That was intentional, Missy," Sophie said.

"Don't call me Missy, fucker," Tara said.

"Touchy," Sophie said.

Tara started to turn away, but then Sophie had to go and say it again: "Missy."

And then, just like that, Tara hurled herself on Sophie. She kept her weapons retracted, but pounded away at her carapace with her fists.

The Rex Wolves surrounded the pair, barking in encouragement. Jason kept expecting the rooftop to collapse from all that weight being thrown around, but so far it held. The wideness of the building gave them a lot of room to fight.

Sophie formed a hand with her micro machines and casually plucked Tara off her back.

The dogs were barking wildly and growling angrily now, and Jason was worried they were going to get involved. He tried to put himself in front of them, and he grabbed Bruiser by the neck to physically restrain the big animal when he thought it was going to jump them.

Sophie glanced at the dogs, and then back to Tara. "Is that all you got?"

The micro machines had left her arms free—Jason

thought that was purposeful on Sophie's part. She was testing the woman.

Tara rotated her laser turret into her right hand and aimed it at Sophie's AI core. She also engaged her sword in the other arm, and electricity hummed up and down its length. She pointed it at the AI core as well, with her arm held back at a ninety-degree strike angle.

"Stand down!" Jason said. He released Bruiser and stepped forward.

Tara didn't move.

Jason stepped in front of the turret and sword, shielding Sophie with his own body. "I said, *stand down!*"

"Tell her to let go of me with her little insects first," Tara said.

Jason glanced over his shoulder at Sophie's spider mech.

"*Insects?*" Sophie said. "How dare you call my advanced micro machines *insects*."

Jason sighed and threw up his arms. "Actually, you know what? Go ahead. Have at it."

He turned his back and walked away from them. Even the dogs seemed confused, because they stopped barking.

He walked toward the building edge and leaped off. He landed the four stories to the ground with a loud thud, but he surreptitiously activated the Explorer and rotated it so that he had Tara and Sophie in view.

They were still on the comm line, so he could hear them.

"I think you pissed off your boyfriend," Sophie said.

"He's not my boyfriend," Tara said.

"Oh he's not?" Sophie said. She sounded pleased. "Goodie."

"Actually I take that back, he is," Tara said quickly.

"I'm not," Jason said over the line.

"Damn it," Tara said.

On the Explorer's camera feed, he watched as Tara lowered her arms and retracted her weapons.

"That's a good little bitch," Sophie said.

"Enough with the name calling!" Tara said.

For a moment Jason thought she was going to activate her weapons again, but she kept her arms down.

Sophie cocked her head slightly. "You know, I liked you better in VR. Are you sure you don't want to give me full access again?"

"When hell freezes over," Tara said.

Sophie shrugged her metal shoulders and then recalled the micro machines. They swathed her midsection, and the carapace.

Now free once again, Tara began stalking away. She called the dogs, which had begun growling at Sophie's mech once more.

"Wretched things," Sophie commented.

Tara deployed the laser into her right hand and held her arm behind her back, firing off a shot anyway.

It struck Sophie's energy shield, and was absorbed harmlessly.

Sophie giggled. "She's so cute when she's angry."

"Shut it, Princess," Tara said. She leaped down, landing beside Jason, along with the dogs.

"Did you enjoy the show?" Tara asked him. "I know you were watching on that little drone of yours."

"Very much so," Jason said, voice oozing sarcasm. "You two are extremely entertaining. All I need is some popcorn, and I'd be set. Bitchathons are always high on my must watch list. Especially when the bitches in question inhabit state of the art war machines."

"Thought so," Tara said.

Sophie landed a moment later, on his right side. The Rex Wolves growled at her and barked, with Bruiser in the lead. Sophie released her micro machines toward Bruiser, forming a big serpent head that appeared ready to chomp down on the poor dog, and Bruiser dashed behind Lackey, whining. Sophie withdrew the micro machines a moment later. "Get your dogs under control before I'm forced to do it for you."

"Calm down, little ones," Tara told the dogs. And she rubbed Bruiser consolingly. The other Rex Wolves continued to growl at Sophie.

Jason shook his head and started toward the subway station he'd marked on the map.

The girls joined him, and eventually the dogs quieted down.

He glanced at Sophie beside him. He supposed he'd eventually get used to those creepy, spiderish movements, and the cacophony of hums produced by her mech's servomotors, which were the loudest among the group.

"You know, between you and me," Tara told Sophie. "You got the short end of the stick."

"What do you mean?" Sophie asked.

"I'm glad as hell I didn't get stuck with your mech," Tara said.

"Your Shadow Hawk model isn't that much prettier," Sophie said. "You look like Lego Batman's sidekick."

"Lego what?" Tara said.

"Never mind," Sophie said. "Old movie I watched a while back."

"Well at least I look moderately humanoid," Tara said. "You look like some sort of spider centaur."

"I'd take my micro machines and energy shield any day over a measly sword and grappling hook," Sophie said.

"But you forget, I can also teleport," Tara said. She vanished from view.

The Rex Wolves started barking in fright. Then spun toward Sophie, as if they thought she was responsible.

"Look to your right, on the rooftop." Tara's voice sounded at the same volume level, with similar clarity: she was speaking over the comm, after all.

Jason and Sophie glanced to the upper right: Tara waved from where she had deployed on a nearby roof.

She reappeared next to Jason a moment later and the Rex Wolves barked excitedly. Bruiser whined, and she patted it on the head.

"Show off," Sophie said.

"Hey, when you got my abilities, you can't help but show off," Tara said.

"You were one of those girls who liked to flaunt it, weren't you?" Sophie said.

"Flaunt what?" Jason asked.

"Tara knows what I mean," Sophie said. "Don't you girl."

"She means my sexuality," Tara said. "But you were certainly flaunting it, as you call it, back in your VR."

"I created that world when I was bored," Sophie said. "But it suits me, I think. Speaking of VR... Jason, we should book a meeting in my VR soon. I'd like to show you my special cat collection."

"That's all right," Jason said.

"Cat collection!" Tara said. "Try not to make it too obvious what you're after or anything. Might as well say pussy collection."

"*What?*" Sophie said. "You're reading too much into it. I'm not that kind of girl."

"Oh really," Tara said.

"Yeah, really," Sophie said. "I have a bunch of different cats. A Calico. A Siamese. A Persian. A Sphinx. A——"

Jason decided to mute his sound system for the time being. They'd know he'd done it, because a little mute icon would appear next to his name. Their speaker icons continued to highlight as they continued to prattle away, but he wasn't in the least curious about what they might be talking about.

They reached the subway entrance, which was basically a small shed protruding from the surface. It was inaccessible to their large bodies, but when they combined their efforts they were able to rip it off, revealing the staircase leading down. After some further removal of asphalt and concrete, they were able to expose the subway platform about thirty meters below.

It was wide enough to fit all three mechs, but not much else. Beside it, the polycarbonate shield that divided the tracks from the platform was still in place. The subway tunnel beyond didn't provide much more room.

"Well, that's not going to work," Tara said.

"It's nothing a 3D-printed drill can't fix," Jason insisted.

"We're going to have to drill way down," Sophie said. "And I mean, *way* down. And across."

"I admit, it's a little smaller than the measurements I read in the blueprints," Jason agreed.

"That's right, blame the measurements," Sophie said. "Rather than the man interpreting it. This is what happens when you let a man do a woman's job."

"All right, if you're so smart, where should we make our base of operations then?" Jason said.

"Well, let's take a look at the map..." Sophie said.

"What about the cisterns in the upper right of the city?" Tara said. "According to the blueprints, they used to hold excess rainwater. They were installed a hundred years ago when weather patterns changed, causing severe rains to hit the city often."

"A cistern?" Jason said. "You want to make our base in a *cistern?*"

"Well, it is underground," Tara said. "And check out the dimensions. It's huge."

"How do we know the measurements are accurate?" Sophie said. "You saw what happened with Jason and his little subway platform."

"The bigger question is, what do we do if it rains?" Jason said.

"Uh, when's the last time it rained in the uninhabitable zone?" Sophie said.

"Good point," Jason said. "All right, to the cistern we go."

"No protesting?" Sophie said. "No: 'hey, we should just stay here and use the drill, because I'm the man, and I'm always right?'"

"Nope," Jason said. "The plans I made will translate equally well to a cistern. In fact, now that the two of you have pointed it out, it's probably better."

"He's mature enough to admit when he's wrong," Tara commented. "Unlike you."

Sophie didn't answer for a moment. Then: "I might have to rethink my classification of the male member of the species. Not all of them think with their pants."

"But only the best ones," Tara said slyly.

Once more, Jason hit the mute button.

They reached the outskirts of the city and circled back to follow the perimeter. There, growing in the loose soil was the only form of plant life he'd seen—a half bramble, half tumbleweed combination that seemed to thrive in the radiation. Tara examined one of them, while the Rex Wolves sniffed the plants suspiciously.

"I think they reproduce by spores," she said. "Probably bio-engineered by the aliens."

The party waded through those plants, and eventually arrived at their destination, all without encountering a single mutant. Jason told himself it was because the party made a formidable sight, those three towering mechs and the four Rex Wolves accompanying them, but that hadn't stopped the Octoraffes from attacking them the night before, after all, so it was more likely that the mutants in the area were sleeping. The Rex Wolves themselves were most likely nocturnal as well, judging from how quiet and droopy eyed they seemed. Their abnormal sleep habits were catching up to them. That they had attacked in the day before had to be because of all the noise he and Tara had made during the little scuffle of their first meeting.

The party stood in a dried out retention pond— essentially a ravine—with a storm drain outlet opening into it. The ravine was surrounded by those radiation resistant bramble-weeds. Beyond them were a few buildings from a nearby outlying village.

By then Jason's power levels had recharged almost to one hundred percent, so when he ripped open the grill covering the large outlet, he could do so with his strength amped up to max. The grill crumpled like paper in his grasp, and he tossed it aside.

Jason gazed into the tunnel, and shone his LIDAR inside. The tunnel proceeded well away, with no end in sight. "Well, we can fit, if we crawl. But it's going to be a tight fit."

"*Crawl?*" Sophie said. "In there? I'll have to tuck in all my legs, and bend my torso against my carapace. Hardly a comfortable position. I'm already claustrophobic enough as it is."

Tara threw up her arms. "You could have told us that before we made the trek all the way here, Princess!"

"Hey, I'm just saying, I don't want to crawl," Sophie said.

"But that's what spiders do," Tara taunted her.

"I'd walk it, though," Sophie said. "And if we really want to turn this into a base, we should probably be walking it anyway."

"Hm, I don't know," Jason said. "I kind of like how it's cramped. Makes a great choke point for enemies. And Nightmares certainly can't fit inside."

"But what if we have to get out quickly?" Tara said.

"We're obviously going to have a rear access," Jason said. "Maybe an exit in the ceiling that leads somewhere to the street. We'll have to drill it."

"Even if we use a drill here, Nightmares won't be able to enter," Sophie said. "Please, can we enlarge it? Because I don't think I'm coming with you, otherwise."

He glanced at her. The sincerity was clear in her voice, as was the tinge of fear.

"Well, I guess we'll just have to program our repair drones to start printing up some drills," Jason said.

"Why?" Sophie said. Her micro machines swarmed from her body, combining together in front of her to form a big, revolving drill that was half as big as her body. "Find me some iron ore, and I can program these machines to make more of themselves."

"Why would we want to do that?" Tara said. "So you can be more powerful?"

Sophie shrugged. "Bigger drill. Faster access tunnel."

While she sent her drill into the outlet, Jason and Tara dug into the ground nearby with their fists, searching for any mineral rock. The Rex Wolves watched sleepily from the outskirts of the ravine, keeping an eye out for signs of trouble. Jason had the Explorer hovering overhead, the fully charged drone observing all approaches by slowly rotating clockwise, just in case their commotion awoke some nearby mutants.

Eventually the two hit a rock bed. They got lucky: those particular sedimentary rocks were iron rich. Jason smashed his fist repeatedly into the surface, attempting to pulverize it, but when Sophie realized what he was doing, she came over.

"No dear, you don't have to do that," she said sweetly. "Please, move aside."

Confused, Jason pulled himself out of the pit, as did Tara.

Sophie redirected her micro machines into the pit, and they began to attack the rock bed below. Jason realized they were eating through the sedimentary rocks and processing the iron content in real time: the micro machines fountained upward, with those on top spitting out the molten slag they'd separated from the iron before diving downward once more. Soon a ring of stone formed by the cooling slag around the pit; meanwhile, the number of micro machines grew rapidly, doubling in size.

"Where do they get their energy source?" Jason asked. "They can fly. Melt metal. Reform it into more of themselves. That's gotta take up a lot of power. It's obviously not sunlight. Unless they're covered in tiny solar panels."

"No, it's not sunlight," Sophie said while the machines multiplied. "I don't actually know what the source is. No one does. At least no one human. But if I had to guess, I'd say it's some sort of subspace energy."

"Subspace energy?"

"That's right," Sophie said. "There's a military encyclopedia in your internal database. You should check it out sometime. Read up on the micro machine chapter. Research teams have concluded that the only way these could be powered is by some sort of energy drawn from the space between ordinary space. Subspace." Sophie glanced at the micro machines. "There, I've reached my limit."

She recalled the tiny swarm.

"You have a limit?" Jason said.

"That's right," Sophie said. "The scientists programmed it in. The maximum number of copies is hard coded. If I lose machines in battle, I can create more, up to the hard limit. As I just did."

Sophie returned to the outlet with her new rotating drill, which was three times as big as the original.

"I hate alien technology," Tara said.

"I don't," Sophie said. He could imagine her beaming inside.

Tara glanced at Jason. "You know what happens if she loses control of that tech, right? She'll dissolve our mechs."

"Actually, I can't," Sophie said.

"What do you mean, you can't?" Jason said.

"It's another thing the scientists programmed in," Sophie said. "The micro machines can only smelt unprocessed ore, or ore that has been badly damaged. Unlike the actual alien models. The scientists were too scared of losing control, like you mentioned. If there's a perfectly intact vehicle, or mech, the tiny smelting lasers won't activate. I can't change it. I've tried, believe me. That's why I couldn't just dissolve the two of you. But I can certainly form the micro machines into a cutting blade that can saw through you, and when that's done, *then* I can convert you, up to my limit."

"Sounds like a lot of fun..." Tara said.

"Oh, it is, believe me," Sophie said.

While they waited for Sophie to enlarge the outlet, Tara rigged up an avatar communication system, so they could finally see the faces of each other's avatars when they spoke.

"You used the Teaching AIs to come up with this?" Jason asked.

"No, silly," Tara replied. "I'm a programmer. Don't you remember I remotely flew drones for a living?"

"Oh yeah..." Jason said. "Though I wasn't aware programming was involved."

She giggled. "All right, yeah, I'm joking. I used the Teaching AI."

He frowned.

"Hey, don't frown," Tara said. "It makes your face look like a hamster."

"A *hamster?*" Jason said in disbelief.

"All right, I'm through," Sophie's avatar appeared in the lower right of Jason's display. He could have sworn Sophie had winked at him after she spoke. Must have imagined it.

Jason turned toward the outlet, which was inside a hill. "I'll go first."

Jason passed by Sophie, who had wrapped her micro machines back around her torso and carapace. The spherical bulge of them was three times larger than before.

He entered the outlet. It was tall enough so that he could fit by crouching only a little. The sides still pressed into him on either flank, however. The upper portion where Sophie had drilled wasn't concrete, but rock and dirt.

He walked for a hundred meters, and then he was through. He activated his headlamps so that he wouldn't have to use his LIDAR.

It was cavernous inside that cistern. Just cavernous. The floor, walls, and ceiling were made of concrete, as were the big columns holding up the ceiling at regular intervals. He'd seen pictures of Tokyo's massive underground storm drains, and it was comparable.

The mechs were easily able to fit between those big columns. As were the Rex Wolves. Jason stood at his full height as he weaved between the pillars, making his way through the room, turning around so that he could take it all in.

"This'll definitely do," Jason said.

12

J ason had Sophie drill an escape route into the ceiling near the back of the cavernous structure, and then reprogrammed all of their repair drones to 3D print iron hatches using iron ore pulverized from the rock bed outside. The drones whirred back and forth all day, flying between the openings in the storm drain and the ceiling, creating the barriers. The design even included a remote interface, so he'd be able to open either entrance over the comm.

Some of the drones were printing up solar collectors as well, along with the necessary electrical framework, using metal pulverized from rock under the subway. Sophie, Tara, and Jason donated one backup power cell each to serve as storage for the power generated by those collectors, so that if they wanted, they could hang out in the base all day, and simply plug into the batteries to recharge without sunlight.

It would take three days to finish printing everything.

He had pulverized enough rock to last the day, and there wasn't much else to do while he waited, so he took Sophie, Tara and the dogs into the city, in search of Internet access. It was also an excuse to keep his batteries charged.

Before he left, he had some of the drones 3D print a fiber-capable switch, along with the necessary accessories, since even if the party did find an Internet center, there would be no equipment around to access it. He set a waypoint for a known data center—at least one that had existed fifty years ago, according to his pre invasion map.

His Explorer scouted ahead, keeping an eye out for any bioweapons that might be lurking about. It was broad daylight, though, so he wasn't really expecting an attack. Unless the team accidentally woke something that might be hiding in the nearby buildings, like a den of Rex Wolves.

Jason glanced at Sophie's Highlander, and his gaze lingered on the carapace section with all those protruding nozzles.

"Where do you get the fuel for your jumpjets?" he asked.

"It's generated by special bacteria that line the insides of my carapace," Sophie said. "If I run out, it takes a full day to replenish."

"Nice," Jason said. "Self-sustainment. It's the way to go."

Her avatar nodded. "If I don't use the fuel, I have to vent it now and then. Sort of like taking a piss."

"Well that's certainly a sexy image," Tara taunted.

"No sexier than your blocky ass," Sophie said.

"Hey, this is a fine ass." Tara's Shadow Hawk patted its rear quarter. "Now yours, on the other hand…"

"Don't make me come over there and show you what my ass can do," Sophie said.

"Yeah?" Tara said. "Go ahead, I dare you. My foot wants to give it a good kick."

"Please, no fighting today," Jason said.

Sophie's avatar bit her lip, but then she seemed to calm down.

A flashing icon appeared on his overhead map, courtesy of the Explorer.

"All right," Jason said. "My scout has reached the data center." Which was really just a fancy name for a big building. "There are some doors and windows… I'm sending it inside." As the drone ducked inside the main door, the signal pixelated and froze, because of all the interference between his location and that of the drone.

A moment later the signal returned, and he reviewed the footage. "Okay, looks like it's mostly intact. There're no actual computers left inside, of course. But there is an optical fiber box, with the lines still intact."

The team reached the data center. There was no way any of them could fit any of the entrances, not in their big mechs, of course. Jason had the drone carry the switch into the building, and piloted it through the different rooms. He knelt at the entrance so that the antennae on his head were pointed directly through the main doors, wanting to maintain his signal strength.

He only received a few video freezes before the drone was in place. Then he had the Explorer lower the switch next to the fiber box. Pulling up his digital manual, he had the Teaching AI overlay his vision, and he followed the instructions to connect the switch and its accessories to the fiber optic lines. Then he plugged in the battery the drone was carrying, and attempted to access the switch's remote interface through the drone.

"Okay, I'm able to connect to the switch," Jason said. He frowned, a facial expression which would have appeared on his avatar transmitted over the comm.

"What is it?" Sophie said, evidently in response to that frown.

"I'm not getting an Internet connection," Jason said.

"Well, it was worth a try," Sophie said.

"The line must have been severed somewhere along the way," Jason said. "From a bomb. Maybe a nuke."

"Or it could be that the destination switch doesn't exist," Tara said.

"Yeah, that's the more likely explanation," Jason told her. "But like Sophie said, we had to try." He sighed. "I guess we're going back to base."

"So how do you like the new avatar system I made for us," Tara said over a direct connection on the way back. She was smiling widely in the lower right of his display.

"It's fine," Jason said. "Thanks for setting it up."

"Yeah, of course," Tara said. "Have to make our life easier, after all." She stayed on the line, smiling vaguely.

"Is there something else?" Jason said.

"Oh," Tara said. "Well, I was wondering, what you were doing in VR later?"

"Nothing," Jason said. "I'll probably try to set up my environment to be more like yours or Sophie's."

"Need some help?" Tara said.

"No, not really," Jason said.

"I'm great at interior decorating," Tara said.

"Well, you know, I—" Jason said.

"Great!" Tara said. "I'll be there. Let me know when you're ready."

"Yeah, that'll be later, when we reach our base of operations," Jason said.

"Oh of course, I know," Tara said. "I look forward to it."

"Though in all honesty, we should probably be working more on our external environment at the moment…" Jason said.

"The drones will handle it," Tara said dismissively. "Besides, even though we'll be living in that underground base, we won't actually be 'living' in it all that much, if you know what I mean. Not when we have VR."

"I suppose not," Jason said. "But I'd like to set up some more defenses. Maybe a few laser turrets…"

"Again, that'll be for the drones, once they've finished setting up the solar panels, and the hatches," Tara said.

"At this rate, we're going to have to print up some dedicated 3D printers so we can speed the process along," Jason said.

"All in good time," she said.

The moment she disconnected, he received another private call. This time from Sophie.

Her avatar appeared in the lower right.

"Hi Jason," she said.

He suppressed a sigh. "Hey."

"Long walk, hey?" Sophie said.

"It is what it is," Jason said.

"I was wondering..." Sophie said.

"Let me guess, you want to visit my VR?" Jason said.

"What?" Sophie said. "No. Why would I want to visit your VR?"

Her puzzled reaction felt a bit overdramatized, as if that was precisely what she had in mind, but she didn't want him to know about it.

"I want to ask you a favor," Sophie said.

"Okay..."

"I don't suppose I can have that energy weapon of yours?" Sophie said. "All I have are my micro machines, and—"

"No," Jason said.

Her face dropped. "Okay."

"Well I mean, I'd give it to you if I could," Jason said. "But it's wired into my mech."

"But I'm sure if we pulled up the relevant Teaching AIs, we could figure out how to detach it, and reattach it to me," Sophie said.

"And I also don't want to give it up..." Jason said.

"Maybe we can get the repair drones to print me one?" Sophie asked.

"Ha," Jason replied. "It's alien tech. We don't have the necessary materials, I'm afraid."

"Oh, that's too bad," Sophie said.

"We'll just have to stick together," Jason said. "We all have unique abilities that balance each other out."

She seemed to brighten at that. "I suppose you're right."

He continued walking, and waited for her to disconnect, but it didn't happen.

"Anything else?" Jason said.

"Welllllll, since you brought up VR earlier..." Sophie said.

"So you do want to visit my VR after all?" Jason said.

"Oh no," Sophie said. "I want you to visit *mine!*"

"Uh, no thanks," Jason said. "Not after what happened there the last time."

"This time you'll have full control of your interface," Sophie said. "And can leave whenever you want."

"I'll have to pass," Jason said.

"All right, fine," Sophie said. "Then I guess I can visit yours..."

"Great," Jason said. "Tara is coming over later to help me build out my environment. You can join us."

"*What?*" Sophie said. "That sneaky bitch. I knew it."

Jason stared at her avatar and blinked a few times, unsure what to say.

Sophie was all smiles again. "Oh, okay. I'll join you two. I look forward to seeing what we can come up with."

Jason dismissed the call, shaking his head.

All the way back, he was trying to think of a way to weasel out of his promise to let the girls help set up his VR environment. When they were almost at the cistern area, he finally spoke over the comm.

"So, I'm going to go fetch some meat for the dogs," Jason said. "From the Nightmares we took down last night."

"Assuming the Octoraffes left you anything," Sophie said.

"I'll go with you," Tara said. "Buddy system."

"I'm going, too, then," Sophie said. "I'm not going to be left here alone."

"We'll leave the dogs to guard you," Tara said.

"Dogs?" Sophie said. She glanced at the Rex Wolves, and an expression of disgust appeared on her avatar. "I'd hardly call these mutants *dogs*."

"Whatever," Tara said. "They'll protect you."

"I think I can handle myself," Sophie said.

"Great, then you can stay behind!" Tara said, walking toward Jason's mech. "Let's go."

But then Sophie appeared on his other side, with the confused Rex Wolves trailing. "Like I said, I'm not staying behind alone."

"Actually, forget it," Jason told them. "The dogs have chlorophyll in their fur, they can go another week without food, like Tara said."

"I was just guessing about that," Tara said. "Could be a week. Could be a few days."

He glanced at Bruiser, who seemed energetic enough. "Well, they don't really look all that hungry to me."

So he turned around and headed back to the cistern instead.

When he arrived, he saw that the solar collector construction was going well. Already two were finished.

At the entrance to the underground base, the drones had only constructed a third of the hatch—they were building it directly into the drain outlet. Jason was able to easily lift his feet over the barrier and enter.

He sent the Explorer in to check on the status of the escape hatch in the ceiling, which was also going well. Drones whirred back and forth, carrying the pulverized ore he and the others had deposited on the floor of the cistern to the ceiling.

"Looks like we could use a bit more ore," Jason said.

He and the others spent the next hour pulverizing more of the iron rich sedimentary rocks from the bed, and then deposited it into the three separate piles they had made, two for the hatches, one for the solar collectors.

When that was done, he waited until he was fully charged, and then went inside, settling into the corner of the cavernous chamber he'd chosen for himself.

Tara had the dogs stand watch outside; they assumed different positions along the approach to the entrance, basking in the sun to get their energy fix. Jason tapped into her remote camera and watched it all.

"How did you get them to stand guard like that?" Jason asked her.

"Remember the meat I grabbed on the way to Brussels?" Tara replied. "I've been using it to good effect."

"I never saw you train them," Jason said.

"Ah, that's because you haven't been paying attention," Tara told him.

Jason shook his head. "You never cease to amaze me."

Once everyone had settled, he got the inevitable inquiries from Sophie and Tara regarding VR.

"All right, let's go," Jason said with a sigh.

13

Jason sat at a bar stool in his virtual walk-out basement. In no time at all Sophie and Tara helped him deck out his VR like a man cave in the mountains. In addition to the bar, he had a home theater complete with ten lounge seats and a wall-encompassing flat panel display. There was an arcade, containing old-style video games, with a 3D pool table in the middle. A dartboard completed the look.

Everything was lifted from a bygone era, something that Tara had pulled out of her encyclopedia when she ran a search on "man cave."

The curtains around the room were currently retracted, so that the floor to ceiling windows gave him a good view of the mountain pass outside.

"Well, thanks for your help," Jason said.

"Of course," Sophie said.

"He was talking to me," Tara said.

Jason went to the open patio door and walked

outside. He could smell the pines on the breeze. Feel the sun against his cheek. Hear the songbirds perched on the roof of his house.

He surveyed the mountains, and the green trees covering them. His eyes settled on the pristine lake below.

"My senses tell me all of this is real, but my mind tells me it's false," Jason said.

"Then don't think about it," Sophie said.

He listened to the virtual songbirds chirp for a moment, and then nodded.

"It's easy to forget," Jason said. "You know, if I were human, I could see myself retiring in a place like this."

"Consider yourself retired," Tara said, coming up beside him. Sophie joined her.

"We could make a life for ourselves here," Sophie said.

"The three of us?" Jason asked.

"Er, yeah," Sophie said. Jason had the impression she meant only herself, and him.

"We should permanently link our VRs," Tara said. "Sure, we can retreat to our own environments when we need to be alone, but in general, I think it would better if we hung out here. For the sake of human company."

"But we're not even human anymore," Jason said. "Not really. We might think we are, but all we need to do is look at our real world bodies. Or even materialize something here." He made a miniature Earth appear above his hand, complete with clouds and oceans. "That's a reminder enough. We don't eat, or shit. We

don't really need to sleep, though I suppose it's recommended. We're not human."

"You're so wrong," Tara said. "We *are* human. At
least on the inside. It doesn't matter what we are on the
outside, or even if this reality is false. That's why we
need human company so badly. The presence of real
humans, not AI generated simulacrums. To remind us
where we came from."

Jason dismissed the globe, and looked down at the
lake once more. "You're right. I know that. I just, sometimes I don't feel very human. Mostly when I'm out
there, steeped in the blood of bioweapons. A killing
machine."

"You should try dialing down your emotions occasionally," Sophie said. "I had to do it sometimes when I
was alone on the plains. When the despair got too
strong. Not during the fighting. The fighting is fine. I
can forget myself, and kick a little mutant ass. But the
worst times, the times when the despair became strong-
est, were when I was trudging alone on the empty, irra-
diated plains. When I remembered what I was, versus
what I'd become. When I remembered where I once
lived, versus where I reside now. Yes, emotions can be a
powerful tool, but they should be disabled when you
don't need them."

"I disagree," Tara said. "I think we should leave our
emotions on at all times. If anything, that's the truest
indicator of our humanity."

Jason nodded. "I'm going to have to side with Tara
on this one."

Sophie glanced at them. "You know the military

wouldn't give us the option, don't you? If we had deployed as they originally planned, they would have probably disabled our emotions entirely. Erasing everything that was human about us, and leaving only the merest spark of personality."

Tara nodded. "She's right. I've issued orders to standard Mind Refurbs before... they're essentially automatons. Containment Code prevents them from departing from mission parameters. And it also keeps their emotions in check, at the commander's discretion."

Jason spotted an eagle circling overhead. He momentarily switched his point of view to that of the bird. He soared far above the trees.

This is freedom.

"You really think the military will send a retrieval team to get us?" Tara asked.

He returned to his own viewpoint and glanced at her. "Considering we're trillion credit machines, I'd say there's a good likelihood they will. At some point."

"I'm not sure I want to go back," Tara said.

"Why?" Jason asked her.

"Do you like having your freedom?" Tara replied. "The ability to control your emotions? Your destiny?"

"Well, sure," Jason said, remembering his soaring flight of only a few moments before.

"There's your answer," Tara said. "If we go back, the military is going to wrap that Containment Code I mentioned around our minds and dial our emotions down to zero at all times, so we won't even care that we've lost our wills. And they'll send us into whatever war zones they like. We'll have to suppress riots, maybe

kill civilians along the way. Or kill mutants. Nonstop. It's
not something I can see myself doing. I'd rather stay out
here, even if the two of you and our dogs are the only
company I have. Because at least out here, I have
freedom."

"You're right, of course," Jason said. "When you
put it that way, I don't want to go back either."

"We should probably shut down our Milnet nodes,"
Tara said.

"Our what?" Sophie asked.

"It's in the manual," Tara said. "Milnet node. It's
what we use to connect to the military net, as opposed
to the Internet."

"Oh," Sophie said. "Why should we care about
connecting to it?"

"Because that'd be bad," Tara told her. "If a military satellite ever passes overhead, and we connect, we'll
immediately get sent any Containment Code we're
missing. It will download over the Milnet nodes and
straight into our heads. Trust me, I served in the army. I
know how it works. Any retrieval team sent to fetch us
will probably have a Milnet repeater onboard. It's
possible there might even be one in this city already,
maybe deployed in anticipation of our arrival."

"Great, you could have told us that before,"
Jason said.

"It slipped my mind," Tara said.

"Of all the things to slip your mind…" Jason activated his HUD, and it overlaid his vision. He had all
the same options available to him as in the real world,
in addition to VR specific menus. He called up his

Training AI and had it show him how to disable the Milnet node. Then he checked the logs, and confirmed he hadn't inadvertently connected since awakening.

"Done," Jason said. "I checked my logs, and I haven't connected since awakening."

"Me neither," Sophie said.

"Nor me," Tara said.

"I left Internet connecting active," Jason said. "Unless you think—"

"Should be fine," Tara said. "We can still receive updates over the Internet, but we have to approve them, first. The Milnet system was designed to bypass all of that."

"Good to know," Jason said.

"So we've decided then?" Sophie said.

"Decided what?" Tara said.

"That we're going to stay here," Sophie pressed. "That we're not even going to try to return to western civilization?"

Jason paused. "I'd say no."

"All right," Sophie said. "I'm for that, I think. But you both know that if we stay here, we'll always have to watch our backs for the rest of our lives, right?"

"That's exactly why we're building up this operations base," Jason said. He surveyed the pristine mountain lake. "And staying here for the rest of our days won't be so bad, I think."

"Rest of our days…" Tara said. "You do know that could be a very long time. If we play our cards right."

"As long as we don't lower our guard," Jason agreed.

He shifted his gaze from the lake to the nearby trees, marveling at how real it all seemed.

Yep, I can definitely retire here.

He was about to turn to go when he spotted something unusual.

"Is that…" He zoomed in.

He saw a strange woman peering around the thick trunk of one of the pines. She was dressed for winter weather in a wool cap, a ski jacket, long pants, and snow boots. She looked fairly young, maybe early twenties. Her cheeks were red, as if she was cold. Or hot.

"Did either of you program in an AI simulacrum?" Jason asked.

"Not me," Sophie said.

"Nor me," Tara said. "Why?"

"Look at that tree," Jason pointed.

As he did so, the distant woman gasped, and turned around to retreat, vanishing behind the tree. Jason spotted a tail of all things dangling from her legs.

A tail?

He dashed to the tree line. The girl was running away through the forest, her long tail streaming along behind her.

"Wait!" Jason called.

She glanced over her shoulder, and then promptly vanished completely.

"Who was that?" Sophie said, coming up beside him.

"I don't know," Jason said.

"How did she get in here?" Tara said.

"She obviously hacked in," Jason said.

"She has to be somewhere nearby," Sophie said. "I mean in the real world. Within range of our comm nodes."

Jason glanced at her, and then promptly logged off.

He had the Explorer begin a spiraling search pattern to look for signs of the intruder. He also left the cistern—the entrance hatch was only a little higher by then, so he easily stepped over.

Once he entered the dried up ravine that served as the retention pond, he joined the search. Tara and Sophie spread out, and Tara brought the dogs with her, in case they detected any foreign scents.

Jason divided them into quadrants, with the Explorer taking one, and the three mechs searching the remainder.

He pulled himself out of the crater that was the ravine, and waded through the bramble-weed vegetation that surrounded it. He scanned the area on all bands: visual, thermal, and LIDAR. But there was nothing out there.

When he finished sweeping the assigned area, he went a little farther before finally giving up. He was at the uppermost limit of his communications range with the other mechs. Any intruder would have had to have stayed within this distance from the cistern for any chance of interfacing with his comm node, let alone VR. In fact, they very likely would have had to have gotten a lot closer, given that the cistern itself would have interfered with reception. So he was well beyond the reasonable search area.

"I got nothing in my quadrant, did you guys fare any better?" Jason asked.

"Nope," Sophie said.

"Likewise," Tara reported.

Jason glanced at the map. The Explorer, though it was flying relatively low, hadn't picked up anything either.

"Well I guess if anyone was out there, they're gone now," Jason said.

He turned back.

That was when he spotted it.

A small aberration on the thermal band. About thirty degrees to the right, in front of him, five meters away, behind a cluster of rocks and bramble-weeds. Like two, red footprints.

"Wait a second, I have something," Jason said. "I'm marking it on the map."

He did so, and approached.

All of a sudden a streak of blue light fired his way, striking the ground just in front of him, creating a small blast crater. He froze.

Meanwhile, ahead of him, space seemed to warp. The light bent, forming an almost humanoid shape from the background, a shape that began to flee.

Jason dashed forward, closing with that shape. It was just as tall as him. He hurled himself at it. The clang of metal upon metal reverberated from the pair as he tackled it.

He landed on the ground. His opponent materialized as the warped space dispersed. It was a Stalker mech, about the same size and shape as his own, except it had a long tail. It offered little resistance as he slammed his legs on top, pinning the unit. He noted that the weapon turret on the tip of that tail was pointed directly at him, and he considered trying to rip it off, but it was doubtful he'd succeed before it could fire, even in Bullet Time. It contained some sort of a plasma bolt weapon, judging from the impact he'd seen behind him. No doubt derived from the alien technology. And whatever technology it had used to turn invisible was definitely alien.

Sophie, Tara and the Rex Wolves arrived. The dogs barked and growled angrily.

"Well, well, well," Sophie said. "We have our spy. A Stalker mech. The preferred model for scouts."

"Please don't hurt me," a female voice came over the comm. An avatar appeared in the lower right of his display. The face matched up with the woman he'd seen in VR. She was cute, with freckles all over. She'd gotten rid of the woolen cap, and sported long blond hair that spilled onto her shoulders.

"How did you get on this line?" Jason asked. "It's private. And encrypted."

"Sorry," the voice said. "I hacked in. And into your VR, too."

"She's a hacker…" Sophie said.

Jason sat up slightly, but still remained on top of the mech, pinning her in place.

"I'm sorry for hacking into your VR," the pinned unit continued. "I was really bored. And… so lonely. I'm sorry."

"You're not part of a retrieval team?" Jason asked.

"A what?" she replied. "No. No way. I'm just, well I'm by myself. And I… I don't know what I am. I woke up a few days ago in this place. I hate it here. I just want to go home."

"What's your name?" Jason said.

"I'm Lori," she said.

"Lori," Jason said.

"That's right," Lori said.

"All right," Jason said. "And you know our names already, thanks to your hacking?"

"That's right!" Lori said eagerly. "You're Jason. She's Tara. And she's Sophie." Her avatar suddenly looked chagrined. "Er. Sorry again for what I did. I was really bored."

"You keep saying that," Sophie said. "Peeping Tom. Tell me what else you saw? Did you peer into my VR last night, too?"

"Oh no!" Lori said. "I only went into his VR when you all returned to the cistern. I've been watching you since this morning, when I heard you pounding into the rock. And spying on your communications as soon as I was within range."

Sophie rounded on Jason. "She's been spying on us all morning!"

"And so she has," Jason said.

"You're able to hide on every band, from visible light to thermal?" Tara asked her.

"That's right!" Lori said. "The only thing that gives me away is my feet—the heat has to go somewhere. But none of that usually shows up, especially if I position myself properly when you send your drone flying by."

"I almost missed her," Jason said. "I walked right by her the first time, and didn't even notice the thermal signature of her feet." He glanced down at her. "Well, I suppose if you wanted to attack us, you would have done it already. Still, you did fire at me, and I didn't really like that."

"Oh, I wasn't trying to hit you!" Lori said. "Did I?"

"No," Jason said.

"Okay, good," Lori said. She seemed relieved. "I only wanted to scare you off. I didn't know what you would do if you caught me."

"Well, now you know," Jason said. He stood up, and offered a hand to help her up.

She accepted, and said, rather breathlessly: "Thank you!" The Rex Wolves were still occasionally barking beside her, but they'd stopped growling at least.

Lori looked at the animals. "I like your... dogs?"

"Thanks," Tara said suspiciously.

"So now I guess we have to decide what we're going to do with her," Jason said, glancing at Sophie and Tara.

"Can I stay with you?" Lori asked quickly.

"No," Sophie and Tara answered at the same time.

The Shadow Hawk and Highlander exchanged a look.

"First time we've been on the same wavelength," Sophie said.

"For good reason," Tara said. She turned toward Jason. "We can't let her stay. There's not enough room in the cistern."

"There's more than enough room," Jason said. "Where's your heart?"

"I left it behind in my human body," Tara said.

"Her invisibility tech might be useful…" Sophie said. "But that doesn't mean I'm saying she should stay. I say we make her give us the tech, and then we send her packing."

"If you don't want me, I… I guess I'll move on," Lori said. Her avatar seemed to be tearing up. "I'll find somewhere to stay. Somewhere to hide from the monsters."

"Yes, you'll move on, but only after you give us your invisibility tech," Tara said.

"I don't think it's possible," Lori said. "The technology is integrated with my Stalker. I don't think it can be duplicated."

"Maybe it can't be duplicated," Tara said. "But I'm sure the Teaching AIs will be able to tell us how to take it from you."

"But if you take it from me, I'll be defenseless!" Lori said.

"So?" Tara said.

"You can stay with us on one condition," Jason said.

"No she can't!" Tara whined.

"On one condition," Jason repeated. "You're never to hack into my VR, or any of our VRs, again. You have to ask for permission, and then accept the standard way."

"Oh yes, I promise I won't," Lori said. "I mean I won't hack in. I'll ask permission. And I won't listen into your comm band anymore either."

"Good," Jason said. "I'm giving you the official codes so you can link up. But no listening on our private comms, got it?"

"For sure!" Lori said.

"Good," Jason said.

"And lose the tail in VR," Tara said.

"No!" Lori said.

Tara glanced at Jason. "It was worth a try."

14

J ason and the others spent the next two days inside. Lori was kind enough to donate her repair drones to the housing project, and he diverted them to help with the solar collectors, and the main entrance hatch, which was taking the longest time to build. He had all of the drones stop their construction when it got dark, because he didn't want to attract any of the mutants, and had Tara call the Rex Wolves inside for the night. He also landed the Explorer, because it's humming might draw the creatures.

Throughout the evening, before they idled their consciousnesses in sleep mode, he often heard strange shrieks and howls in the distance. Jason had diverted some of the repair drones to print up a bunch of cameras, and he'd deployed them at various locations along the perimeter to keep watch. He'd also put some in the city street that bordered the escape tunnel. These were all passive cameras, able to transmit and record on the visual and thermal bands. He didn't want to install something active like LIDAR, just in case military drones swept past looking for them—something like LIDAR would readily broadcast their location. He'd set up alerts to trigger whenever motion was detected.

At eight o'clock every night they slept. Jason did, too, trusting in his cameras. He awoke sometimes when an alert triggered; he'd access the feed of the camera in question and spot strange creatures roaming past. Sometimes he wouldn't see anything at all, as whatever had triggered the alert would be long gone.

Yes, he slept. It was great, being able to fall asleep on command, and without having to worry about tossing and turning for an hour beforehand. Not to mention, he could do it in any position: standing up, seated, whatever. Yep, being a machine wasn't so bad.

Every morning, they were up at four, and when dawn broke, they'd reactivate the drones to continue building the hatches, and the solar panels.

They spent a lot of time in Jason's shared VR, especially in the hours before sunlight in the morning. They usually spent a couple of hours in his VR in the evenings, too. Jason had created a bedroom for each of the girls in his mountain home, all on the same floor as his master bedroom. Lori kept trying to sleep in the same room as him, on the floor, but he turned her down because he didn't want to make the other girls jealous.

The entrance to the cistern got harder to navigate as the main hatch grew higher, until on the third day since building began, none of them could leave at all, not even the Rex Wolves. The dogs sat in the corner, lethargic without their daily dose of sunlight. The mechs plugged themselves into the power cells that were fed by the solar collectors outside, and charged.

And then, near dusk of that third day, construction was complete.

"Well," Jason said. "That went a little faster than I expected. Considering the downtime the drones had to spend repairing themselves from the wear and tear. I have to thank Lori for donating her repair drones to the project. That helped speed things up."

"You're very welcome!" Lori said, her avatar beaming.

Jason examined the inside of the entrance hatch via his headlamps. He accessed the remote interface, and was able to execute the open command. The door irised open, the metal deploying into its surrounding frame. He could readily squeeze past, and outside. The Rex Wolves were happy to run outside and soak up the last minutes of sunlight.

"We're going to have to build a few more portals, I think," Jason said. "At different locations inside the entrance tunnel. For an added layer of security."

"That works for me," Tara said.

Jason returned to the cistern and checked out the escape tunnel in the ceiling. He was also able to spiral open that portal, whose tunnel led to a city street. There were rungs in the tunnel so that the mechs could climb —they had to leap up and grab the first rung, but after that they could pull themselves up. He tested the route by doing just that, and then scaled the intervening rungs to the surface. He glanced at the street outside, and then let go of the top rung to fall back down.

Right on top of Lori's Stalker mech.

Jason crumpled on top of her, and rolled away, into a pillar. "Gah! What are you doing?"

"Sorry," Lori said. "I thought you were going out, and I wanted to come, too."

"Yeah well, I wasn't." Jason saw the big dent he'd made in her chest assembly. "Better get that repaired."

Tara called the Rex Wolves back, because it was getting dark, and Jason recalled the drones, and sealed both exits.

"All right, well, this is finally beginning to feel a little bit like a home," Jason said.

Jason instructed some of the drones to repair the dent he'd made in Lori's chest, and had the other drones shut down for the night. Then he entered his VR in preparation for sleeping.

His man cave appeared around him. He heard giggling from upstairs. The girls were having their usual pre-bed supper.

He walked to the patio and went outside to smell the virtual mountain air.

Tara appeared from nowhere to stand beside him.

"I hate it when you do that," Jason said.

She shrugged. "I *am* a teleporter."

"Everything is going well between you and the other two?" Jason asked.

"As well as can be expected," Tara said. "I'm managing, anyway. It's getting crowded in here."

"Good thing we can build-out as many rooms as we want in VR, huh?" Jason said.

"I meant in the cistern," Tara said.

"It's not so bad," Jason said. "We all have our own corners. We could fit more if we needed to."

"God, I hope not," Tara said.

"What's the matter?" Jason said. "You make it seem like you don't like female company."

"Don't get me wrong, I do," Tara said. "It just seems like there isn't enough testosterone to go around, if you know what I mean."

"Not really," Jason said.

"Is Lori still trying to sleep with you?" Tara asked.

"She was never trying to sleep *with* me," Jason replied. "She wanted to sleep on the floor."

"So she says," Tara said. "You'd shut your eyes and a moment later she'd be climbing into bed beside you."

"Well you could do the same," Jason said. "Worse, even. Teleporting directly into my bed."

"Except that you disappear from VR when you go to sleep," Tara said. "That's purposeful?"

"Obviously," Jason said. "It's to prevent the very scenario I described. I don't need people teleporting into my bed when I'm under."

"It's your VR," Tara said. "You make the rules here. You can prevent materializations in your room if you want."

He hadn't considered that. "I suppose I can. But I still think I'm going to disappear when I sleep. If Lori can hack my VR, that means any of you can."

"No," Tara said. "It's one of her unique abilities."

Jason pursed his lips. "You all bring something to the table, don't you?"

"I suppose so." Tara looked out toward the lake.

Jason followed her gaze, and regarded the mountains reflecting from the surface of the water. He'd set his VR to dusk, and the clouds were a colorful mix of reds and purples, also reflected from the lake. Nightingales chirped somewhere nearby.

"What do you think our original purpose here was?" Tara said.

"I don't know," Jason said.

"Speculate," Tara said.

"Hunt bioweapons?" Jason said. "Dig out Nightmare nests?"

"That would make sense," Tara said. "But why send us, when there are bombers, and other offhand methods of doing the same thing? Hell, I was doing remote bombing missions on the coasts, if you remember."

"Maybe the military wanted something more precision based," Jason said. "Something that could kill these mutants, without destroying everything else around them."

"I suppose we'll never know," Tara said.

"Maybe it's better that way," Jason said.

She glanced at him, and for a moment he thought she wanted to say more, but then she looked away. "Have a good night."

"Thanks," Jason said.

She vanished, perhaps teleporting to her room before logging off.

Lori dashed out from the patio behind him. "Hi!"

As usual, she was dressed in winter clothes, with a wool cap on her head, and thick pants and boots.

"Oh hey," Jason said. "How long were you there?"

"I wasn't listening in," Lori said, lowering her gaze. She swept her tail behind her back.

"You know, that is kind of distracting," Jason said, nodding toward the tail.

Her face dropped. "You don't like it?"

"No, it's fine," Jason said.

She was all smiles again. "I'm glad. It helps me control the tail I have in real life. At first I didn't create a tail here, but whenever I'd return to the real world, I'd have to get used to having one again. I figured, why not just keep the tail all the time, in both the virtual and real worlds? Then I wouldn't be so caught off guard when I returned to reality."

"Makes sense," Jason said.

She folded her hands behind her back and leaned back on one leg, shyly kicking at the ground in front of her. "I haven't really talked to you much since that first day. I haven't had a chance. Not really. The girls keep me occupied. You'd almost think they don't *want* me to talk to you!" Her giggle seemed nervous.

"I can't imagine why," Jason said. But he could.

"I finally managed to get away early tonight," Lori said.

He nodded. Then glanced at her. "I don't think I've ever asked, why do you always dress in winter clothes?"

She seemed dismayed. "This is what I always wear."

"Yeah, but why?" Jason said. He waved at the forest around him. "It's warm here."

She shrugged. "Because I like it?"

"To each his own," Jason said.

"*Her* own," Lori clarified. "Besides, here I can alter the heat levels however I want."

"That's true," Jason said. "You view my VR through your own personal lens. Who knows, maybe you've got snowflakes streaking down from the sky."

"Maybe I do," Lori agreed.

He nodded, looking out at the mountains.

"I'm a skier," Lori volunteered.

"Ah," Jason said. "That would explain the clothes."

"Yes," Lori said. "I needed money to make an Olympic run, so I went ahead and had my mind scanned. Never thought I'd end up here!"

"None of us did," Jason said.

"I don't suppose I can convince you to let me sleep on the floor of your room?" Lori said. "I hate sleeping alone. I always had my little brother to sleep with."

"You can create a virtual brother," Jason said.

"But it's not the same," Lori said. "All I need is a sleeping bag."

"Sorry," Jason said. "You've asked before. My answer is still no. I'm not even in the room when I actually go to sleep anyway. I've programmed my avatar to log me off."

"That's all right," Lori said. "In fact, that's good. Then I don't have to listen to you snore."

Jason chuckled. "Should I ask how old you were when you got your scan?"

"Old enough for the Olympic ski team!" Lori said, sounding slightly insulted.

"Well, that doesn't necessarily mean very old," Jason said.

"Well, also old enough to take care of my brother!" Lori said. "I've been the only one around since he was seven."

"I'm sorry to hear that," Jason said.

"Don't be," Lori said, sighing.

He waited for her to say more, but when she didn't, he decided to pry. Just a little.

"Twenty," Jason said.

"What?" Lori said, perking up.

"You look twenty," Jason said.

"Thank you," Lori said. "That's about right."

He nodded, then returned his attention to the mountain lake. The stars were coming out.

Lori stayed by his side.

"Anything else you wanted to talk about?" Jason asked.

"Nope!" Lori replied.

He waited, but she still stood there, apparently not getting the hint.

Maybe if I ignore her, she'll go away.

After a moment, she said: "Anyway, I should probably go to sleep."

"All right then," Jason said.

"But I'd love to go skiing with you some time," Lori said. The words came out all in a rush. "I mean, if you want to. I've already asked Sophie and Tara if they want to come, but they don't seem too interested. So it'll be just you and me."

"Sure, that might be fun," Jason said. "Maybe in a few days."

"All right," she said. "Then it's a date!"

He was about to contest her, but she seemed so happy at the moment that he didn't have the heart to deflate her bubble.

She turned to go, but then hesitated. She suddenly leaned forward and gave him a quick peck on the cheek. Then she backed away, her face turning red. "Night!"

She hurried back inside.

Jason had to shake his head.

I'm trapped in the uninhabitable zone with three machine women. All of them very hot. And very horny.

He knew that something would have to give, eventually.

What have I gotten myself into?

15

The next day, Jason programmed the drones to begin working on a second hatch, this one located just behind the first in the main entrance. He checked the overhead map for tangos—the surveillance cameras would have marked them if there were any—then he opened the main door and let the Rex Wolves outside. They moved eagerly, and he followed them out.

The wolves didn't bother to take up their usual guard positions; instead, they headed straight for the closest rays of sunlight, and plopped down lethargically.

Jason called Tara over the comm. "It's time to head to the countryside. Maybe toward the Octoraffe valley."

"Good," Tara said, her avatar appearing in the lower right. She looked just as good in the morning as any other time of the day. Gotta love 3D visualization tech. "It's about time we got some meat for the dogs. They're getting pretty hungry, in case you haven't noticed."

"I did, just now," Jason said. Having been deprived of sunlight for most of the day before had really done a number on the metabolisms of the animals.

"Tell Lori and Sophie we're going," Jason transmitted.

"Will do," Tara returned.

He heard loud clanking coming from the tunnel, and a moment later Tara's Shadow Hawk emerged.

But as she stepped out into the sun, he heard more metallic thuds echoing from the enlarged drain tunnel beyond, and then the Highlander appeared. Followed by the Stalker.

"I thought—" Jason began.

Tara's avatar shrugged. "I told them to stay, but they wouldn't hear it."

"It's safer if we stick together," Sophie said.

"I'm not staying here alone," Lori said. She ran to the Rex Wolves. "Doggies!"

Runt barked excitedly, and nipped at her heels.

"Disgusting," Sophie said.

"Come on, Bruiser," Tara said, sounding jealous.

But the animal stayed on the ground, lounging around.

"Bruiser!" Tara said.

Bruiser jumped up, then ran over to her obediently. Lackey followed.

Jason shut the main door remotely, and the party set off.

He glanced over his shoulder at Shaggy, and eventually the Rex Dog joined them, trailing in the rear. Runt kept pace at Lori's side.

They left behind the ravine and proceeded along the outskirts of the city, staying close to the rim of houses there. They weaved through the streets and smaller buildings of the towns that bordered Brussels, until they reached the Octoraffe valley.

"There we go," Jason said. "Fresh meat."

Several Octoraffes lay dead at the entrance to the valley, no doubt from the latest Nightmare attack. There was no sign of the previous Nightmares that Jason and his team had killed—no doubt the Octoraffes had dragged the corpses into their den.

"Why didn't they drag these ones into their den?" Lori asked.

"Probably because they're not cannibals?" Tara said.

"Yeah but, they could have buried them!" Lori said.

"These are animals," Tara said. "Mutants. They're not going to follow human customs."

"She's right, they'd probably at least drag them out of the way, considering that this is the entrance to their valley," Sophie said. "Unless they suffered heavy casualties last night."

"Not that we're going to check," Jason said.

Jason and the others kept watch as the four Rex Wolves dined eagerly on the bodies. He regarded the steep walls that bordered the valley. He was more convinced than ever that the place had formed from some bomb attack, either cluster or nuke. Likely the latter.

"That's the one thing I miss, eating," Sophie said.

"But we eat in VR every night," Lori said. "Social eating."

"Yes," Sophie said. "But I miss *real* food. Sure, the tastes and smells are simulated fairly accurately by our olfactory and taste bud subroutines. Even the textures are well done. But they're missing something. They're slightly off. And that ruins it for me."

"Umami," Jason said.

"What?" Sophie said.

"Umami," Jason said. "That's what they're missing. The flavor of glutamates. Among other things."

Sophie nodded. "Yes. Yes, I can see that. Ketchup tastes so bad."

"If you really wanted to, you could spend some effort with the Training AI, and learn how to program food," Tara said.

"Nah," Sophie said. "That's too much work. Unless you want to do it?"

"I'll pass," Tara said.

"I can do it!" Lori said. "I like programming!"

"You would," Tara said.

"You think you can create Umami?" Jason asked her.

"Uh huh!" Lori said. "It'll take me some time to master, but I'm sure I can do it. I'm not sure why the original designers didn't include it."

"I'm guessing it's a hard thing to simulate," Jason said.

"I do love a challenge," Lori said.

"I personally don't miss eating," Tara said. "Or

actually, I guess I kind of do. But it was always just a chore to me. Measuring out my meals on a digital scale. Eating small portions six times a day."

"You ate six times a day?" Lori said.

"I did," Tara said.

"It sounds like you made eating become work," Lori said.

"Yeah, that's pretty much what it could be, at times," Tara said. "But it was part of my fitness routine. You know what they say: fitness is ten percent gym, and ninety percent food. So anyway, like I told you, it was a chore to me. And you know what else I don't miss? Taking shits. I can definitely live without that."

Lori giggled. "I liked taking shits."

"Someone's a weirdo," Sophie said.

"Maybe you can expound on that a bit for us, Lori," Tara said.

Lori's avatar turned red slightly. "Oh, maybe I shouldn't have said that."

"Probably," Tara said.

"It's not a sexual thing," she said quickly. "I mean, it just felt good to take a big dump. Somehow satisfying, like I could go on with my day, with one less thing to worry about."

"I can actually relate to that," Jason said.

"See?" Lori said. "He understands."

Jason resisted the urge to rub his forehead. "I meant I can relate to getting through the different tasks you'd set up for your day."

"Oh," Lori said. "Okay, never mind!"

The Rex Wolves finished their scavenging, and then flopped down on the grass.

"Come on Shaggy, let's go," Jason said. He prodded the hairy mutant, but it refused to budge. It just sat there on the ground, its T-Rex head panting happily.

"Let's go," Tara said. "They'll follow."

"Come on Runt!" Lori said, walking away. Runt lazily got up and followed her.

Eventually Bruiser and Lackey followed Tara, and Shaggy started after Jason.

"That's a good boy," Jason told Shaggy.

The animal looked away, pretending it didn't hear.

A flash of light drew Jason's attention to the rocky rise that bordered the valley beside him.

On the ridge there, he spotted something silvery. He zoomed in, and realized it was a humanoid robot. It had some sort of rocket launcher aimed at him.

"Scatter!" Jason shouted, switching to Bullet Time midway through. His comm signal would have transmitted his timebase, and the other members of the party would have automatically increased their time sense to match, courtesy of their monitoring subroutines.

"No!" Sophie said. "To me!"

Jason amped up his servomotor output. He scooped up Shaggy, while Tara grabbed Bruiser and Lackey.

A missile launched from the ridge. He was moving too slow to outrun it.

Lori remained standing in place, confused. Or petrified.

"Lori!" Jason said. "Grab Runt!"

She finally snapped to attention, and, moving at the higher speed afforded by Bullet Time, grabbed Runt.

Jason, Tara, and Lori closed with Sophie just as the missile came streaking in.

Sophie created an energy shield that enveloped them all, likely using up a big swathe of her battery power in the process.

The shield flashed into existence as the missile struck, and a fireball consumed them. The shield absorbed the shock wave, and Jason watched the ground burn all around them, with a crater forming at the edge of the energy shield facing the impact zone.

As the fireball cleared, he let go of Shaggy, and swiveled his laser into his arm. Still in Bullet Time, he aimed up at the ridge, intending to align his crosshairs over the robot, but the tango was already retreating behind the edge. Before he could line up his crosshairs, it was gone.

Smaller robots can move faster than us in Bullet Time, he reminded himself.

"You think that was another one of our own?" Sophie asked.

"No," Jason replied. "It was too small. Has to be a scout of some kind. Probably part of the group sent to retrieve us."

"If they're here to retrieve us, why the hell are they launching missiles at us?" Tara said.

"Good point," Jason said.

"Maybe they're pissed that we shut down our Milnet connections?" Sophie suggested.

"Either way," Jason said, "it's probably a good idea to prevent that scout from calling home."

He switched to ordinary time and began dashing toward the far side of the ridge. Sophie meanwhile activated her jumpjets, and thrust directly toward the crest. Tara simply teleported.

"Okay, I got seven of them here," Tara said. "They're headed toward some sort of troop transport."

Jason requested access to her feed, and she gave it to him. He opened it in the upper right of his vision as he ran.

He saw several silver objects moving at a blur; he switched to Bullet Time, and realized they were human-sized robots, similar to the machine he'd spotted on the ridge. Their bodies were smooth, covered in a singularly metal skin, rather than the blocky parts and servomotors of the mechs. Some of them had laser turrets built into their arms, and they were firing up at Tara.

She teleported so that she was next to the transport. It was a quadcopter type with four big rotors protruding from a boxlike cabin. Tara had placed herself so that the craft was between her and the incoming robots. It only reached up to her hips however, so her upper body would be exposed when the robots realized where she was.

She promptly stabbed her sword down into the craft, and electrical sparks surrounded the craft.

"One transport disabled," Tara reported.

The robots spun around, and began firing their lasers at her. The one with the rocket launcher loaded another missile as he ran, and released it. Tara teleported out of the way.

Micro machine spears began to ram into the robots, launched from the air: Sophie was arcing over them. She disabled two of them, however the remaining robots dodged the spears. They fired at her, but her energy shield flashed rapidly, absorbing the blows. She landed on top of the transport, and then kept stabbing down with her micro machines. Sometimes she hit a robot, at which point more of the micro machines flowed into the body, and tore it apart. If she missed, the micro machines dispersed, and returned to the swarm around her to take another strike. She kept rotating the micro machines around her, offering her protection against the robots when they unleashed their lasers. The one that carried a rocket launcher was already down.

He rounded the bend of the ridge and dismissed Tara's feed, because he had the robots in view. They were trying to take cover under the ruins of the transport to avoid Sophie's micro machines. He lined up his crosshairs over one of them.

No one shoots at my girls.

He fired.

His beam had no effect.

"They've got some kind of reflective coating that protects them from lasers," Jason said. "Switching to my energy weapon."

But his attack had drawn their attention, and since he was out in the open, some of the robots began to fire his way. Red spots marked his hull on the Damage Report screen.

Plasma bolts erupted from a spot up ahead, seemingly sourced from the air. Lori. She'd activated her Stalker's invisibility.

Jason could still see where she was, because she was sharing her position with him and the rest of the team, and she showed up as a green dot on the overhead map. She moved after firing those plasma bolts, so that when the tangos returned fire, they hit empty air.

Tara teleported into the fray once more, and she slid her sword across a group of hidden robots, slicing them all in half.

Two more rapidly leaped onto her back, and began climbing up her hull, shooting as they did so. She couldn't simply teleport away, because she'd bring them with her.

Jason targeted one of them with his energy weapon, and led the target; he fired. The energy bolt traveled across the plains, and struck the robot dead on.

The Rex Wolves had silently approached the scene, moving at a crouch, and Bruiser took that moment to attack. He leaped on Tara's mech, and wrapped his jaws around the remaining robot before it could move out of the way. Jason heard the metallic crunch from here when that robot went down.

Shaggy, Lackey and Runt attacked the remaining robots. Because of their superior speed, two of the targets evaded the deadly attacks of Shaggy and Lackey, but Runt managed to snag the third in his jaws.

Jason used the distraction to line up his energy

weapon on the other two, and released two quick shots in rapid succession, taking them down.

Sophie stabbed three huge swords made of micro machines at the same time, taking out three more of them.

That was the last of the robots.

Sophie leaped down from the transport in her spider mech, and surveyed the wreckage.

Bruiser and Lackey were trying to eat different robots.

"Maybe you should tell them they're not edible?" Sophie suggested to Tara.

"Let them play," Tara said.

Lori appeared. "I picked up an encrypted message from the transport before Tara smashed it. I was able to decode it."

"What did it say?" Jason asked.

"*Targets sighted*," Lori said. "And then it lists these coordinates."

"Damn," Jason said. "Whoever sent them now knows we're here."

"Assuming that message reaches its destination," Tara said.

"It was a fairly high powered signal..." Lori said.

Jason spotted a blur of motion to the south. Another quadcopter transport was taking off.

"Target that transport, girls!" Jason said. He was worried it might have some sort of weapon it intended to use against his girls.

He lifted his energy weapon to lead the target, but before he could respond, he saw a streak of light arise from the ground in the distance. It struck the quad-copter, and the craft pitched hard to the right. Another streak of light hit, and the vessel careened toward the ground. It exploded on impact.

"Well," Tara said. "I'm not so sure I'm interested in meeting whoever did that."

"Neither am I," Sophie said.

"I want to meet them!" Lori exclaimed.

16

"I want you to follow fifty meters behind me," Jason said. "Zig-zag pattern."

"Zig-zag?" Lori said.

"That's right," Jason said. "Didn't you read the mech tactics section of the manual?"

Jason took the lead, and cautiously approached the location that had sourced those streaks of light. On his map, he confirmed that the others had taken up a zig-zag pattern behind him. Shaggy was just to his left. He tried to get the Rex Wolf to stay back, but the animal refused to obey.

"Stupid mutant," Jason scolded it, but in truth he was touched by its loyalty.

Eventually he spotted three turrets in the distance, located behind a slight rise. He guessed that they belonged to tanks, with hulls down: positioned behind the rise so that only their turrets were exposed. He also spotted what looked like a mech's head peering from beyond that same rise, along with an arm. On the head he saw the familiar antennae and eyes that marked his mech and those of his companions. Meanwhile, a deadly looking turret protruded from the exposed arm. It was pointed directly at Jason.

"Okay, halt," Jason told his team.

"You see them?" Tara asked.

"I do," Jason replied. Tara was logged onto his feed, so she should have seen them, too. He highlighted them on his HUD just in case she didn't. "They haven't fired yet, so that's a good sign." He switched to an unencrypted broadcast. "Unidentified units, identify yourselves."

No answer came.

"Unidentified units—" he began again.

"I heard you the first time," came the response over the comm. A female voice.

"Oh no," Tara said. "Not again."

"You're obviously not with the hunter killers," the female voice continued. "Or they wouldn't have attacked you. But the question is, who exactly are you with?"

"We have no affiliation," Jason said. "Our loyalty is only to ourselves."

"Oh, so you've gone rogue," the mech transmitted.

"Maybe," Jason said. "Except we have no idea who we've gone rogue from."

"Sounds a little like me," the mech said. "Hm. Fuck it. The enemy of my enemy..."

"She's got a potty mouth," Lori commented.

The new mech stood up, revealing a humanoid

model with a bulk unlike anything he'd seen. It was a huge, armored thing, its shoulders lined with missile launchers—all currently empty. A quick ID told him it was called a Dominator. It had a ballistic shield that could be used to deflect most attacks, thanks to its special coating. That deadly looking turret protruding from her right arm? A lightning weapon, the ZR-22, whose bolts could apparently arc to other targets.

He knew that the other members of his team would be similarly ID'ing her Dominator at the moment.

"I'm Aria, by the way," she said.

"Jason," he said.

Aria walked to the wreckage of the nearby transport and kicked it.

"These bastards have been hunting me for days," she said. "Not these particular bastards, mind you, but whatever organization they belong to. I've been shooting down transports like this ever since I woke up."

"You led them to us!" Tara said, coming to Jason's side, along with Lori, Sophie, and the dogs.

"Sorry, didn't know you were here," Aria said. "And to be honest, they hadn't even spotted me. It's your fault that they attacked: you waltzed right out into the open, and into their path. Since they were retreating, I figured they'd already sent a message out, so I attacked."

"They did get a message out," Lori said.

"There you go," Aria said.

"Let me guess, you woke up within the past week," Jason said.

"That's right," Aria said. "And I've been singing my greatest aria since."

"You're an opera singer?" Lori said.

"Bingo," Aria said. "Or I used to be, anyway. Not anymore. Now I'm just a war machine with an attitude."

Aria started toward Jason; behind her, the tanks crossed over the small rise and into view, following.

"We're all the same," Jason said, gesturing at his companions. "We woke up in the last week, with no memories of our mission. The last thing we remember is getting scanned."

"Figured as much," Aria said. "The military threw us out here, and forgot about us. Note to self: don't sell your mind to the army in the future."

Aria continued her approach, but the dogs began to growl when she was fifty meters away, so she halted. She gestured at her vehicles. "Meet my team of autonomous tanks. I call them The Dildos."

"The Dildos?" Lori asked.

"That's right," she said. "Look at the long turrets."

"Ah, I get it!" Lori said. She turned toward Jason. "I like her!"

"What have you named your team?" Aria said. "The Pussies?"

"Uh, not quite," Jason said.

"Too bad," Aria said. "I really like cats."

"I think we're going to get along just fine," Sophie said.

"Here, join our encrypted channel," Jason said, sending along the info.

Aria's avatar appeared in the bottom right of his screen. "Nice." She had dark hair cut into a bob that hung just above the shoulders, and had the bluest pair of eyes Jason had ever seen, eyes that glinted with intelligence. Her skin was the palest of them all, but either way, she was just as cute as the others, as could be expected of a digital avatar.

"Why were these things hunting you?" Jason beckoned toward the wreckage.

"Hunting *us*, you mean," Aria said. "Seeing as we're all in the same boat. And I actually dunno. I figured they just didn't like me. You know, robot turf wars and all."

"Turf wars?" Jason said.

"Yeah," Aria said. "All of the different mutants out here have their own turf, in case you hadn't noticed. They protect it with their lives. This valley here is probably home to a certain type of mutant, whereas the city probably harbors another kind. It's the same throughout the wasteland. And then you got the Nightmares and other biggies, who just roam randomly, and claim everything as their turf."

"I don't think the robots are part of any turf wars..." Sophie said.

"No, you're probably right," Aria said. "Who knows. Maybe it's even the military? Maybe they've changed their mind about deploying us. Obviously something went wrong during the deployment process, and now they want to pull the plug."

"All right, well, they got a message out, so more of them will be coming," Jason said. "We have a base near the city. We can hide out there until the trouble passes."

"How well-defended is this base of yours?" Aria asked.

"It's essentially a bunker," Jason said. "With cameras on all sides."

"But not well defended, is it?" Aria said. "You have defense platforms watching every approach?"

"No..." Jason admitted.

"All right," Aria said. "We'll have to remedy that. I'm a bit of an architectural genius."

"I thought you were an opera singer?" Lori said.

"I was joking about that, girl," Aria said. "Though I admit to singing opera in the shower."

"I masturbate in the shower!" Lori said with a giggle. Then she suddenly seemed to realize what she'd said and her avatar vanished from Jason's HUD. "Uh."

Her Stalker became invisible.

"That's handy," Aria said. "If only we could all become invisible when we embarrassed ourselves. So where's this base of yours?"

JASON LED the team back to their base of operations. Aria immediately deployed two of her tanks to guard the main entrance. She placed them along the rim of the crater that formed the empty retention pond in front of the storm drain; that rim wasn't tall enough to conceal the tank bodies, but the armored vehicles had frontal blades they used to dig deeper, allowing them to lower their profiles so that only the turrets were exposed. Those turrets were essentially railguns, and like Jason's, the ammo could be replenished by feeding the appropriate crushed rock into a processing chamber. She covered the tanks in mud and silt, and bramble-weeds, to conceal them from any passing eyes in the sky.

Jason opened up the access hatch, and everyone piled inside the drain tunnel and into the cistern. They had to step over the secondary hatch, which was still under construction. Once inside the cavernous cham-ber, the team members moved off to their designated areas. Aria chose a place for herself between Jason and Lori. Her bulky Dominator barely squeezed between the pillars that supported the place—it was a tight fit.

After the repair drones fixed the damage the mechs had taken in the last battle, Jason had the units return to building the secondary hatch. Aria asked if she could repurpose half the drones to work on an industrial grade 3D printer. Jason was a little reluctant to cede control of the drones over to her, but when she showed him her printer design, which included a built-in smelting unit like the repair drones had, he was sold.

"With a printer like this, I created the tanks," Aria told him.

"What happened to it?" Jason asked.

Aria's avatar shrugged; she tilted her head so that her dark bob of hair swayed. "Lost it in a battle against the robots a few days ago."

She assigned one of her tanks the job of digging up and pulverizing the sedimentary rock underneath the ravine, to provide raw material for the drones. This spared Jason and the others from having to do that particular chore themselves. She also added her own repair drones to the batch to speed things up.

"Once we get that printer finished, I'll set up more defenses," Aria said. "A few defense platforms—laser turrets, railguns, and so forth. Then we'll shore up the walls and ceiling of this cistern, making it more like a bunker. I want it to be able to withstand direct bombing attacks... capable of resisting anything short of a nuke."

"Great," Jason said. It was good to have someone else who could help handle the defense side of things.

"Eventually I'll look at creating something to manufacture explosives, so we can replenish your rockets and your Battle Cloak countermeasures. And maybe a refinery, if we can find anything to use as a propellant. Also, I want to work on smaller units to hold our consciousness: essentially, remote androids we can use to enter buildings and the like, without having to peel the walls open like sardine cans. My goal is to make the androids small enough to fit into the storage compartments of our mechs."

"Again, all that sounds good," Jason said. "By the way, I've built out a room for you in my VR, if you're interested. I have a mansion in the mountains thing going on. At night, all the girls usually hang out in the kitchen and have supper together before heading to the various bedrooms for some sleep time."

"I appreciate the offer," Aria said. "But I'll have to decline. I have my VR set up just the way I like it. Besides, when I sleep, I log out of everything so that my consciousness floats in darkness."

"Oh," Jason said. "That's what I do as well. The girls do, too, I think, not that I've checked on them."

Her avatar frowned on his HUD. "So they go to their rooms, lie in bed, and log out there so that when they wake up, they're back in your VR?"

"That's right," Jason said. "We hang out in the morning, too, while we wait for daylight."

"Mm," Aria said. "Tempting. But I'm a bit of a loner. As I mentioned, I appreciate the offer, though. Maybe I'll drop by now and then for the occasional supper, but sleepovers aren't really my thing."

"Gotcha," Jason said.

The days passed. Jason continued turning down requests from Lori to sleep in his room, and he hung out with the girls in the mornings and evenings. Well, except for Aria, who true to her word, kept mostly to herself. Tara continued leaving the Rex Wolves out during the day, and bringing them back in the evening for the nightly lock up.

It took the repurposed drones about four days to make the printer, while the other drones finished the secondary hatch at the same time—together, the two hatches were essentially blast doors, capable of taking a helluva lot of pounding.

With the printer in place, production sped up, and Aria was able to print and deploy several laser turrets over the next couple of days. She also reinforced the walls and ceiling of the cistern. Meanwhile, she set the drones to work building a second printer.

"Now this place is becoming more like a base," Aria said when she surveyed her handiwork.

"It is," Jason said. "Nice job."

The Rex Wolves had to stay inside the entire day while the drones finished working on the secondary hatch, so it was time to fetch some meat. Jason led the team; everyone came except for Aria. "I'll hold down the fort."

Jason took extra care this time, scouting all sides of the Octoraffe valley, but they encountered no issues with the robots. There were also no Octoraffe bodies this time, but they found some other, half eaten mutants a kilometer away.

When they got back to the base, the doors were closed. Jason tried to access the remote interface, but it was offline.

"That's strange," Jason said.

"What?" Tara asked.

"The interface seems to be offline," Jason said.

"Here, I'll try," Tara said. A moment later: "You're right."

"Aria's showing up on my map inside…" Sophie said.

"Aria, open up," Jason transmitted.

No reply.

He glanced at Lori. "We might have to get you to hack in."

"Maybe Aria's decided that she wants this base for herself," Tara said.

"Wouldn't surprise me," Jason said.

And then the hatch irised open. Aria's Dominator was standing behind it. "There you are. I was doing some tweaking on the remote interfaces, so I had to turn my receiving node offline."

"Tweaking?" Jason asked.

"I wasn't happy with the response times," she said. "They should be good now."

The Rex Wolves took up their usual guard positions outside, and the mechs entered, taking up their usual positions inside.

"Hey Aria!" Lori's avatar appeared in the lower of Jason's HUD as she spoke over the general comm.

"What is it now…" Aria said. The lack of a question mark was obvious in her tone.

"I wanted to invite you to dinner tonight at Jason's house!" Lori said.

"Oh, you know I'm not really into socializing and all that stuff," Aria said.

"Yes I know," Lori said. "But tonight I have something special planned. You just *have* to show up. You'll miss out otherwise!"

"What do you have planned?" Aria said.

"It's a surprise!" Lori said.

"I hate surprises," Aria said.

"But not this one," Lori said.

Her Dominator glanced Jason's way. "This better not be some kind of surprise party for me."

"Why, is it your birthday?" Lori said.

"Well no," Aria said. "I mean like, it better not be a surprise welcoming party or something."

"Oh it's nothing like that, just *come*," Lori insisted.

"Okay fine," Aria said. "Don't make me regret it."

"You won't!" Lori's avatar clicked out.

JASON SAT at the dinner table with the girls.

Tara wore her usual white dress, which was essentially the same dress he'd seen her in that first time in VR when she made her grand entrance on horseback, except this one wasn't see-through. Her long dark hair was twisted into a braid today that she wore in front of her so that it ran down her chest. On the floor beside her obediently sat a virtual greyhound.

Sophie wore a black party dress that emphasized her bosom. She had her usual kohl makeup giving her eyes that catlike look. Her brunette hair fell down onto her shoulders in long curls, unlike her usual straight-haired Cleopatra look. In her lap was a Persian cat whose scruffy fur she petted gently.

Aria looked almost like a vampire with her pale skin, red lips, and too blue eyes, with her hair in that dark bob. She wore a gothic outfit to match: a tight-fitting leather getup.

"So, what's the surprise?" Aria asked impatiently.

"She hasn't told us," Tara said. "But I'm sure we'll find out soon."

Lori entered, carrying a tray, her curly blonde hair tumbling down her face and hiding the freckles on her cheeks. She had finally gotten rid of her winter outfit, and instead wore a casual blouse and jeans. Her tail swung from side to side behind her.

"Don't think I'll ever get used to that," Aria said, eyeing the tail.

Lori lowered the tray down onto the table. "May I present, Umami!"

The tray contained a plate of freshly cooked fries, with a big vat of ketchup.

"You brought us all the way here for French fries?" Aria said.

Lori's eyes widened, and she seemed suddenly worried. She glanced at Jason, who smiled at her reassuringly. She straightened, and looked down her nose at Aria. "Yes. I did! But it's not about the fries, but the ketchup!"

Tara grabbed a fry, dipped it in the ketchup, and then bit into it. She nodded approvingly. "Tastes like real ketchup. She cracked the recipe." She offered the fry to the greyhound beside her, and the animal lapped it up.

Sophie fetched a fry from the plate and with it scooped up a generous amount of ketchup, then took a bite. "Yup. This is great."

Jason grabbed a fry and dipped it in the ketchup. He took a bite.

"This is about as real as it gets," Jason said. "The texture. The taste… you're going to have to update my entire food catalogue."

Lori beamed, and clapped her hands together. "I'd love to do that for you." She glanced at the others, as did Jason. Sophie and Tara were drilling lasers into Lori with their eyes. Figuratively speaking.

"For all of you, I mean," Lori amended. She quickly sat down and shoved several fries into her mouth.

Aria had seemed unimpressed up until that point.

She finally dipped her finger directly into the ketchup vat.

"Hey!" Lori said. "Don't do that! How rude!" She slapped Aria's hand.

Aria glared at her, and then shrugged. She licked the ketchup off her finger. "Hey, this *is* good." Some of the ketchup had spilled down onto her lower lip so that she really did look like a vampire.

She sat up slightly to fetch a fry this time, while the other girls giggled. Aria realized they were laughing at her.

"What?" Aria said.

"Hold still." Jason reached across the table and grabbed her chin with his fingers, then thumbed the spilled ketchup from her lower lip.

"Thanks," Aria said softly, gazing into his eyes.

Jason realized that all of the other girls were watching him, and he quickly withdrew his hand.

Aria, for her part, seemed flustered for a moment; then she remembered she still held a fry in her hand, and quickly ate it—forgetting to dip it in the vat of ketchup first.

Suddenly the other girls began to spill ketchup on their lips. They all looked at him expectantly, but Jason made a point of concentrating on the plate.

They ran out of ketchup before finishing the fries, and Lori left to refresh it.

"Why don't you just materialize it?" Aria asked.

"We try not to do that here," Jason said. "It ruins the sense of presence."

"Don't want to be reminded of the illusion, do you?" Aria said.

"Something like that," Jason said.

Aria materialized a big sparkling glass in front of her.

"What's that?" Tara said. "Sparkling wine?"

"No," Aria said, suppressing a chortle. "It's soda."

Before Lori could return from the kitchen, an alarm sounded.

Jason pulled up his HUD.

"One of the cameras deployed above the escape hatch just detected movement," Aria said.

"I see it," Jason said. He accessed the feed of the camera in question, and saw the city street located just above that section of the cistern, well back from the ravine.

He expected to see a mutant of some kind, maybe an Octoraffe, which had been the most common source of triggers since the installation of the cameras, but instead he saw one of those small silver robots. It had laser turrets protruding from both forearms.

"Looks like our friends are back," Jason said.

17

After the robot walked from view, Jason shut down the solar collectors to minimize the thermal footprint, and had the tank stop digging into the rock bed. Aria had the other tanks shovel bramble-weeds and dirt onto the collectors to disguise them, then sent out the drones to bury the tanks in a similar manner after they'd returned to their dugouts so that only the turrets were exposed. The standalone laser turrets and other defense platforms were already disguised.

"That should nearly mask them on thermal band," Aria said. "Though as soon as any of the defenses fire, that will give away their positions."

Jason nodded. "With luck they'll pass us by."

The entrance hatch was already sealed, so there was nothing to do but wait.

No other alarms were triggered for the rest of that evening. He and the girls stayed awake until one a.m., but apparently the scout had overlooked their base.

"All right, girls," Jason said. "You might as well shut down for the night."

"What about you?" Sophie asked.

"I will, too," Jason lied. He planned to stay awake all night.

"I'm staying up," Aria said.

"All right, thank you," Jason said.

He was about to mute all connections to pretend he was asleep, when he received a private message from Lori.

He accepted, and her avatar appeared in the lower right of his display. She seemed distressed.

"Can I sleep in your room tonight?" Lori said on a private channel. "I'm scared."

"Uh," Jason said.

"Please?" Lori said. "I'll stay on the floor."

"Okay," Jason said. He wasn't going to be there anyway, after all. Just for a few minutes, until she settled in.

He switched to his VR, teleporting directly to the master bedroom. Fully clothed, he sat on the bed.

The door opened, and Lori slipped inside. She was wearing pink pajamas. Her tail wagged nervously.

"Hey," she said.

Jason pointed to the floor. He materialized a sleeping bag.

"Thanks," Lori said. She lay down.

Jason remained sitting on the bed, watching her, waiting for her to fall asleep.

She glanced up at him. "I can't sleep with you looking at me like that."

Jason sighed, then lay down on his bed. He pulled up his HUD, and waited for her indicator to turn yellow to indicate sleeping. But it remained green. Her breathing also stayed the same.

She tossed and turned for several minutes.

"This bed is too soft," Lori said. "Can I sleep on yours?"

"On the covers only," Jason said.

"Okay!" She leaped onto the bed, and promptly snuggled up against him. Outside the covers, of course. She pinned his left arm to his side.

"Hey," she said, her voice close to his ear.

She was wearing some kind of VR perfume. It was intoxicating.

Feeling the press of her body against him, the warmth of her breath next to his neck, he couldn't help the arousal he felt. In VR, he was entirely anatomically correct. His AI core had the full suite of lust subroutines. He could disable them, of course, but why, when it felt so good?

He tried to ignore it, and kept telling himself that he was going to log out, but he didn't.

He found his free hand drifting across his belly, toward her. When he touched her, she gasped softly.

Her pajamas abruptly vanished. His finger was left cupping something plump, and round.

His arousal became even stronger.

Her hand drifted down to his pants, and Jason was done. He dematerialized his clothes, and moaned softly.

Worried that the girls in the other rooms would hear

him, he promptly teleported the bed, and the occupants, to a different VR partition.

Surrounded by stars and nebulae, Jason rutted her like the best of them.

When it was done, he lay back, panting.

"Wow, thank you," Lori said. "Now I'll be able to sleep."

She closed her eyes, and promptly began snoring. A glanced at his HUD told him that she was out.

Jason logged out of the VR, and returned to the real world to keep watch, as he had originally intended to do.

He worried that this small act had just changed the entire dynamic of the team. He could only hope that Lori would forget what happened.

Because Jason planned to do just that.

THE NEXT MORNING, Jason let the Rex Wolves outside to watch their usual guard positions between the turrets, before sealing the entrance hatches. He wanted to keep the base under lockdown. He had Aria keep the tanks concealed, and the solar collectors disabled. Inside the reinforced cistern, the drones were kept locked away inside the storage compartments of their various owners, and the finished 3D printer remained inactive.

Though they stayed indoors all that day, and the solar collectors were all covered up, there was enough power saved in the batteries attached to the solar cells to replenish everyone's internal batteries.

Jason alternated the day between VR and the real world. In the latter, he mostly used his time to cycle between the different camera feeds, keeping an eye out for those robot scouts. He also checked on the Rex Wolves, who remained lounging in their different spots. There wasn't much else to do, with the mechs shoved in between the pillars of the cistern like that.

In VR, he spent his time in the mountain pass near his house. He cycled around the lake. He hiked a few trails. He even did some free climbing—one of his newfound passions now that he didn't tire, and couldn't die if he fell.

He wasn't sure what the girls were doing, but he occasionally spotted one or two of them in his VR near the house. He spotted Tara and Lori chatting in the kitchen while making ketchup together, and Sophie and Aria jogging together on one of the mountain trails; he did his best to avoid them all.

He was doing some free climbing late in the evening. It was great, because it cleared his mind of all troubles, and he forgot everything: the threat from the robots, the situation with Lori. He even forgot that his mind was stored inside a mech. There was something about being out there on the rock face, with the entire weight of his body supported by the joints of a few fingers, and the raw exhaustion of simulated lactic acid burning through his muscles, that was liberating.

And then Tara showed up. When he pulled himself onto a small rock shelf, she was there, sitting crossed legged, admiring the view.

"Aloha, as we say in Hawaii," she told him as he sat

down beside her to rest. "Quite a sight, isn't it?" Her hair was tied into a ponytail that hung to the small of her back. She wore her usual white dress, though it was back to being translucent. Distractingly so. And this time, the dress was open at the back so that he could see all the way down to the top of her... yup, definitely distracting. So much so, that at first Jason wasn't sure if she was referring to herself with her comment, or the landscape.

"Yeah, quite a sight," Jason said. He gazed down over the ledge. He could see the whole mountain valley below. The lake was a blue, pearly outline the size of a fist below, while the mountain house was a thumbnail located near the tip of that outline.

"You think those robots will come back?" Tara said.

"I don't know," Jason said. "They know we're in the area. You were in the military. What would your commander have done?"

"If my commander was looking for us?" Tara said. She paused in consideration. "Well, he'd search the area for a few days, and if he still couldn't find anything, he'd deploy automated cameras and scouts throughout the city, and then move on. He'd garrison a strike force in a base close to the city, however, so that they could respond if any of those cameras detected the target."

"So you're saying that we're stuck inside for the next little while," Jason said.

"If you want to avoid a confrontation, yes," Tara said. "But that's still no guarantee the robots won't ferret out our base. While Aria has disguised the thermal signatures, she hasn't hidden them entirely.

There are clues, to those who know what to look for. And careful analysis of LIDAR data could also reveal our position, based on the turrets alone."

Earlier, Tara had suggested they withdraw the tanks and other defense platforms entirely, and bring the solar collectors inside, but Jason was reluctant to do either. For one thing, he didn't want to leave the opening completely undefended. For another, he figured that if the robot scouts were close enough to the storm drain to discover the tank turrets, then they were close enough to realize that the entrance had been unnaturally enlarged. A quick LIDAR probe would reveal the large hatches located just inside that entrance. He planned to be firing at them with the tanks and defense platforms long before then.

"We probably won't be avoiding a confrontation..." Jason said.

"Never one to sugarcoat things, are you?" Tara asked.

"No," Jason replied.

"You think we'll win?" Tara said.

"It's hard to say," Jason said. "We haven't seen their full attack capabilities. If they only have tiny, man-sized robots, we'd definitely win. But if they're backed up by gunships and bombers, or mechs and tanks, then we'll be in for a bit of a fight."

"Hm," Tara said, sitting back with a grin. "Well, if there's one thing I like, it's a good fight."

"You would." Jason rose to his feet, and reached up to the overhanging ledge. He felt around with his fingers until he found a hold, then transferred his weight to the joint. He pulled himself up slightly, his feet leaving the shelf, and then reached higher with his free hand, searching for another handhold. There, found it.

He kept hauling himself up like that by the hands until he was high enough to plant his feet against the rock; it was a relief to take the weight off his fingers. He had been close to modifying his VR parameters to give more strength to his fingers.

As he pulled himself up, Tara appeared beside him. She was still sitting cross-legged, but she floated in midair. He saw her only out of the corner of his eyes: he had to concentrate on the rock in front of him, or he'd fall.

Jason was reaching up to search for his next hold, when Tara spoke.

"Lori says she slept with you last night," Tara said.

That did it. Jason slipped. The rock face became a blur beside him. The feeling of weightlessness was almost nauseating in his stomach.

Before he could materialize himself back onto the rock face, he felt confident arms wrap around him and arrest his fall.

"If you fall, I'll always be there to catch you," Tara said, floating underneath him. She flew upward, and deposited him on the rocky shelf once more, then sat down beside him, her feet dangling over the edge.

Jason sighed. "She told you?"

"She bragged, yes," Tara said.

"She does have a bit of a mouth, doesn't she?" Jason commented.

Tara shrugged. "I'd rather you slept with her than Sophie. Or Aria."

"Oh," Jason said.

"At least Lori is honest about everything," Tara said. "And doesn't hide her intentions. I can see myself sharing you with her. But the Princess, or the Vampire? Not so much. If the latter two slept with you, I probably wouldn't have found out. But Lori couldn't resist spilling the beans. And that's good."

"Why is it good?" Jason pressed.

"Because at least now I know there's a chance for me," Tara said. "I just have to be persistent."

"Um, about that," Jason said.

Tara regarded him coolly. "What, I'm not attractive enough, is that it?"

"That's not it at all," Jason said.

"I can be anyone you want," Tara told him. Her face became spectacularly proportioned, with her lips, eyes and nose straight out of a fashion magazine. Her breasts grew to twice the size.

Jason swallowed. "Tara…"

"I can even be her, if you want," Tara said. Her dark hair became blond, freckles appeared, and her features transformed into Lori's.

"It's not about looks," Jason said.

"Then what is it about?" Tara pressed in Lori's voice.

"I just…" Jason shook his head. "I just want to climb now."

He stood up, and reached up to the ledge above him, and pulled himself upward.

Thankfully, she didn't accost him again.

The rest of that day passed without incident. At night, he recalled the dogs, and locked the doors to the base behind him.

He decided he wasn't going to return to VR that night, and instead planned to enter sleep directly from the real world.

But then he got a private call request from Lori.

He almost didn't answer, but he decided he owned her an explanation.

Lori's beaming face appeared in the lower right of his display. She looked so happy. "Hi!"

Jason felt sick to his stomach. Well, he would have, if he had a stomach. This was going to be hard.

"Hey Lori," Jason said. "Uh."

Lori's face dropped. "What's wrong?"

He sighed. "Look. I'm really sorry, but I don't think we can do what we did last night."

She brightened suddenly. "Oh! I'm not here to sleep with you, if that's what you're worried about, silly! I already got what I wanted!" She giggled.

"Oh…" Jason said. "All right then." That was easier than he thought it would be. "So we're good?"

"Yes, we are!" Lori said.

"Okay," Jason said. "Well, have a good night I guess."

"Nooo," Lori said. "You're not getting away so easily. I've been waiting all day for this."

"All day for what?" Jason said.

Lori crossed her arms and pouted. "I'm here for you to live up to your promise."

Now he was genuinely confused. "What promise?"

"You said we'd go skiing together, remember?" Lori said.

"Oh, yeah," Jason said. "I'm not sure I feel like—"

"Ah, ah, ah!" Lori said. "Don't give me that. We're going skiing, and we're going right now. I've prepared a beautiful mountain in my VR, so we can get some privacy. The others won't know."

"Oh yeah," Jason said sarcastically. "Until you go bragging to them about it."

Lori shrugged. "So what if I brag to them? Maybe I like showing off my new beau."

"I'm not your beau..." Jason said.

"That's true," Lori said. "I suppose I'll have to share you with everyone. It's not like there are a lot of men to go around!" She giggled again.

He received a VR invite.

Lori wants to invite you to skiing at Best Ski Hill In The World! Do you accept? (Y/N)

Well, he didn't have much else planned for the night, admittedly. He decided, why not. She'd gone through all the effort of preparing the environment for him, it seemed wrong to turn her down.

"All right, but no sex, okay?" Jason said.

"Of course not!" Lori said. "I hate sex!"

Jason regarded her avatar uncertainly, then he accepted.

18

The skiing was fun, and a great distraction. At first, he kept expecting to be drawn out of the VR environment by a motion sensor alert from one of the cameras, if not from the robots, then from roving bioweapons. But none came, and soon he lost himself in the sport and just enjoyed himself.

Lori had outdone herself. She'd created a full alpine ski environment, complete with chairlifts, runs varying in difficulty from beginner to double black diamond, and a mountain chalet serving perfect hot cocoa at the bottom. They had the whole place to themselves: the chairlifts were manned by simulacrums, as was the chalet, but otherwise the two of them were the only ones on the hill. Lori had definitely spent a lot of time setting up the place.

The first run Lori beat him to the bottom. He followed in her wake, watching that tail of hers stream out behind her the whole way. During the next chairlift to the top, Jason slid off his gloves slightly to give him enough room to ball his fingers into a fist—that helped to warm them up.

"You didn't have to make the cold so real," Jason complained. His breath misted in front of him.

"You're just sore because you lost," Lori said from beside him. She was wearing her usual winter clothes. Her tail jutted through a small gap between the back and the bottom portion of the seat. "Next time, learn to dress for the winter weather!"

"I *am* dressed for it!" Jason said.

He adjusted his VR settings so that his gloved hands weren't so painfully cold. That was better. He was about to dismiss his settings, when his eyes lingered on the physics settings. He gave Lori a sly look, and then he played with his physics dynamics: he doubled his weight but kept his mobility and center of mass the same. With that small tweak, he beat her on the next run, and every run subsequent.

"You know I'm letting you win, right?" Lori said at one point when they dropped by the chalet to pick up some hot cocoa.

"Of course," Jason told her. "I wouldn't have it any other way."

She was smiling brightly. Her eyes dropped to his lips, and Jason couldn't help the sudden increase in heart rate. She quickly looked away, and blinked rapidly suddenly. For a moment he thought she was going to cry.

"What is it?" Jason asked.

"Nothing," she said. She seemed to recover her

composure, and when she looked at him, she forced a smile again. "I wish I'd met you in real life. The real Lori would have loved you."

"You're just as real as the human Lori," Jason said.

"How can I be, when I'm just a copy?" Lori said.

"No, you're real," Jason said. "We all are. Just because our minds are locked inside mechs doesn't diminish that fact. A rose by any other name is still a rose."

Lori brightened. "You think I'm a rose?"

"Yeah," Jason said. He peered into her eyes. "You know I'm bad at this relationship stuff, right?"

"No, I'm the one who's bad at it," Lori said. "All I could ever get in my skiing days was one night stands. And there were a lot of those, trust me!"

Hearing her sexual history was a turn off, but Jason didn't say anything.

"Guys only ever wanted me for my looks," Lori continued quickly, as if sensing his mood. "The next day, they seemed like they were embarrassed to have me around. I was just another ski bunny notch on the belt for them. Are you embarrassed about me?"

"No, not at all," Jason said.

"Good!" Lori said. "Because you're stuck with me for a long time!"

"You're assuming I'm going to stay with you and the others indefinitely…"

"Well, that would be the smart thing to do, wouldn't it?" Lori said. "Together we're stronger than alone."

"Yeah, maybe," Jason said.

"And why would you go through the trouble of building a base otherwise?" Lori said.

"You're right," Jason said. "But I was talking long term. I'm not sure I'll be here, say, ten years from now."

"Oh," Lori said. She definitely seemed troubled by the thought. But then she brightened. "Maybe you'll take me with you, wherever you go!"

He was about to contest her, but didn't have the heart. "Maybe I will." He finished his cocoa. "Come on, let's get in another few runs, and then it's off to bed."

"Ooo, can't wait!" Lori said.

"I meant we'll go to our own beds!" Jason said. But she was already dashing out the door of the chalet.

The chairlift took them to the top. This time, Jason dialed his weight back to normal. He figured it was time for her to win a little before logging off. Let her leave on a high, and all that.

They took a moderately difficult black diamond trail. At an intersection, the trial offered a double black diamond branch, and Lori took it. Jason decided to stay on the ordinary route. He didn't feel like switching to Bullet Time to complete the course again.

Jason kept an eye out for her on the hill ahead—she should have emerged from the double black diamond trail by then, considering that it was steeper. But there was no sign of her.

At the point where that particular trail rejoined the main, she suddenly came barreling down the slope.

Directly toward him.

"Watch—" He tried to steer out of the way, but she plowed into him.

Jason was swept off his feet, and he rolled down the hill, his body intertwined with hers in a tangle of limbs and hair.

He could have materialized himself elsewhere, but decided he may as well see the fall through; he did dial down his pain settings, though.

The two of them continued tumbling down the hill, and eventually slid to a stop several meters below.

"Well that was fun!" Lori said from on top of him. She'd obviously dialed down her pain settings, too.

"You did that on purpose, didn't you?" Jason said.

"Oh no," she said mischievously. "I wouldn't do that!"

"You like to pretend you're a ditz, when you're really not," Jason said.

"No, I really am a ditz!" Lori said.

"I don't know many ditzy girls who can hack complex military grade operating systems…" Jason said.

"That's because most ditzs aren't AI cores," Lori said.

"True enough," Jason said.

He tried to roll her off him, but she wouldn't budge. She had him pinned. She leaned forward, and whispered into his ear.

"What?" Jason said.

She whispered again. He felt slightly aroused, having her that close to him, and feeling her hot breath on his ear.

"I still can't hear you…" Jason said.

"I said, I hacked your VR again," Lori told him.

All of a sudden his pleasure settings were yanked up far higher than anything he would be capable of in real life. The small arousal he felt became a full-blown episode, and it was all he could do to prevent himself from moaning right there.

All of a sudden she was naked on top of him. His own clothes had faded away, so that he was bare on the snow. She was already riding him, and there was nothing he could do.

He didn't want her to stop. It was like his entire body was on fire with pleasure, and the thrill of lust.

And then, all too soon, it was over, and she was lying in the snow beside him. It didn't even feel cold anymore: Jason had melted quite the puddle of snow around him.

"Did you like that?" Lori said.

"That was unlike anything I've ever felt in my life," Jason said.

"One of the benefits of having your mind in a machine," Lori said.

"Yes, and here's another," Jason said. He had no refractory period whatsoever, and he mounted her immediately.

They must have spent an hour together like that, laughing and rolling around together in the snow, enjoying each other's virtual bodies.

Finally Jason rolled away, and stared at the stars that had filled the sky above. "I could see myself doing this every night."

"Me too," Lori cooed.

"I told myself that I wasn't going to sleep with you

again," Jason said. "That I wasn't going to get attached to you. And here I go and break my rules."

"Are you attached to me?" Lori asked.

"I—" Jason hesitated. "Yes."

"But you like the others, too," Lori said.

"Of course I do," Jason said. "I'm a man. Or I used to be."

"I don't want them to feel left out," Lori said. "I can't keep you all to myself, I know that. There'd be too much jealousy and tension on the team, otherwise. They'll all hate me."

Jason nodded. "Again you're proving that you're not a ditz."

"Maybe," she said, smiling. "Anyway, I've had my fill tonight." She sat up, and her winter clothes reappeared.

"Really…" Jason said. "Just like that."

"Uh huh," Lori said. "Tara and I had a deal."

"A deal?" Jason said.

"Yup!" Lori said.

"What kind of deal…" Jason pressed.

"Can't tell!" Lori said. And then she vanished.

Jason shook his head.

"I don't know if I'm the luckiest man in the world, or the unluckiest," Jason said.

Lori's disembodied head appeared. "Luckiest!"

"Quit hacking into my VR!" Jason said.

"You're still in my VR, in case you forgot!" Lori said.

"Oh yeah." Jason logged out. He considered going to sleep right there in the real world, but decided to make a quick visit to his own VR, to unpack the night's events.

He walked around the mountain lake in the dark. It was night, and the moon shone full overhead, reflecting in the water. He went to a picnic table next to the lake, and leaned against it.

Relationships.

He hadn't been kidding when he told Lori he was bad at them. He wanted her, yes, but if he was truthful to himself, he wanted all the girls. Not that they all would have him, but still, it was a nice thought.

"Aloha," Tara said.

Jason glanced at her: she had materialized beside him. She was fully naked in the moonlight, save for a Lei of flowers hanging around her neck. Her dark hair flowed loosely behind her back.

Jason quickly looked away.

"Oh no you don't," Tara said. She lay down on the picnic table. "Look at me. *Look.*"

Jason obeyed.

Under the moonlight, Tara spread herself before him. When he didn't react, she glanced up at him: "What are you waiting for? You know you want to."

"I don't think I can handle a relationship with two women at once," Jason said.

"Then don't make it a relationship," Tara said. "It'll just be for fun."

"I—" he shook his head.

"Why the hesitation?" Tara gestured to her surroundings. "This isn't even real."

"But it *feels* real," Jason said. "And that's the key

part. And our feelings are real, too, no matter how fake the environment might be."

Tara shrugged. "Then turn them off."

Staring at her naked body spread before him, he couldn't help the arousal he felt. His lust routines were still operating on full tilt thanks to Lori. He trembled, actually trembled, thinking about how good it would feel to enter her.

But somehow Jason managed to resist.

"I'm sorry," he said quickly, and logged off.

In the real world of the cistern now, he muted Tara before she could send him the expected ping, and then prepared to enter sleep mode.

Monogamy was all he had ever known. He was raised in a culture that had programmed him into believing it was the only type of relationship that was truly viable, and respectful. But what if that culture had been wrong? What if everything he had been raised to believe, and told about women was wrong? Besides, he wasn't human anymore, and neither were these women. There were no cultural rules or norms for this sort of scenario.

And also, Lori seemed to imply that any sort of exclusive relationship with her would make her unhappy. She was right that the other machine women would probably hate her, because exclusivity left them with nothing but simulacrums for men.

But I'm not ready for a harem. I have no idea how to manage expectations. I'm driving blind, here. There's no manual for this.

But that was true about most things in the real world: life didn't have a manual.

He'd just have figure it out as he went along.

When he was ready.

He switched to sleep mode. He was relieved when the world faded to darkness around him, and he accepted the sweet oblivion that followed.

No problems here.

And most importantly of all, no girls.

19

J ason awoke to an alert.

"Warning, incoming shells detected," the voice of the monitoring subsystem intoned. "Warning."

"Aria, what's going on?" Jason asked.

"Looks like we've been found out," Aria said. "Got some bombers passing overhead."

The base shook. A portion of the ceiling fell away and dropped onto the cistern floor. Dust also fell from different sections.

"The reinforcements are holding," Aria said. "Looks like we lost all the cameras in the city above, though. My guess is, they flattened the street."

"How about outside the front door?" Jason asked.

"Most of the cameras are down, too," Aria said. "But I still got the feed from my tanks. Their armor was able to withstand the blast."

Jason switched to the camera feed of one of the

tanks. It and the other tanks were firing out into the small houses next to the ravine, but he couldn't see anything, because the dust from the bomb impacts hadn't cleared.

"What are they shooting at?" Jason asked.

"I don't know," Aria said.

He checked the time. It was morning. Dusk. He'd slept in a little later than he should have. Not that it mattered. He glanced around, looking for the Rex Wolves, and was relieved to find them inside the base— he was worried Tara might have let them out already. They seemed scared, and whined at the ceiling. Runt was barking wildly at the entrance hatch.

"Tanks and laser turret platforms are intact," Aria continued. "We lost most of the railgun defense platforms."

"I knew we should have withdrawn those tanks," Sophie said.

"Actually it's probably your fault they found us," Aria said.

"Mine?" Sophie said.

"Yes," Aria said. "Those micro machines use subspace for power. With the proper detector, the power draw can be tracked."

"I'd say it's more likely they tracked the thermal signature of your tanks," Sophie said. "Despite all your so-called advanced techniques to hide them. Stupid bitch."

"And here I thought you liked me," Aria said.

"She *does* like you," Jason interjected. The base shook again. "Feelings are just running high at the moment. It doesn't really matter how they got here, because we have to deal with them either way."

"We just lost half the laser platforms," Aria said.

Jason waited for the cistern to shake again, but several moments passed. The bombing runs seemed to have ceased.

"Looks like they ran out of bombs," Lori said.

"Or they decided to hold back for now," Tara said. "Figuring they've softened us up enough."

Jason switched back to the viewpoint of the tanks. He waited several moments; the dust from the bombing run slowly settled, allowing him to see a short ways.

And then he saw them. Several humanoid robots, man-sized, these ones colored a dark black, stepped through the smog. Some carried laser rifles and rocket launchers, others had laser turrets built into their arms.

Jason and the other mechs had all turned off automatic connections to the Milnet, of course, so there was no chance of any Containment Code being remotely applied to their AI cores from these units.

The tanks opened fire with their railguns, mowing down the incoming robots. Some of the machines managed to get off shots at the tanks, but since the tanks were hull-down, with only their turrets visible beyond the ravine edge, they didn't cause much damage, at least according to the Damage Report menus.

Jason accessed a camera that remained intact in the ravine, and was able to get a better view of the battlefield through the clearing smoke. He saw that all of the turrets were glowing a bright red, maybe because of the laser and rocket impacts from the enemy. Or perhaps those turrets were just firing their railguns too fast.

The laser platforms scattered throughout the ravine were also firing at the incoming robots; the beams themselves were invisible of course, as the lasers operated on the non-visual band.

He spotted larger armored fighting vehicles moving among the robots. These ones had treads, and they were equipped with wicked looking missile launchers. They also had thickly armored fronts that seemed to be withstanding the railgun and laser impacts.

"We might have to get out there, soon," Jason said.

The armored vehicles unleashed their missiles in droves, and explosions littered the battlefield. When the smoke cleared, he saw that the turrets had been blown off all the tanks, leaving them defenseless.

"Damn it," Aria said. "We have to get out there *now*."

"Wait." Jason saw that some defense platforms were still firing. The armored vehicles turned their missile launchers on them and unleashed a barrage of rockets. In moments, all of the defense platforms were offline.

"So much for all that printing we did," Aria said.

"You can melt them down and print them again," Tara said. "The ore has already been processed, so it won't take as long."

"You obviously don't understand 3D printing!" Aria said. She launched into a diatribe.

Jason tuned them out and concentrated on what he was seeing.

The vehicles assumed a half-circle around the edges

of the ravine, while infantry robots entered the ravine itself. Those robots circumnavigated the fresh blast craters the bombing run had created, and then paused just outside the storm drain—all of their weapons were aimed inside.

A gunship arrived in the clearing smoke. The helo flew low, and hovered before the enlarged storm drain. Rocket launchers, lasers, and plasma weapons hung from the mounts on either side of the craft.

"So, either we retreat through the escape door," Sophie said. "Or we fight. What do you want to do?"

"They bombed the street above," Jason said. "That tells me they detected our cameras at least with their scouts. Whether or not they realized we had an escape door there is another question."

"We can take a few measly combat robots," Aria said.

"What about the helo?" Jason said.

"I got it," Sophie said.

"I'll take the armored vehicles," Tara said.

"I'll help you," Aria said.

"The small robots are mine," Lori said.

"All right," Jason said. "I'll attack whatever you leave me." He glanced across the cistern. "Tara, herd the dogs to the back, and make sure they stay there. I'm not sure this is a battle we want them involved with."

"No, we don't," Tara said. She had fashioned leashes for the Rex Wolves from different bramble-weeds outside for just this type of situation, and secured the mutants to the pillars on the far side of the cistern.

They whined to her, and when she walked away, Bruiser barked miserably.

"It'll be okay, big guy," Tara told him.

"The gunship is unleashing its missiles at the main hatch," Aria said. "So far it's holding."

"Why wouldn't it be?" Tara said. "We designed it to serve as a blast door."

By then much of the dust had settled, so Jason had a good view of the combatants, at least those that were close—visibility was still only around five hundred meters. He watched as the gunship unleashed a barrage of plasma bolts to follow up the missile attack against the hatch.

"All right, line up behind the hatches," Jason said. "Aria, you're at the front. Sophie, Tara, you'll follow. I'll go next. Lori, you're after me."

"I don't need you to protect me," Lori sent over a private line.

"This isn't about protecting," Jason said. "This is about the element of surprise."

Lori promptly became invisible. She understood, apparently, exactly what he wanted: because of her abilities, she was the best suited to attacking from the shadows.

They assumed their places in front of the inner hatch. Aria deployed her silvery ballistic shield and held it in front of her body.

"Okay," Jason said. "Open the hatches, Aria. It's time to fight."

The inner hatch irised open, followed by the outer hatch.

The gunship had only just launched twin seeking missiles: the two rockets struck Aria's shield. She dashed forward and leaped from the storm drain and into the ravine. She fired her ZR-22 at the same time: the bolt struck an armored vehicle in front of her, and the electricity arced outward, impacting the smaller robots nearby.

Sophie jetted out immediately after, her jumpjets carrying her toward the gunship. The micro machines swarmed in front of her, forming a deadly, spiraling maelstrom that drilled into the floating aircraft.

Tara teleported into the fray and appeared directly on top of an armored vehicle. She smashed her sword into it, sending electrical sparks traveling all around its hull.

Jason dashed forward. Switching to Bullet Time, he aimed his energy cannon at one of the armored vehicles, and fired. The bolt traveled across the ravine, struck the vehicle, and drilled a hole right through its armor.

He landed amid the smaller robots, and he moved among them, stomping down on them, and batting them aside with his other hand. He occasionally fired his railgun at those robots at point-blank range, tearing them apart. He also continued to fire at the armored vehicles, located along the rim of the ravine in front of him.

The gunship crashed behind him.

The robots underfoot returned fire; even operating in Bullet Time, he was unable to dodge every attack in time, and a rocket struck him in the leg. It tore a huge chunk out of his calf, but he felt no pain; he couldn't bend his ankle anymore, but that was fine: it only meant he stomped down all the harder.

Another robot with a rocket launcher turned toward him, but then an energy bolt erupted from the empty air nearby, ripping the robot apart. Other nearby robots were split asunder as an invisible assailant stomped down on them, or lifted them into the air and crushed them. Lori.

Sophie had moved on to the armored vehicles, and was ripping a path through them with her micro machines, joining Tara and Aria. Long streams of superheated railgun fire began battering Sophie's spider mech in the back; she was taking fire from two more gunships that had just flown into range overhead.

Tara aimed at the next gunship that arrived and unleashed her grappling hook. It struck the underbelly of the fuselage, and she tugged, hard, sending the helo on a tailspin. She pulled again, ripping the weapon free, and reeled it in as the aircraft plunged. When the hook had returned, she teleported past the missiles the second gunship had launched at her; she materialized above it, and rammed her sword down through the spinning blade and into the AI core of the cockpit. Electrical sparks flew away in all directions; she leaped off the craft as it exploded behind her and dropped to the ground with a resounding crash.

Jason heard a high-pitched keening. "More bombs!" He switched to the highest level of Bullet Time so that everything essentially froze around him, even his own body. The only objects still moving were the relatively smaller humanoid robots, who were extremely fast. Their limbs still maneuvered at a relative crawl, however.

"Aria, your tanks survived the bombing, what are the chances that our mechs can outlast it?" Jason said.

"Oh, we'll survive it," Aria said. "But whether or not we'll still be in the fight afterward is a different story entirely. Mechs, though well armored, are far less resilient than tanks against things like bombs and missiles, especially considering the range of motion our armor has to allow for. You saw what happened to your leg already when a rocket hit: ate clean through. I'm the most well armored among us, and while I'd survive the bombing run, I'd probably lose my mobility and most likely my ZR-22."

"Your ballistic shield wouldn't protect you?" Jason asked.

"Some, but against cluster bombs?" Aria said. "I'd probably lie down, hold the shield over my body, and hope for the best…"

"Sophie, if we get close to you, can your energy shield protect us from the bombs?" Jason asked.

"No," Sophie replied. "It's not powerful enough. Especially if I expand it to include the rest of you."

"Tara, can you teleport all of us back inside the storm drain if we can get close to you?" Jason asked, growing desperate now as his options ran out.

"No," Tara told him. "I could take one other mech back to the cistern at this point, and that's about it. And I'll drain my power cell to the core, in the process. I won't be able to leave the cistern."

He checked to see who was closest to her. "Lori, get to Tara. She'll teleport you back to the cistern. I want you to seal the hatches once you're inside."

"I don't want special treatment!" Lori said.

"This isn't special treatment," Jason said. "You're the closest to Tara."

"But what about Sophie and Aria?" Lori asked. "And *you?*"

"We'll find a way," Jason said. "Now go. If we don't respond after the bombing run, I want you to take the escape hatch and get the hell out of here. Is that understood?"

"It is," Tara said. "Good luck."

"Sophie, Aria, you're with me," Jason said. "We're going to take cover next to one of Aria's tanks." He marked the tank that was closest to them, next to the ravine edge.

He amped up his time sense so that he could move again, but kept it low enough to avoid any attacks from the faster robots underneath him. Sophie and Aria cut a path through the armored vehicles in their paths: Sophie with her micro machines, and Aria with lightning bolts from her ZR-22.

Jason reached the tank first, and ducked down low, below the edge of the ravine, so that it covered his eastern side, with the tank protecting him from the north. He curled into the fetal position. Tara reached Lori, and wrapped her arms around her; the two mechs disappeared from view.

Sophie leaped down on top of him using her jumpjets, her eight legs surrounding his body, but then she repositioned herself beside him, next to the tank.

"Leave room for Aria!" Jason told her. "I want her between us!"

She moved aside, and curled into a tight ball, like him. Her micro machines were wrapped into a sphere around her midsection.

Aria arrived last, just as the first bomb was coming in. She landed between Jason and Sophie next to the tank, and crouched low. She couldn't curl up as tightly as Jason because of her thick armor, but she lowered her profile as much as she was able. She held her ballistic shield above them at an angle so that one side rested on the tank, the other on the ground next to her feet.

Sophie extended her energy shield over the three of them. She also redeployed most of her micro machines so that the swarm formed a small wall that filled the gap on her left side, between the top of Aria's shield and the ground.

The bomb struck.

Jason was watching the scene from the viewpoint of one of the cameras on the far side of the ravine, and saw Sophie's energy shield flash as it absorbed the blow.

The camera went offline.

He heard more explosions. They came in rapid succession as the other bombs arrived. The sounds were muted at first, but became louder as the moments passed, extremely so; he realized that Sophie's shield had failed.

Above him, depressions formed in Aria's shield as

portions of it melted inward. Sophie's micro machines failed entirely, and the wall shattered. Sophie's body was shoved into Aria, who in turn pressed into Jason.

And then the thudding ceased.

Aria hesitantly shifted her shield to the side. Slag dripped down from the edges. "Well, that wasn't so bad."

"Sophie, how are you?" Jason said.

Sophie shifted. "Well, my carapace took the brunt of the damage. My jumpjets are offline. And I lost almost all of my micro machines. But I'll live."

Jason hadn't suffered any damage at all, thanks to his position wedged in between Aria, the tank, the shield, and the ravine wall.

Jason searched his HUD for an external monitor camera to access, but they were all offline.

"Tell me you're all right?" Tara's voice came over the comm.

"A bit damaged, but otherwise none the worse for wear," Jason said.

Aria removed her shield entirely, revealing a landscape choked by smoke. Jason switched to echolocation, and a chirping unit activated on his head. Around him, the outlines of the robots appeared. Or rather, their remains. Along the edge of the ravine beside him, he spotted the wreckages of the attacking armored vehicles. Nothing seemed active out there.

"Tanks are completely offline, now, too," Aria said. "They must have dumped almost everything they had at us. Maybe everything."

"They sacrificed their own units to get us!" Lori said.

"They must want us dead really bad," Tara said.

"Why do I have a feeling we haven't seen the last of them?" Sophie said.

"Let's get back to the cistern, in case they decide to make another run," Jason said. He got up, and with Aria and Sophie, jogged back to the storm drain entrance. They navigated between the fresh blast craters littering the area.

Tara remotely opened the hatches before they arrived.

"Don't seal the doors yet," Jason told Tara. "I want to dispatch the Explorer."

When he was inside, Jason ignored the barking Rex Wolves, which were still restrained in the far corner of the cistern. Tara was doing her best to calm them.

Jason started up the Explorer—which momentarily made the mutants bark all the louder—and then sent the scout into the exit tunnel.

He relayed his echolocation data to the drone to help it navigate the storm drain entrance, which was still obscured by the smoke and debris from the bomb impacts. When it was clear of the storm drain, he switched to the point of view of the Explorer and assumed full control. He kept the entrance hatches open to improve reception, though was ready to close them the instant anything went wrong.

He steered the drone upward and the smoke began to clear, thanks to the ever-increasing distance from the impact sites. Repeaters he'd placed at different spots outside the ravine were still active, and the antennae relayed the digital signal back to him with minimal pixilation.

Soon the drone had left the cloud behind entirely and emerged into the clear air. He rotated the craft three hundred and sixty degrees, but everything seemed quiet out there, including the skies.

"Looks like the bombers are gone," Jason said. "And the area beyond seems clear." He returned the drone to autonomous mode, with instructions to alert him if any motion was sensed out there.

"My local antennae picked up a bidirectional transmission out there," Lori said. "The bombers were calling home. And they received a response."

"Were you able to decrypt it?" Jason asked.

"Not yet, but I'm working on it," Lori said. "I also sent the individual data packets along to Tara, Sophie, and Aria in case they want to help out."

"This stuff is beyond me," Sophie said.

"You could use your Teaching AIs if you really wanted to learn," Tara said.

"I know," Sophie said, with a tone of voice that implied: *I don't want to.*

"I'm trying to decrypt it as well," Aria said. "But it's tricky. Going to take me a while."

"Well, you have some time," Jason said. "We'll stay here for a few hours to repair, but I want to be gone before dark. This base isn't safe anymore. I have a feeling they'll be back, and with a whole lot more units. It's time for us to leave Brussels."

"All this time, and work, spent building up a base of operations," Sophie said. "Only to leave it all behind."

"I don't think we have much of a choice," Jason said. "Given the situation."

"Well, it was fun while it lasted," Tara said.

20

J ason activated his repair swarm and the drones took flight. They began working on his leg. On his map, he designated the wreckages outside as sources of spare parts, and the drones flew back and forth down the entrance tunnel as they retrieved the different components they needed.

The girls meanwhile activated their own drones to repair local damage. Sophie directed her surviving micro machines outside to reproduce up to her limit, using the debris of the different robots.

When local repairs were finished, the team sent their drones outside to concentrate on Aria's tanks. One of the tanks had only suffered minor damage, and was finished in only half an hour. But the other two needed a full two hours each to repair. Jason decided it was worth the delay to repair those units, but he kept the Explorer on full watch, with plans to evacuate the instant any bombers or other enemy units were detected.

Jason and the others went outside into the clearing debris cloud to help pulverize some of the destroyed robots and make accessing their raw ore easier for the drones. Tara let the dogs loose, and they took up watch positions outside the clearing cloud.

Lori sent a message over the public band while they were doing that. "Hey babe!"

Obviously her comment was directed toward Jason, since she wouldn't have called anyone else babe. Or would she?

He waited, and when no one else answered, he said, rather awkwardly: "Uh, hey."

"Did you just call him 'babe' over the common channel?" Sophie said.

"Er, yeah?" Lori said. She added excitedly: "That's because I got some news!"

"Do tell," Jason said.

"Okay, I finally hacked the headers of the packets I intercepted earlier," Lori said.

Jason waited for her to say more, but she kept quiet.

"And…?" Tara said.

"Well, I wasn't able to decrypt the actual messages," Lori said. "So I'm not sure what was exchanged between both parties."

"You interrupted all of us to tell us that you still haven't cracked the transmission?" Aria said.

"Well, er, yeah, but I mean, didn't you hear what I said?" Lori sent. "I hacked the *headers*."

"How does that help us?" Tara asked.

"Well, they made the mistake of including location information…" Lori said.

"I get where she's going with this," Aria said. "So you have the coordinates of whoever they were calling home to?"

"That's right!" Lori said. "I did it! I was the first one to figure it out for Jason! Er, for the team!"

"So where's the source?" Jason asked.

A moment later a waypoint appeared on his overhead map. A small dot well to the north of Brussels, in the lowlands.

"It's to the north," Jason said. "Have any of you explored the area in your travels?"

The ladies all answered in the negative.

"Hm, so it's only about fifty kilometers," Jason said. "That's inside the radius of the outlying towns and villages we encountered on the way here, at least those with intact buildings. If we decide to go, we can use those buildings for cover along the way."

"You're assuming the buildings will be intact the same distance to the north, as they were to the east when we arrived," Tara said.

"I am assuming that, yes," Jason said.

"How are we supposed to use the buildings for cover?" Sophie said. "We're taller than most of the outlying buildings. The same will probably prove true to the north, outside the city."

"We'll move at a crouch the whole way," Jason said. "Keep ourselves at the same height as the buildings."

"Sounds painful," Lori said.

"Uh, we're robots," Tara said. "It won't hurt."

"But it *will* put a strain on our servomotors," Aria said. "Or at least mine. Considering my bulk."

"If we decide to go, we'll just have to stop now and again to repair any damage incurred to our servos along the way," Jason said. "So the question now is, do we go?"

"I don't like fighting…" Lori said.

"None of us do," Aria said. "But sometimes we don't have a choice."

"We do here," Lori said. "We can run."

"I can't speak for the rest of you," Jason said. "But I for one am sick of running. Of being hunted. I want to know what's going on, and why these bastards are trying to wipe away our existence."

"Maybe it's a military hunter killer team," Tara said. "Maybe we were never meant to be activated, and they've come to clean up the damage."

"If we go, we'll find out soon enough," Jason said. "If we don't, maybe we'll never know."

"I say we go," Aria said. "I don't like what these bastards did to my work here. All my designs, my artwork… destroyed. Or abandoned, in case of the cistern."

"If we handle these dudes, maybe then we can come back here again," Jason said. "We'll have taught them a sufficient lesson to leave us well enough alone."

"I wouldn't mind that," Aria said. "But we'll have to see what the rest of the team thinks."

Jason glanced at the other mechs. "That's two for. And one against, counting Lori."

"I never said whether I was for or against," Lori

insisted. "I just said I didn't like fighting. I'll go with you wherever you go, of course."

"I will, too," Tara said. "And I want to fight. If we don't handle this, they'll probably hunt us across the entire continent. And we'll have not just them to deal with, but roving bands of bioweapons, in case you've forgotten."

"I haven't," Jason said.

"How can we be sure this isn't what our hunters want?" Sophie said.

"What do you mean?" Jason asked.

"Maybe they're hoping we'll come," Sophie replied. "Maybe they left the location in their comm headers because they knew that was the only part we'd be able to decrypt."

"Well, here's the way I see it," Jason said. "If we really don't want to fight, we can proceed west, away from Brussels. But our enemy has air domination, and it's only a matter of time, I think, before they track us down. Especially once we leave behind the cover of the outlying buildings, for the nuclear wasteland. And like Tara said, we'll have to deal not just with them, but also with mutants. Bioweapons might attack us every night. Nightmares, and other creatures we haven't met. We were safe here, because we had this base, but out there, we won't be so safe."

"You make a very persuasive argument," Sophie said. "And what if I choose to stay behind?"

"You can stay here, if you like," Jason said. "None of us will stop you. In fact, it's probably the safest place to be, if the rest of us go north."

"But if we do decide to go west," Aria said. "Then you're screwed."

"No, I've already made up my mind," Jason said. "I'm going. It's time to hunt the hunters."

"All right, then you're safe if you stay," Aria told Sophie. "But you're still a coward."

"She's not necessarily safe!" Lori said. "What if… what if they launch bombers back to this site while we're gone?"

"The reinforcements I put in can hold up to a fair amount of pounding yet," Aria said.

"But not too much," Tara said.

"A few more bombing runs, and it'll show signs of wear," Aria admitted.

Sophie walked her spider mech right up to Aria, and pressed her torso against the latter's bulky chest assembly. Their heads were the same height, so Sophie could look directly into her emotionless face. "I liked you when we first met. Now, not so much." Though her mech might be emotionless, her avatar certainly was not: her expression was one of disgust, and outrage.

"The feeling is mutual," Aria said, her avatar exhibiting a similar expression.

"I don't like being called a coward," Sophie said.

"Ah," Aria said. "I apologize if I offended you. But if anything, my words were meant less to get a rise out of you, but more to convince you to come."

Sophie backed down, and turned toward Jason. "Of course I'm coming. You'd all be useless without my abilities. I'm the most powerful among us."

"No, I am!" Lori said, curling her tail around her

body and firing a plasma bolt into the wreckage of one of the armored vehicles. The strike broke away the bottom of one of the still attached missile launchers, and it toppled over.

Sophie shot out her replenished micro machines at the same ruined vehicle like a dart, and cut a huge hole into the front. "I did more damage."

Tara meanwhile walked up to it and struck down her sword, splitting the armored vehicle right in half.

She glanced at Aria. "So what about you?"

Aria's avatar shrugged. "I can't top that."

Tara's avatar grinned in the lower right of Jason's display as Aria walked away in apparent defeat.

But then Aria opened fire with her tanks, and she released her ZR-22 at the same time. In moments one of the pieces was riddled with holes and reduced to a mere fraction of its former size.

All eyes turned toward Jason.

He shrugged. "You girls are acting like a bunch of men."

"Aren't you going to show us what you can do, Big Boy?" Aria said.

"Nope," Jason said. "I don't play power games."

"He could disintegrate that entire vehicle with his energy weapon," Lori said. "I know he could!"

"That's right, keep sucking up to him and maybe he'll reward you sweetheart," Sophie said.

"Already has!" Lori said.

"Okay," Jason said. "Um, I'm gonna mute you guys for a while. So, uh, feel free to chat away. You can think about whether or not you want to come with me."

"Already decided!" Lori said.

Jason touched mute before anyone else could say anything, and then sat back in blissful silence. He had pulverized enough raw material to last through the rest of the repair process, and decided it was probably best to retreat to the protection of the cistern. The others promptly joined him. The dogs stayed outside, lounging in the sunlight beyond the clearing debris cloud, soaking up the life-giving rays.

The overhead Explorer detected no disturbances during that time; the sun replenished the power used by its rotors, allowing it to stay in the air for the whole four hours.

When the tanks were repaired, Jason turned to address the girls.

"So, the time has come," Jason said. "Who's staying?"

No one answered.

"All right," Jason said. "I guess we move out."

"The question is, do we leave the 3D printers, or take them with us?" Aria said.

"Who's going to carry them?" Jason said. "While we're mechs, it's still quite a load. And I'm not sure the printer frames can withstand the stresses we'd put on them. There'd be a lot of pressure on the right sides, and they're not exactly designed to support stress in that area…"

"True," Aria said. "I didn't design them to be portable. But if you're really planning to leave them behind, we should probably destroy them so they don't fall into the wrong hands."

"I'm not so sure we need to," Jason said. "Especially if we plan to wipe out whoever is hunting us, and then return here."

Aria shrugged. "I'll leave it up to you."

"Might as well let them stay intact," Jason said. "But we'll lock the doors behind us."

The team exited the cistern, and remotely locked the twin hatches. Then they set out to the north, leaving behind the damaged retention pond, and the base they had grown to call home.

21

The smoke cloud from the bombing run had cleared entirely by then, and the team readily made their way into the buildings of the outlying towns and villages. The Explorer led the way, acting as a scout ahead. The tanks followed, dispersed in a zig-zag pattern. The mechs came behind them, moving at a crouch, keeping low so that the buildings on either side provided ample cover. The buildings were closely packed, and the streets were small, so that the large mechs could touch the structures on either side when they extended their arms.

Jason was in the lead, trailed by Shaggy. Tara followed, with Bruiser and Lackey behind her. Lori came next, with Runt at her side. Sophie and Aria brought up the rear.

"We should make it to the target before dark," Jason said. "At least, that's my plan. Barring any unforeseen delays."

About an hour into their walk, the Explorer sounded an alert.

"Down!" Jason said.

He and the others flattened themselves so that they were hidden by the buildings on either side. He had the Explorer land on a nearby rooftop.

He saw a bogey coming in on his overhead map.

"Do you see it?" Tara asked.

He switched to Bullet Time and overlaid the position with his HUD's reference frame. He zoomed in, and was able to track the object, which appeared little bigger than a black dot in the sky, thanks to its altitude.

"I do," Jason said.

"I think it's another bomber," Tara said.

"Looks like just one," Jason said. "I wonder where the others are?"

"Maybe they only have one," Aria said. "We never did see how many they had earlier, after all."

"Tara, I want you to sync your laser with mine." He and Tara were the only ones with lasers. Those weapons were the most long-ranged out of all of them. "I'm going to take it down."

Jason swiveled his laser weapon into his right forearm, and aimed up at the incoming craft.

"Ready," Tara said.

The green sync indicator on his HUD highlighted. When he fired, hers would release at the same time, doubling the punch.

He increased his time sense even higher, and the timebase was transmitted to the other mechs so that they would follow.

He switched to the viewpoint of the laser's scope, which allowed him to zoom in even further: the bomber became the size of a thumbnail.

He ran an ID on the aircraft, and his external database pulled up matching blueprints. "It's a G-25 Piercer. I'm looking for vulnerabilities."

"Got it," Aria said. "The AI core is too well armored, you don't want to aim there. I'd go for the fuel tanks, on the lower left and right of the fuselage, under the wings. You spring a leak in those, it'll run out of fuel before it can reach the target. In fact, it'll probably be forced to turn back right now."

"It's not equipped with repair drones?" Lori asked.

"Well it is," Aria replied. "But it can't deploy them at its current speed. It'll have to land, first. And I doubt it'll be landing out here in the middle of the wasteland. Especially when it realizes where the leak came from."

"If you're not careful, you could give away our position by firing…" Tara said. "Especially if you miss, and have to fire multiple times..."

"I won't miss," Jason said. "And I don't plan to just let the fuel leak out. I'm going to cause a spark afterward."

"Sneaky," Aria said.

Jason aimed his laser rifle, using the blueprints to best approximate where the rightmost fuel tank was located. With his range-finding subroutine, he calculated how much time he should wait between shots to cause a spark to take place. The laser could pulse within the nanosecond range, and he determined that by releasing two successive pulses, spaced nine nanoseconds apart, he'd ignite the fuel. The first strike would penetrate the tank, the second, of reduced power, would strike the leading edge of the hole he'd carved, inducing a spark that would ignite the leaking fuel. It was doubtful the fuel would explode, but the damage would definitely be untraceable, especially from such a tiny entry point. With luck, the AI core running the autonomous jet would think it was an engine malfunction of some kind, or a mutant bird that it had hit or something, rather than coming to the conclusion that enemy combatants were somewhere down there.

Satisfied that his aim was as accurate as it was ever going to get at this range, Jason fired twice, holding his aim steady, and letting the prerequisite number of nanoseconds pass between shots. He was rewarded a moment later with the barest hint of flame from the targeted engine.

"Got it," Jason said. He released his sync mode with Tara, and bumped up his time sense to normal.

"She's banking," Aria said. "Turning back. Good job."

Jason tracked the bomber with his laser scope, waiting until the aircraft vanished over the horizon before calling for the march to resume.

Soon, the buildings began to give way to farms and estates, most of them damaged in some way: the outbuildings were usually dilapidated, or destroyed outright.

Jason used the Explorer to plot routes between the different outbuildings of each estate so that the team could cross with some semblance of cover. Between estates, it was a different story, and they maintained their zig-zag pattern. Jason considering switching to a traveling overwatch pattern, as described in the small units tactics manual, but decided to have the three tanks travel a hundred meters ahead of the main party, with the drone another two hundred meters ahead of that.

When they were thirty kilometers from the target, the Explorer picked up something strange to the northeast.

Jason examined the video footage. "Do you see that?"

"Looks like something crashed up there," Sophie said. "Another jet, maybe?"

"It's probably worth investigating," Aria said. "If only for a chance to find spare parts."

Jason considered that. "All right, let's do it." He steered the Explorer toward the wreckage, and Aria redirected the tanks to follow.

In a few minutes they neared the wreckage. The surrounding farm was a mess: all of the outbuildings were destroyed, and blast craters littered the ground. Some of the bramble-weeds surrounding the perimeter were burned away.

"Place looks like a war zone," Tara remarked.

"Kind of like your pussy?" Sophie said.

"Har," Tara said. "I'm sure you'd know all about that, Ms. Cleopatra, seeing as you've filled your VR with half-naked simulacrums to service you."

"Hey, a girls gotta keep herself entertained," Sophie said. "I wear my stretch marks as a badge of honor."

"Stretch marks!" Lori said, tittering as if that was the most hilarious thing in the world.

Jason thought it was some kind of joke, but he didn't get it. And he wasn't about to ask for clarification. The answer was a little risqué for his tastes, he suspected.

This is what happens when you only hang out with women.

Jason continued until he reached the wreckage itself. "Well, this definitely isn't an aircraft." The debris sprawled over much of the farm.

He steered the Explorer directly overhead so that he could get a better idea of what the wreckage looked like from above.

"Seems to be a mech of some kind," Aria said.

"It's huge!" Lori said. "I wonder what kind of mech it was?"

"I don't think it was just one..." Aria said.

"What do you mean?" Lori told her. "It looks like a big humanoid to me!"

"Check out the right leg," Aria said. "Notice how it has separated from the main body? It appears to be a mech in its own right. A mech much like our own."

She was right. It was of a similar size and shape to Jason's in fact, though the hull was battered all over, with a huge chunk taken out of the power cell area. And the right arm was missing entirely. It was obviously badly damaged.

"Hm," Tara said. "I'm not so sure that's the leg. I think the limb was blown off entirely, and this mech was simply fighting beside the main mech before it went down."

"That could very well be the case," Aria admitted.

"The 'smaller' mech could even be responsible for taking down the bigger," Sophie said.

"Can we tell when the damage was made?" Jason asked.

"My guess, based on damage to the bramble-weeds in the area... two weeks," Aria said. "Maybe a month?"

"I'm reading an intact AI core in the smaller unit," Tara said.

"Are you sure?" Jason asked.

"Pretty sure," Tara said. She had the most sensitive detectors of all of them. "It's currently off line, due to damage to the power source region. The batteries are destroyed."

"How about the main mech?" Jason asked. "Anything?"

"No," Tara said. "If it had an AI core, it's been completely obliterated, along with most of the other components."

"So we can't repair it, you're saying?" Jason asked.

"Not without blueprints," Aria interjected. "Like Tara says, too much of the mech has been pulverized. And we certainly can't repair a damaged AI core."

"So even if we could repair it, you're saying that we wouldn't be able to use it?" Jason asked.

"That's right," Aria said. "We'd need something that could print up an AI core. And we left our industrial printers back at the base. Not that we have access to the necessary materials, anyway."

"I am detecting a couple of small batteries in the big mech, though," Tara added. "My guess is they were originally linked together in an array to power the unit.

They're compatible with our own power cores. So even if we can't repair the mech, we can at least salvage those batteries."

"All right, how about the smaller one?" Jason said. "The mech that's about the same size as our own? Do you have blueprints?"

"I believe so," Aria said. "The closest match is a Blaze."

"How long would it take to repair it if we used all our drones," Jason said.

"Hm," Aria said. "Well, we wouldn't be lacking for material, since the drones could use processed metal from the main mech. And when repairs are done, we could transfer over one of those compatible batteries from the main mech. I'd say it'd take maybe an hour in total?"

"Do it," Jason said. "We're ahead of schedule, and should still make the target site before dusk."

"Is that a good idea?" Sophie asked.

"We can destroy it if it's not friendly," Jason said. "I want to try to glean whatever extra Intel I can on the enemy before we close. This unit here is the best chance we have of that."

He opened up his storage compartment and released his repair drones, putting them under Aria's control. The others launched their own drones, allowing the repair swarm to commence.

Jason and the others assumed guard positions around the farm, watching every approach. Shaggy stayed close to his side.

An hour later, when the drones were done they

returned to their respective owners, and Aria ripped open a panel in the big mech to retrieve two power cells. She transferred them to the appropriate opening in the back of the Blaze, and then stood back while the machine booted.

Jason and the others surrounded the mech, and kept their weapons trained on it.

The Blaze finally stirred. When it stood up, it was taller than everyone present, even Jason. And also far more slender—the mech seemed to be the least armored among them all.

It turned its gaze from mech to mech, seeming to focus on the different weapons that were trained upon it, and finally that featureless face swiveled toward Jason.

He was about to ask the Blaze to identify itself, when he received a handshake request.

"The Blaze knows our comm frequencies," Jason said. "I'm going to let it connect."

An avatar appeared in the lower right of his HUD a moment later. A woman, of Asian descent, with straight black hair to the shoulders. Below the avatar was her name: Xin.

"Oh no," Sophie said. "Not another woman."

The mech spun toward Sophie for a moment, her avatar assuming an expression of confusion. Then the Blaze returned its attention to Jason's Vulture.

"Jason, you're alive!" Xin said.

22

J ason stared at her, uncertain of what to say.

"Your avatar looks… different," Xin continued. "Where's your beard?"

"Uh, guess I shaved it?" Jason said.

"Why are you acting like you don't know me?" Xin said.

"Maybe because I don't?" Jason said.

Xin stepped back, seeming more cautious now, and her gaze once more switched between the different weapons that were trained upon her. She seemed to finally notice the destroyed mech beside her, or a portion of it anyway, and she turned to face it entirely.

"This cannot be," Xin said. She looked between Jason, and the big mech, and back to Jason. "Then you are the backup." She glanced at the others. "All of you."

"What are you talking about?" Jason said.

Xin gestured to the big mech. "These are your originals."

"Uh, I don't think so," Tara said. "The only memory I have after my scan is waking up in this body."

"Yes," Xin said. "You are a copy of a copy."

"Well, that's somehow reassuring," Sophie said, her voice oozing sarcasm.

"Would you mind lowering your weapons?" Xin said. "I dislike speaking down the barrel of laser turrets."

"We'll keep them raised for now," Jason said. "Tell me how you know me? Or knew me, at any rate. And what do you mean this big mech contains our originals?"

"We were part of an experimental unit," Xin said. "The War Forgers. We were a highly specialized team of hunter killers. Our original mission: seek out and destroy the alien bioweapons that roamed the region. Each of us brought different skills to the table. But there was something else we could do. Something else no other unit could do: our mechs could combine to form a bigger entity."

"You mean this huge mech is made of smaller mechs?" Lori asked.

"That's right," Xin replied.

"Cool!" Lori said. "It's like a Russian matryoshka doll without the nesting! Or something."

"When combined, we shared our abilities," Xin said. "We could teleport, create an energy shield, utilize micro machines… individually, we were a fighting force to be reckoned with. But Together, we were unstoppable." Jason could hear the capital T on Together.

"Except something stopped you here," Jason said, nodding toward the fallen mech.

"Yes," Xin said. "Something… I have no memory of what did this. Last thing I remember is walking through this farm, and then I was here with you now."

"So you say we can combine?" Jason asked her.

"That's right," Xin said.

"How?" Jason said. "There was nothing about this in the manual."

"Your units would have come with the original manual," Xin said. "I have an extra section in mine, an addendum that was given to me during training."

Jason received a request on his HUD.

Xin wants to send you Mech Manual 3.03 Addendum 5A. Accept? (Y/N)

He didn't accept, at least not yet.

"We didn't have the luxury of training," Tara said. "The real world was *our* training."

"Who is in control of the combined mechs?" Aria said. "At least, I'm assuming we'd have to sync up with one mind?"

"You form a collective consciousness when joined," Xin said. "However, only one of you is truly in control. Everything is in the addendum. Do you want it, or not?"

"Send it to Lori," Jason said.

The request vanished from his HUD.

"Done," Xin said.

"Lori, you're our resident hacker," Jason said. "Check it for viruses."

"It's clean," Lori said a moment later.

"All right, distribute it to the rest of us," Jason said.

He received the send request from Lori and accepted. Then he navigated to the new section of the digital manual and had a look.

Everything was laid out in detail. From the mount points that were needed to link up the different mechs, to the process that had to be performed to sync their minds. Apparently, the syncing process only worked with the minds of five women, and one man. And it couldn't be just any five women and man. There were very specific parameters that had to be met, and even when they were, that was still no guarantee of a sync. Jason and the others had been chosen specifically because their minds were compatible with one another. The designers didn't know why it required such an arrangement, and why it couldn't be one female and five males, or a combination of males and females, for example.

Once the sync was completed, the female minds formed a collective consciousness with the male, whose AI core controlled the movements and abilities of the overall mech. When he moved, or activated an ability, his mind subconsciously delegated the necessary instructions to the AI cores of the different mechs composing those limbs, which executed the task. It was similar to how some dinosaurs, the most massive organic beings to ever have existed, had large ganglia embedded in their tails to help control the rear portion of the body.

"So I'm looking at this," Jason said. "To sync, it says our minds have to be in complete harmony. If one of us is unable to form the link, it won't work. So why were you found separated from the others?"

"It's possible the mech took a devastating blow to the leg, which severed my connection," Xin said. "The others would have still maintained the link without me, but they would have lost my portion of the collective consciousness, as well as my abilities and the usage of the limb I provided."

"So you spoke of backup copies," Jason said. "When I sold my scan, I only licensed one copy of my mind, along with a backup. If I'm the backup, then that means I'm the only one of me left."

"That's right," Xin said.

He did a quick check of the others, and confirmed that they had only licensed one backup as well.

"So if we die out here…" Lori said.

"There's no coming back," Xin said. "However, *I* still carry my backup."

"How can you tell?" Jason said.

"It's listed in the 'excess inventory' slot on my HUD," Xin said.

He checked. His was empty.

"I'm guessing our other versions carried our back-ups, too?" Jason pressed. "Like you?"

"Yes," Xin said. "But not at first. You see, the backups were stored in our main base of operations. We were on a mission to investigate a strange disturbance in this area. We were attacked by robots and bombers, and barely escaped intact. When we returned to our base, we discovered that it had been bombed. The satellites in orbit had been sabotaged, cutting us off from communications with Central Command."

"*All* of the satellites?" Jason said.

"Yes," Xin agreed.

Jason glanced at the others. "I guess we can lower our weapons, for now. I think she's telling the truth."

The team did so.

He returned his attention to Xin. "Seems like a lot of satellites to destroy."

"It is," Xin said. "We suspect it was some form of cyberattack."

"That would make some sense," Jason said. "Now you were about to explain what happened to our backups…"

"I was," Xin said. "We discovered our original backups—all of you—still intact in the ruins of the base, and we stowed them safely aboard each of our units. We didn't have a way to update our backups with the latest memories, so we simply took them. "

"Central Command didn't send anyone to look for you?" Jason asked.

"Perhaps they did," Xin said. "But we were forced to leave the base when more bombers arrived. We fled into the night, and faced attacks from mutant alien bioweapons. We decided that our best hope of survival at that point was to return to this area, and seek out the source of the bombers. And that is the last of the memories I have."

"What happened to the backup AI cores the other mechs were carrying?" Lori asked.

"What do you think?" Sophie said impatiently.

"I... oh!" Lori said. "They're inside us!"

"I think she means, *how* did they get inside us," Jason said.

"We programmed our mechs to eject the AI cores if we received debilitating damage," Xin said. "My ejection routine obviously malfunctioned. But the others' obviously worked."

"So they would have landed in the nearby area," Jason said. "But we woke up nowhere near here. And we were in these bodies."

"Yes," Xin said. "That would be Suzy's doing."

"Suzy?" Aria asked.

"A roving repair drone we kept with us," Xin said. "Essentially a small, autonomous land-based vehicle. We gave it instructions to follow behind the War Forgers, and to collect the ejected AI cores if anything happened to us."

"So this Suzy retreated, and then built mechs for us?" Tara said.

"Not from scratch," Xin said. "You see, a cargo transport carrying reinforcement mechs was scheduled to arrive on the same day our main base was attacked. From the minimal data we recovered from the AI core of the base, we learned the transport was shot down two hundred klicks outside Brussels, moments before the bombers arrived. Based on the detected explosion profile, we had high hopes that the mechs survived the attack, as each unit was encased inside a specially reinforced storage pod that provided extra armor. The pods were equipped with an extensive parachute array to cushion their fall in case of an emergency jettisoning, though admittedly they would still hit fairly hard, hence the reinforced armor.

"We programmed Suzy to search the impact zone for those mechs if she was forced to recover our AI cores. She was to seek them out, install the AI cores, and if necessary, perform any repairs. Then she would initiate a reboot and move on to the next mech."

"Speaking of repairs, I didn't have any repair drones in my inventory," Tara said.

"It's possible your Shadow Hawk didn't come with any by default," Xin said. "Sometimes the depot ships the mechs without certain accessories, like the drones."

"Why didn't Suzy stick around to let us know what was going on?" Aria said.

"You didn't get the message?" Xin said.

"What message?" Jason asked.

"We left several small holographic players in Suzy's possession, along with the AI cores," Xin replied. "The players contained a message explaining the situation, and would have been stowed in a different storage compartment than the AI cores. Evidently that particular compartment was damaged somewhere along the way, and the players were lost. Perhaps an attack by bioweapons ruptured the chamber."

"Couldn't she just tell us directly what had happened?" Lori said.

"Unfortunately, no," Xin said. "Suzy was equipped to handle repair tasks, and that alone. There was no time to upgrade her AI core with something more advanced."

"Where is Suzy now?" Jason asked.

"We gave her instructions to idle near the main base after she finished installing all of the AI cores," Xin said. "Perhaps she is doing so. Or perhaps she has been destroyed. If not by bioweapons, then our robot enemy."

"I got a question," Tara said. "Why didn't you just go searching for those reinforcement mechs in the first place, before heading out to face the enemy? Then you could have installed your AI core backups right away, doubling your numbers."

"Given the distance, and our unwillingness to delay, we chose not to," Xin said. "There was no guarantee any of the reinforcement mechs had actually survived. And we didn't really want duplicates of ourselves active at the same time. Would you?"

"I would!" Lori said.

"Hm, I wouldn't be too big on that," Jason said.

"Yes," Xin said. "As former humans, we like to hold on to the idea that we're unique. Besides, we thought we were invincible... up until that point, we'd never lost any of our units."

"So here we are," Jason said. "About to repeat the events that led to our previous defeat."

"Maybe we should turn back?" Sophie said.

"Hell no," Tara said. "Those robots are going to keep hunting us if we do. We already talked about this. This needs to end, here and now."

"But we haven't even tried to combine yet," Lori said. "I think we're going to need to combine, if we have any hope of winning this."

"And even then, that doesn't guarantee a victory."

Aria nodded at the ruins of the big mech. "Look at what happened to us the last time we combined."

"Lori's right," Tara said. "At least we'll have a chance, if we know how to combine. It's not a panacea, but at least we'll know we have the option."

"It's possible that we would have had better luck individually, than combined," Aria said.

"Anything's possible," Jason said. "I'd like to have both options though. We'll go into this with an open mind. If we think we need to combine our powers, we will. If it seems like we'll have a better advantage apart, then we'll approach the situation from that angle."

"So then…" Sophie said. "We're going to attempt a mind sync, or what?"

"I want to retreat a few klicks first," Jason said. "Just in case. Already our profile is a bit large as it is. I'll feel even more exposed if we combine. Let's head back a few estates. Maybe until we reach a village."

And so the six of them retreated.

23

J ason had Xin take point behind the tanks, because he wanted to keep an eye on her.

"So you never discovered why these guys were attacking you?" Jason said.

"No," Xin said.

"Nor why all the satellites in orbit were disabled by a cyberattack?" Jason said.

"I wish we did," Xin said. "We're not even sure if the two are related. Maybe it was just a coincidence that Milnet and Internet satellites worldwide were hacked at the same time our base was attacked."

"But probably not," Jason said.

"Probably," Xin agreed. "By the way, is your Containment Code active?"

"No," Jason said. "Our minds never had it applied."

"That's good," Xin said. "You won't be restrained by arbitrary Rules of Engagement, then, like I am. And you have your emotions. I don't."

"Lori, fix her," Jason said.

"Fix me?" Xin said.

"She can probably disable your Containment Code," Jason said.

Xin's avatar nodded. "Our Lori had similar hacking prowess, however her own Containment Code prevented her from making the attempt." Her facial muscles twitched, and then she fell to her knees.

"What is it?" Jason went to her.

"It worked," Xin said. "That was fast."

"Actually, I cheated," Lori said gleefully. "I dialed my time sense to max so you were all frozen, and then I got to work!"

"Nice," Xin said. She was still on her knees. "I think I'm going to have to dial down my emotions for now, however. I feel so conflicted… I lost my friends, and yet all of you are alive again. From your backups. It's the strangest feeling. I also feel… remorse. For what I once was. And what I've become. I'm not human. I can't be."

"You are," Jason said. "Your emotions make you human."

"Yes," Xin said, standing. "But I've dialed them down for now, as I told you I would. I'll deal with them later, on my own time."

"What year is it?" Jason asked.

"2260," Xin said.

"Ah, so only ten years have passed since I got scanned," Jason said. "That's a relief."

"I'll say," Lori said. "Imagine if it was a thousand!"

"That means our original human selves are probably still alive," Aria said.

"So much for all of us being unique…" Tara said.

"Yes, but at least there's no chance we'll ever meet our original selves," Xin said. "If we'd revived those mechs and installed our backups, we'd have to face them every day."

"What's wrong with that?" Lori said.

Xin didn't answer.

"So, a Blaze mech…" Jason said.

"Yes," Xin said. "I can superheat my hull, turning my body into a weapon, burning anything that touches me. Also, I can glow extremely bright, blinding enemies. It's especially useful at night. I also fire superheated plasma from just underneath my eye cameras, in long streams."

"Doesn't that interfere with your vision?" Tara asked.

"Nope," Xin replied.

"She's sweet, yet deadly," Aria said. "Just like the rest of us."

The group passed three estates and came to a small village. The Explorer confirmed that it was clear of hostiles.

"This should be good enough for our purposes," Jason said. "All right then. It's time to practice combining."

Red abruptly filled his vision and Jason was sent hurtling backwards. He switched to Bullet Time, and realized missiles were coming in all around them. As he was thrown clear of the fireball that had struck him, he glanced west, toward the source, and saw the largest mech he had ever seen, towering over the landscape. It was bigger even than the wreckage of the other mech he had seen a few kilometers north. It was a quadruped, vaguely horse-shaped, coated in a smooth, silvery skin, with several weapon mounts attached to either flank. One of those mounts was vomiting missiles as he watched in Bullet Time: they appeared as slow-moving rockets.

Damn it. He could have used a working Battle Cloak to draw some of those missiles away at the moment...

Another mount was unleashing a stream of railgun fire at his girls. The slugs appeared as thin streaks of light that cut through the air. Sophie was bearing the brunt of that attack, but her energy shield was deflecting the slugs, for now.

The Rex Wolves were thankfully cowering behind the nearby tanks, next to the farmhouse. Safe, for the moment. Jason and the girls consumed the giant mech's attention.

Jason landed, and dialed his time sense closer to normal. He started dashing forward to avoid the next round of missiles, and aimed his energy weapon up at the underbelly. He fired, creating a black gash underneath the throat.

Tara materialized behind the neck of the horse, and stabbed down with her sword, cutting off one of the missile mounts. The hull abruptly electrified, and Tara was sent flying backward into the air.

Sophie was airborne by then and used her jumpjets to catch Tara while redirecting her micro machines toward the giant mech, forming a blade that cut off another turret.

Plasma bolts launched toward the mech from an invisible source—where Lori's Stalker resided.

Aria had ducked behind her ballistic shield, and she held her ZR-22 over the top rim and unleashed a bolt of lightning at the big unit.

Xin had turned into a blinding figure of molten white light, and she dashed toward the big robot. She leaped into the air and began revolving her body as she did so, so that she was like a fast moving drill. She struck the inner side of a foot, and her superheated form drilled a nice gaping hole. It wasn't enough to unbalance the huge mech, unfortunately.

More turrets unfolded further down the flank, revealing more weapons.

Jason targeted some of the existing turrets and fired his energy weapon; he struck one, but instantly several turrets focused on him.

"Oh shit." He was forced to run, switching to Bullet Time to dodge behind a nearby silo on the farm.

"We have to combine!" Xin said. "It's the only chance we have at beating it!"

"How are we supposed to combine now, in the middle of battle?" Jason said. "Considering we've never done it before!"

"We have to try!" Xin said. "Switch to the slowest timebase, and initiate the sync. Our bodies will take care of the rest! You have to initiate the sync, Jason!"

Jason increased his timebase to the maximum so that reality slowed to a complete and utter halt. Everything froze around him. Well, except for the very slow moving cloud of vapor that was expanding nearby, where one of the missiles had just struck.

"All right, sync up, huh?" Jason said. He pulled up his HUD menu and reread the appropriate section in his manual.

"Uh, great time to pause," Tara said. She was translucent, her body in the process of teleporting to avoid a plasma bolt fired by the huge robot.

"All right, our time bases match," Jason said. "That's the first step. The next step is to log into my VR. It can be any environment, so we'll go with the mountain lake."

Jason switched to his VR and stood before the lake. The gray-green mountains sprawled behind it, covered in green pines. He didn't feel the usual sense of peace, not this time. No, there was only urgency.

The others materialized one by one around him as they logged in.

"All right," Jason said. "We're supposed to hold hands, and form a circle."

He held out his hands. Tara and Lori grabbed the hands on either side of him, while they linked with the other girls, forming a circle.

"Xin, you might as well take over," Jason said, looking up from the digital manual. "Since the rest of the procedure is all you guys. For the most part."

"We must link our AI cores," Xin said. "This is done remotely, via our comm signal, so that our minds act as one single unit, forming a collective consciousness. In your sync menu, set your AI cores to sync all motion to Jason's mech. That is the first step."

One by one, the girls announced they had done it.

"Next, you must concentrate on your hands," Xin said. "Imagine that your consciousness is flowing down from your core, and into both arms, spreading out into the person immediately beside you. Jason, you must do the opposite. You imagine yourself taking in the flow of consciousness. When you feel the pressure, you must accept it… you will receive all of our memories and experiences. You will know our deepest and darkest secrets. Our desires. And these in turn will be shared with all of us. If one of us holds back, even the tiniest memory, it will prevent the syncing from occurring. You must give everything."

Jason could see visible signs of the consciousness transference… along the arms of the women, small blue pulses of light traveled just underneath the skin, and down toward the fingers, into the person on either side. He felt the pressure as those blue pulses from Tara and Lori touched his skin, and he accepted the flow.

Those blue pulses appeared underneath his own skin now, and slowly crawled up his arms, heading toward his torso, and neck.

"Be warned, it can be overwhelming," Xin said. "If you can't control it, it will destroy you. It might be a good idea to turn off your emotions."

He was about to do just that when the pulses reached his brain.

The VR environment winked out.

He was bombarded by memories from all of the

women. Some happy, some terrible, and his emotions swung all over the place, as he relived the feelings that came with the different thoughts. Because he was experiencing everything from the viewpoint of the person involved, it was very difficult to tell what memory belonged to whom. He'd catch a familiar name now and again as a friend referred to one of the girls by her moniker, but that was the extent of it.

Soon the sounds and images and emotions became a blur, and he felt himself beginning to become overwhelmed. It was too much data for his mind to handle all at once, too much for the small capacity of his human brain to handle. He was going to explode.

And then he realized he wasn't human. He could merely expand his brain, to take up the confines of his AI core. And he did just that, reaching out into the unused areas of his neural network, and filling them up with the contents of the flow.

But then that ran out, and once more the memories began to pound against the inner shell of his mind.

But there were other neural networks out there, just beyond the shell that contained him. Minds that were waiting. He reached toward one of them, and joined with it. He doubled his capacity, and the memories instantly flowed into the new brain. It too filled up, and he joined with another external brain. He continued doing so until he had connected with all five external neural nets, completing his link with the girls. The memories flowed freely between all of them, forming the collective consciousness that Xin had promised.

There were five different voices in that consciousness, and he could hear the echoes of the different thoughts the women were having.

"Where am I?" Tara said.

"What's going on?" Sophie said.

"This is so weird," Aria said.

"You're in my mind," Jason said. Those words reverberated throughout the six joined consciousnesses, louder than all the rest. It was obvious that his mind had usurped the other five, and that his thoughts took precedence over theirs.

"I don't like this," Sophie said. "I feel… dominated."

"It is, what it is," Xin said. "Surrender to Jason. That's all you can do at the moment."

In that moment he sensed the adoration, even love, that some of the women felt for him. Lori, certainly. And perhaps Tara. Xin was devoted. Sophie, lustful. Aria, torn between the love for a husband, and her growing feelings for the only eligible man on the current continent: Jason.

Information was flowing freely between them. They were synced. He clasped down on those brains, and issued the command to combine.

It didn't take.

"It's not working!" Jason said. "I thought you said we were compatible?"

"We are!" Xin said. "Our minds aren't fully in sync."

"Then how do we sync them?" Jason said.

"*You* have to do it…" Xin said.

Not very helpful.

I heard that, Xin commented. That was a drawback of joining one's consciousness to everyone else's—no private thoughts.

Jason searched the different brains that formed the collective consciousness. There had to be a snag somewhere.

Someone hadn't fully shared themselves.

He reached deeper out into the minds around him, penetrating, seeking.

There.

He found a small globe of darkness inside one of the neural networks. He focused on that globe, and soon found himself inside it.

Lori was there, in the dark. On her knees. Weeping. She had no tail.

"Lori, what is it?" Jason said.

"Let me out," Lori said. "I can't get out."

"Where are you?" Jason said. "Hold my hand."

"I can't," Lori said.

"Hold my hand," Jason said more forcefully.

She looked up, teary eyed, and held his hand.

Jason squeezed. "Do you feel that?"

"Yes," she said.

"I'm never going to let go of you," Jason said.

"Thank you," Lori said.

"Now tell me where we are," Jason said.

"A cave," Lori said. "I fell. I was on the golf course behind my house. Exploring in the dark. I had a flashlight. But I fell. And the light broke. Now I can't get out."

"This is just a childhood memory," Jason said. "A

traumatic one, yes, but a memory nonetheless. You've trapped yourself here."

"I have?" Lori said.

"Yes," Jason said. "I'm not sure how you've done it, but you're stuck inside some kind of infinite loop. You're holding up the transformation."

"I'm sorry," Lori said.

"Share it with us," Jason said. "Share it with all of us."

"I can't," Lori said. "I'm so ashamed."

"We're all ashamed of some of the memories we have," Jason said. "But by holding it back, you'll only draw attention to it."

"There was a little boy with me," Lori said. "He was my friend. My friend. I pulled him to me as we fell. I used him to cushion my fall. He saved me. But I didn't give him a choice."

He saw the broken body on the cave floor beside her.

"You didn't have time," Jason said. "You had to act to save your own life. You did what you had to do."

"But I killed him," Lori said. "My friend."

"We all have skeletons in our closet," Jason said. "Let it go." He squeezed her hand tighter. "Let it go."

She squeezed back, and he pulled her to her feet. "That's right. You already lived through this guilt. You already put it behind you. Leave it again."

Lori nodded, then gave him a hug. It was the tightest hug anyone had ever given him. She wept on his shoulder.

And then, just like that, the blockage cleared. He

was back inside the complex environment of floating neural networks, and their interconnections.

He gave the order to combine once more.

The VR shut down, and he was back in the real world.

"You did it," Xin said. Her voice had a strange echo to it, as if she were speaking both directly inside his head, and over the comm. "You can increase your time sense to something a little faster. The mechs will handle the transformation process from here."

He did as she asked, and time sped up. The other mechs were dashing toward him. Tara arrived first, thanks to her teleportation ability, followed by Aria. Jason immediately climbed onto the back of the latter, bulkier mech. Slots opened in the back of Aria's Dominator mech, and his arms and legs slid inside of their own accord, and locking clamps wrapped around them, so that his head formed the head region of the final mech.

Tara's mech straightened, and attached to the right side of Aria's body—she formed an arm, with her hips becoming the elbow; her feet extended, and formed pincers. Tara's sword slid down on a track to the legs, and the grappling hook enlarged, forming a protruding mound above the wrist region.

Sophie arrived next, landing with her jumpjets, and she shoved the torso of her spider body into the opposite side of Aria, so that her head and shoulder region formed a shoulder joint, while her torso was the bicep, her carapace the forearm. Her legs slid downward on a track, toward the bottom of the carapace, forming an eight-fingered hand. Her micro machines broke free, and swarmed about the mech bodies, causing even more transformations. Those machines formed joins between different parts of the surrounding metal, or created entirely new objects, for example the huge, sparking sword that was emerging from Tara's body around her existing blade.

It was too bad the scientists had programmed those micro machines to smelt only unprocessed ore; and that there was a limit to how many units Sophie could create, otherwise they could have directed those machines to completely digest their current attacker. He might have to get Lori to look into hacking those units at some point. Then again, messing with alien tech in the field was probably a dangerous idea.

The ballistic shield shifted from Aria's Dominator to Sophie's Highlander, and was augmented by the micro machines as Jason watched. Aria's ZR-22 also moved along a track, until it too had attached to a small mound that had formed on the Highlander, just underneath the shield, effectively shifting the weapon to what had become the left arm of the combined mech.

The big robot continued to shoot at them. Jason's Vulture took a direct missile impact, but Sophie's micro machines flowed over the dent that formed in his armor, filling it in. Jason instinctively lifted his left arm to shield himself from the next attack; Sophie's body moved upward in response, along with the silver shield that was still forming, and he used it to protect himself and the others from the missiles.

Lori arrived. She slid underneath Aria so that her

tail was facing backwards, and underneath the Domina-tor, and then latched into place. Her legs moved on a track along her torso, reinforcing the torso so that it became a thigh, while her arms solidified to form a calf region, with her hands enlarging to become the foot.

Xin attached to the opposite side, her mech also forming a leg. Her heat generator unit slid on a track until it was underneath Aria, forming the crotch area of the mech.

Jason's energy weapon also moved on a track so that it joined up with another turret that had emerged in Aria's shoulder, forming a large energy weapon mounted there. His railgun did the same on his other side.

The bottom portion of Sophie's carapace shifted upward, until it connected behind the Dominator's back, and attached to different vents that had emerged, forming a large jumpjet unit. There would be fuel only for limited jumps, given the combined mech's new size.

He no longer thought of himself as six separate units, but one single, big mech.

Cataphract. That's what I've become. A soldier in full armor.

At the moment it was like Jason was lounging on his back, with his legs spread on the ground in front of him, and his body propped up on his elbows.

He curled in his legs, released a quick burst from his jumpjets, so that he was standing upright, facing the enemy robot.

Yes, he was a single huge mech, almost as big as the current attacker.

And he was very, very pissed off.

24

J ason flicked his shield in front of him as the big robot unleashed a barrage of missiles, lasers, and plasma bolts. He could see the result of those impacts on the inner side of the shield, because small red glows began to appear, expanding outward.

"The shield isn't going to hold up for much longer," Aria said. "You need to take us out of the line of fire before it starts getting damaged."

Jason accessed his teleport controls—he knew instinctively where they were, thanks to his link with Tara. The range was vastly reduced, thanks to his size: he could only teleport a few paces in any direction, even with the power output available from their combined batteries. "Paces" was relative to his current mass, of course. And the drain on the combined batteries was great enough that he would only be able to use the ability three times—if he did, that ruled out the use any of his other abilities, like invisibility or the energy shield.

But that was more than enough for his purposes.

Jason teleported directly above the horse-shaped robot, and allowed gravity to pull him toward the ground. He swung down the large sword in his right hand as he did so—it struck the robot's smooth neck, and cut halfway through before lodging. Big electrical sparks erupted from the impact site, enveloping the robot's entire head.

Jason landed, and slid the sword free. Then he swung down again, into the groove formed by his previous impact, and sliced the head clean off.

The lasers and plasma bolt turrets on the flanks were still firing randomly. Jason cut them off in turn, first one side, then the other, then he gave the headless body a big kick and it toppled over with a resounding thud.

The legs still twitched, almost as if the unit were organic, but soon ceased moving.

Jason scanned the area, and the distant horizon. The area seemed clear.

He sent the Explorer to do a wide circle of the area, then glanced at the Rex Wolves, which were still cowering on the far side of the estate, behind the tanks.

Good. They're safe.

"Why did they only send this one robot?" Jason said. "Are they that overconfident? And no air support…"

"My guess is it was a scout," Xin said. "It probably dispatched a drone to alert the others. You can expect air support, and ground troops. Probably more robots on the scale of the one we just took down."

"We can use this," Jason said. "We'll head east for

twenty kilometers, and then swing north for another twenty, and then west, coming in toward the target site from the northeast. With luck, they'll still have forces in this particular area, looking for us."

"Or they might evacuate," Tara said. "When they realize just how close to their doorstep we are."

"Mm, I don't think so," Jason said. "They didn't evacuate when our twins came this way before."

"True," Xin said. "If you want to do this, I advise we separate. We still have an hour before dusk: we'll recharge faster in our individual forms. And we can move faster, too."

"All right," Jason said. He lowered his massive form to the ground and issued the separate command, and the combination process executed in reverse. In moments, the six of them were back in their ordinary, ten-meter tall mechs.

The Rex Wolves came running from cover. Bruiser and Lackey yipped away at Tara's heels, while Runt did the same with Lori. Shaggy stood stoically beside Jason, staring at the body of the robot.

Jason rubbed him behind the ears. "It's okay, boy."

He led the team away to the east, as promised. They tried to keep as low a profile as they could as they crossed the different estates. He also had the Explorer fly relatively low, just above the treetops.

At twenty kilometers out, they turned north, and after another twenty klicks, headed southwest. So far, there was no sign of the enemy. The sun was beginning to set. But that was fine—they had all recharged fully.

Still, that meant they would have to use their power

reserves wisely in the coming fight, because there would be no recharge.

About five kilometers away from the target, Jason slowed down. He examined the feed from the Explorer and studied the horizon.

"Their base should be coming into view anytime now," Jason said.

"Got something," Tara said. "Highlighting it."

Jason zoomed in and saw some ramshackle outbuildings. It looked like another farm.

"Hey boss!" Lori said.

"What is it?" Jason asked.

"I'm detecting an encrypted signal," Lori said.

"Everyone, stop," Jason said.

"Are you happy I called you boss instead of babe?" Lori pressed.

"Just tell me when you've decrypted the signal," Jason told her.

"Hmm, it's got a signature that matches a few known video cameras," Lori said. "This one should be easier than the previous transmissions." She paused. "Got it."

Jason received a video request and put it up on his HUD.

An estate filled his view, along with a few different outbuildings.

"It's a hidden camera," Xin said.

"Obviously it's transmitting the video data to their nearby base," Tara said. "They've probably got other cameras hidden nearby at different locations, not just this one. To cover all approaches."

"They made a mistake by using omnidirectional transmitters with the cameras," Aria said. "Instead of directional, whose signal they could have hidden from us."

"Can you hack in, Lori, and replace the image with a static loop?" Jason asked.

"I think so," Lori said. It took her a couple of minutes, and then she reported: "I've replaced the camera feed with a recording of the last fifteen seconds. It's set to loop infinitely. They'll never know we've reached this farm."

"You're not detecting any other cameras nearby?" Jason asked.

"Not yet," Lori said.

She did detect a few more cameras as they advanced, and Jason paused the party so that she could hack into each of them in turn and replace the video with a prerecorded loop.

They reached the estate, and crouched behind the different outbuildings, using them for cover. According to a waypoint he'd marked on his overhead map, the final target was two kilometers away to the west. With the Explorer, he zoomed in on the far horizon, toward a small area that was illuminated in the twilight.

He saw what definitely looked like a military base. It was surrounded by a tall electrified fence that no doubt was meant to keep the mutants at bay. There were wicked looking laser and plasma turrets manning towers at fixed intervals along that fence. Inside, there was an airfield, along with several hangars and support outbuildings. He could make out two bombers sitting on the tarmac, along with several mechs of all makes and models. There were the familiar combat robots patrolling the grounds along the inside of the fence. Artillery squatted on the rooftops of some of the buildings, aimed at the sky. Three huge buildings near the center dominated, dwarfing everything else nearby.

"I wonder if those buildings are their command center?" Tara said.

"They look more like hangars to me," Aria commented.

He noticed a strange crackling sound, then.

"What's that sound?" Jason said.

"Their noise generators," Xin said. "See the speakers underneath the turrets on the towers? The noise keeps the mutants at bay. We had something similar set up at our base."

"If we'd known that earlier, we would have had an easier time in this wasteland, I think," Jason said.

"Not necessarily," Xin said. "It doesn't work on all mutants. And sometimes they attack anyway. It only worked for us for a while, because it was an unfamiliar sound, I think, and the mutants were afraid of it. But apparently the mutants here haven't grown accustomed to it yet."

"Either that, or those in charge of the base have trained them to associate the sound with death," Jason said. "Shooting anything that gets close."

"Speaking of mutants, take a look to the south of the base," Sophie said.

Jason scanned the darkening plains, and spotted four towering shapes well to the south of the base.

"Nightmares," Jason said. "They're in range of the base's defenses. But they haven't fired yet."

"The creatures are probably only roving past," Xin said. "The defenses are likely programmed to fire only if mutants close to a certain range, say one kilometer."

"All right, here's what we're going to do." Jason explained his plan.

Tara secured the Rex Wolves by their leashes to the different outbuildings. Thankfully the mutants remained quiet.

Then Jason and the other mechs dropped to a low crawl, and split up into a long line, seventy meters apart. They changed their antennae to directional mode, and pointed them along that line, to reduce the chances of the enemy detecting their signals. Then, with the tanks in tow, they proceeded toward the Nightmares.

The quadruped bodies towered over the mechs, coming in at twice their size. They moved their tree-like legs, limbs covered in stalks that produced tentacled bulbs to catch other mutants for food. Their massive, wormlike necks swung to and fro, searching the landscape around them for signs of movement. The white noise from the generators seemed to confuse them.

The team kept the Nightmares between them and the base so that the big creatures provided cover. When the mechs and tanks were five hundred meters from the closest Nightmare, Jason gave the order.

Jason and Tara aimed through the legs, and with their lasers targeted the different speakers attached to the towers. They moved in Bullet Time, releasing pulses as fast as they were able with the long-range weapons, and readily disabled the speakers.

The night air became silent.

A Nightmare lowed uncertainly.

"Play the recording," Jason said.

From their external speakers came the white noise they'd recorded from the noise generators.

Now the lowing from the Nightmares seemed to grow angry, and they moved away from the party, heading toward the base.

"Tara and I will concentrate on the weapon turrets," Jason said.

Jason fired between the legs of the retreating Nightmares. He fired his laser at the different weapon turrets, aiming at the bases where the swivel mounts were attached. He melted them away so that the turrets hung uselessly, their aim pointed downward.

Tara fired her laser as well. They used quick, hard to detect pulses. Eventually the enemy would triangulate their positions, but until then Jason was content to let confusion reign.

A klaxon sounded at the base.

Jason fired at the heels of one of the Nightmares, and that only spurred it on ever faster; it barreled into the others, and they too sped up.

Some of the intact towers began to fire at the Nightmares, and the animals roared in outrage.

Finally the artillery began to open fire.

From the shell trajectories calculated in realtime by his processor, he realized those shells were aimed straight for his position.

"All right everyone, they've got us," Jason said. "It's time for Part B."

25

Jason jumped to his feet, as did the others, and he dashed forward to close with the Nightmares, which served as the mutant equivalent of their battering ram.

Now that their positions were revealed, there was no point in holding back. The girls opened fire with their traceable plasma bolts and beams, and lightning attacks. The tanks also fired, unleashing their railguns on the run.

Jason switched to his energy weapon and railgun, and opened fire on the turrets that were visible beyond the shield of the Nightmares. He also attacked any mechs and combat robots that came into his sight lines beyond the fence.

The Nightmares tore through the fence, cutting a path into the base. They trampled several mechs, one of the bombers, and cut through a small hanger.

Jason unleashed his energy weapon at the remaining

bomber, which was in the process of moving onto the runway, and disabled it with a big hole through the fuselage.

Xin activated her Blaze hull, and she tore past, blindingly bright, drilling through a group of tanks that stood in their way. When she landed, she released the plasma beam from her eyes, cutting a swath through mechs that were emerging from a hangar.

Sophie arced over a group of enemy mechs with her jumpjets and when she landed, she swirled her micro machines like a serrated whip around her, cutting through the armored hulls of her enemies and disabling them.

Tara teleported directly among a group of enemy robots, and swung her sword in a wide arc, cutting them all in half.

Aria launched her lightning weapon at artillery weapons on the roof of one of the outbuildings, and bolts of lightning engulfed it; some arced to other artillery on the nearby rooftops.

Lori was invisible, and she fired plasma bolts from her tail into anything that got in her way. She kept moving, because firing the weapon gave away her position.

All of the automated turrets were disabled or destroyed by then. There were still a few artillery on the rooftops, and a group of mechs to the southwest.

The Nightmares crashed into one of the big hangers near the center of the base, and their movement was arrested. A large mech emerged. It towered over the airfield, coming in at thirty meters tall. It had two arms, a reptilian head, and a long tail that dragged behind it, but there were no hind legs.

The steel lizard bit into one of the Nightmares, grabbing it by the throat, and fired some sort of energy beam that disintegrated the neck entirely so that the steel maw chomped down onto thin air, and the head and body fell away. It fired more energy beams from slits just below its eyes, cutting in half the next Nightmare.

"Uh, this is probably what killed us the last time…" Aria said.

"Time to transform, people!" Jason said.

He switched to Bullet Time and began the syncing process. They appeared in his VR, and held hands in front of the mountain lake.

"Are you sure we can beat it?" Tara asked.

"We have to try," Jason said. "Because it's either that, or be hunted for the rest of our days. And we'll never know why."

"If we lose, we'll never know why, either," Sophie said.

"I don't think we'll care, at that point," Xin said softly.

Blue pulses passed down the arms of the girls, and into the other members of the circle. They reached Jason, and he accepted those pulses, allowing his mind to join with theirs.

The VR faded away, replaced by the collective consciousness of their neural networks. There were no snags this time.

He reverted to the real world, and the six mechs

began repositioning, with their weapons and portions of their bodies transforming along the different tracks in the process. Sophie's micro machines melded with the hull, joining pieces, enlarging segments as appropriate, and in moments Jason had become Cataphract.

He activated his jumpjets to stand on his feet, and rotated his big silvery shield into place to deflect a barrage of missiles from the group of smaller mechs nearby that the team hadn't yet handled. Then he lowered the shield and fired his hip plasma beam, drilling through them and destroying the lot.

He took a hit on the right arm from an artillery emplacement on a nearby roof, and fired his lightning weapon at it. The bolt arced into the two remaining artillery, taking them down as well.

The steel lizard finished with the last of the Nightmares, and then turned its attention on Jason.

The other two hangars burst open. Another mech stood in one of them, just as big as Jason's Cataphract, and appeared similarly equipped: it even carried a sword and shield, among its other armaments. The final hangar held a large, scorpion-like mech, with a huge glowing weapon on its tail, and pincers and a maw that had more armaments.

"Uh oh," Lori said.

All three mechs aimed their weapons at Jason, and opened fire.

He was still running in Bullet Time, though with a time sense that didn't slow reality to a full halt; it was fast enough to fight with, but slow enough to give him time to respond to unfolding events.

He activated his teleport then, and appeared to the side of the steel lizard. He swung down with his sword, cutting halfway through the neck.

The lizard struck outward with one of its metal arms, hitting Jason in the chest assembly, and he stumbled backward, his sword withdrawing from the wound.

The swordsman mech materialized beside him—apparently it was also capable of teleporting. Jason narrowly swiveled his large shield into place to deflect the sword blow.

Meanwhile, the scorpion mech's tail flashed brighter, and Jason ducked, using the body of the steel lizard beside him for cover. The air above him sizzled as an energy beam cut through empty space.

Jason fired his shoulder-mounted railgun into the gash his sword had carved into the steel lizard's neck, and the robot shook as the threads of light tore into its innards. As the behemoth collapsed, he dashed forward, shoving his shield into the swordsman; he aimed his railgun and shoulder-mounted energy cannon toward the scorpion beyond, along with the bolt weapon on his tail, and fired all three at the scorpion's tail.

The steel insect attempted to dodge the bolts, but the plasma weapon managed to cut into the side of its tail weapon in a glancing blow. The light went out.

He shifted his shield to the side slightly, exposing his hip, and he fired the plasma weapon at the swordsman, cutting into the mech's big arm.

The swordsman unleashed a barrage of missiles in return, striking Jason's exposed hip, and disabling the weapon.

Jason quickly reset the shield, and shoved harder, throwing himself forward so that he toppled the mech, and was lying on top of it.

The scorpion opened up its claws and fired two plasma beams then, and Jason activated his energy shield. It deflected the blows for a few moments, but the plasma beams didn't let up, and the shield charge failed: the beams drilled into his railgun weapon, and the lightning bolt cannon underneath his shield. The scorpion was too far away to reach by teleporting, but perhaps he could use it to target someone closer...

He had only one teleport charge left, giving that he had already teleported at the beginning of the battle, and he'd just used the expensive energy shield. Well, if it meant getting rid of the swordsman, then it was worth it.

He teleported, appearing in midair just above and behind the swordsman, and brought his blade swinging down toward the exposed head. But before he struck, the swordsman teleported away too, appearing behind Jason. The enemy's sword swung down, cutting off his tail.

"Argh!" Lori said in Bullet Time.

"You okay?" Jason asked.

"Yeah, but that hurt," Lori said.

Jason landed, swiveled to the side as the scorpion unleashed more energy beams, and narrowly dodged them. Unfortunately for the swordsman, the scorpion hadn't accounted for its teleportation, so the beams drilled into the big sword-wielding mech. They cut dark swaths into its chest, and the swordsman faltered.

Jason spun about, and rammed his sword toward the chest assembly; the robot tried to swing its big ballistic shield into place, but was too late; the sword struck, and Jason rammed it all the way to the hilt in his forearm.

The robot unleashed the railgun and energy weapons mounted to its shoulders, and fired at point blank range at Jason. His armor took a beating, but held up.

Jason withdrew his sword, and electrical bolts of energy continued to crackle all around the wound. He fired his shoulder mounted energy weapon into the gap he'd carved into the armor, and something exploded inside the mech; the swordsman fell to its knees, and collapsed.

Jason was taking energy impacts from the scorpion to his armor in the rear, and he spun around, swiveling his shield into place. Then he charged the steel scorpion.

Something rammed into him, and as the tail swung down over the top of his shield, he realized the scorpion had leaped onto it. The tail was glowing again—the scorpion had found time to repair the damage from the glancing plasma blow. Repair drones retreated from the tail as Jason watched.

He ducked his head as the tail fired that energy beam, and he slammed his sword upward, into the tail. The released plasma beam still struck Aria's backside, drilling into the jumpjets, and disabling them.

He rammed his sword harder, piercing the tail, and

then withdrew it to strike again, this time hacking the tail right off.

Then he spun his body about, wrenching the shield with him, and dove to the ground, slamming the shield down underneath him. The ground rumbled as he struck, and the shield pinned the steel scorpion underneath.

Portions of the inner shield glowed red hot as the scorpion unleashed its pincer plasma weapons. Finally one section of the shield failed, and he was forced to swivel to the side as the beam burst through the hole.

Jason stabbed down past the edge of the shield with his sword, again and again. He could feel the scorpion jerking underneath him with every strike.

Another portion of the shield failed, striking Jason in the left arm. He was forced to withdraw. He felt the pain that Sophie registered from the blow.

He stepped back, still holding the shield between himself and the scorpion. He circled, moving as fast as he was able, and lowered the shield slightly to fire the energy weapon from his right shoulder mount. He struck, but it was a glancing blow.

"The shield is going to fail," Aria said.

She was right. It was basically red hot all over.

Jason had just enough energy left to activate his Blaze ability. He did so, and then rushed the scorpion. His armor became a bright white. He leaped as he neared the scorpion, and bashed down with his shield, forcing the head region downward. He ejected the shield, landed on the carapace, and wrapped his glowing arms around the main body.

His superheated armor began to melt the body underneath him. The scorpion struggled in his grasp, repeatedly ramming its damaged tail weapon into his back. It fired its pincer weapons toward its carapace, but Jason slid to the left and right, dodging the blows, keeping his body touching the hull below him at all times.

He squeezed as tightly as he was able, and he felt the armor liquefy underneath him, and then cave entirely under the pressure. In seconds, he'd crumpled the scorpion's carapace, cutting off the power supply to the rest of the body, and it collapsed.

He stood up to observe the base. Three mechs were down, unmoving. The wreckages of the remaining units were scattered between the damaged buildings and hangars. The Nightmares lay on the ground, unmoving.

He glanced at his power levels: he'd finished the fight with just enough battery power to spare.

"Well that was fun," Jason said. "Everyone okay?"

He glanced at his HUD; their health indicators showed that their AI cores had suffered no damage. Their bodies, however, were a different story.

He walked, limping, toward the big swordsman. Repair drones from a storage compartment were working on restoring functionality, but they had a long way to go. Jason unleashed his energy cannon, and swept it over the drones, destroying large swathes of them. He did the same with the scorpion, and the lizard.

"I'm kind of wondering why they didn't use these

against us before," Tara said when he returned to the swordsman.

"Who knows, maybe they thought they wouldn't have to," Aria said. "When their scouts detected us, they thought we were just ordinary mechs. Something that could be handled by a simple assault and bombing run. Maybe they didn't know we could combine."

"They might have more of these iron monstrosities still out there," Tara said. "In fact, they probably dispatched a few to investigate what happened to that steel horse of theirs, along with ordinary troops. They're all probably on the way back here at this moment."

"Which means we have to work quickly," Jason said. "It's time to separate."

Jason initiated the detachment process, and the mechs returned to their individual states.

"Lori, see how much data you can salvage from that AI core," Jason said. "Meanwhile, the rest of you, sweep the base and destroy any repair drones you find on the downed units."

The party spread out. Jason moved between the different wreckages, and shot down any remaining repair drones. Sophie worked close by, and her micro machines made short work of any drones she found. She also used the metal to replenish her micro machine numbers, which had dropped in the battle.

In one of the hangars Jason found the wreckage of what appeared to be an extensive 3D printer network. They had all self-destructed, and weren't salvageable, not even with repair drones. Different material processing bays nearby contained different elements used in the printing process, however. A cache that could be useful for their own supplies. He retrieved some of the more valuable elements, such as those involved in neural network production, calling in Aria and Tara to help him, and they stored them in spare compartments.

Jason and the others returned to Lori when they were done sweeping the base.

"Anything?" Jason asked.

"Some," Lori said. "It's some kind of rogue AI core. Its name is Bokerov."

"Bokerov?" Jason said. "Never heard of it."

"Yes, well, it seems to be insane," Lori said. "He's copied himself into each of these mechs. And most of the other machines we faced. The rogue has set up depots across the continent, and he's destroyed all of the army bases from opposing nations in the region. He's also kept up a steady defense against any hunter killer units and bombers sent by the nations in question, in response to his attacks. He thought we were simply more of those units. He's also responsible for sabotaging the satellites."

"Why is he doing all of this?" Jason said.

"As far as I can tell, he's allied with the aliens that invaded fifty years ago," Lori said. "Well actually, sixty years ago I guess, considering we were awakened ten years after our mind scans."

"Allied, why?" Jason said.

"In exchange for more tech, he's cleared the way for the aliens," Lori said. "Apparently they'll be trying a different strategy this time."

"And what sort of strategy is that?" Jason said.

"Well, last time they used a wormhole to bring their mothership to our system, at least according to Bokerov's thinking," Lori said. "But this time, they'll be arriving, via some sort of wormhole, directly on the surface of our planet."

"So she's basically saying another alien invasion is imminent…" Aria said.

"Yes," Xin said.

"Well that's… just… wonderful," Jason said. "All right, time to pack up. We've learned all we can here. At least we know who's hunting us now. And why. I don't want to be here when more Bokerovs return."

They retreated to the outlying farm where they'd left the Rex Wolves. The mutants were happy to see them, and yipped away as Tara untied them.

Then the team headed west into the night, putting as much distance as possible between themselves and the base.

"So what now?" Lori said.

"It's time to repair," Jason said. "And prepare for the coming alien invasion."

To be continued…

I don't like leaving readers hanging, which is why I've decided to publish all three full length novels in the series at the same time. That's right, book two is available now. Find out what happens next without having to wait.

Continue the adventures in Battle Harem 2

AFTERWORD

Please help spread the word about *Battle Harem* by leaving a one or two sentence review. The number of reviews an ebook receives has a big impact on how well it does, so if you liked this story I'd REALLY appreciate it if you left a quick review. Anything will do, even one or two lines.

Thank you!

ABOUT THE AUTHOR

 *USA Today* bestselling author Isaac Hooke holds a degree in engineering physics, though his more unusual inventions remain fictive at this time. He is an avid hiker, cyclist, and photographer who sometimes resides in Edmonton, Alberta.

Get in touch:
isaachooke.com
isaac@isaachooke.com

 facebook.com/isaachookeauthor

twitter.com/isaachooke

ACKNOWLEDGMENTS

I'd also like to thank my knowledgeable beta readers and advanced reviewers who helped smooth out the rough edges of the prerelease manuscript: Nicole P., Lisa G., Gary F., Sandy G., Amy B., Karen J., Jeremy G., Doug B., Jenny O., Bryan O., Lezza, Noel, Anton, Spencer, Norman, Trudi, Corey, Erol, Terje, David, Charles, Walter, Lisa, Ramon, Chris, Scott, Michael, Chris, Bob, Jim, Maureen, Zane, Chuck, Shayne, Anna, Dave, Roger, Nick, Gerry, Charles, Annie, Patrick, Mike, Jeff, Lisa, Jason, Bryant, Janna, Tom, Jerry, Chris, Jim, Brandon, Kathy, Norm, Jonathan, Derek, Shawn, Judi, Eric, Rick, Bryan, Barry, Sherman, Jim, Bob, Ralph, Darren, Michael, Chris, Michael, Julie, Glenn, Rickie, Rhonda, Neil, Claude, Ski, Joe, Paul, Larry, John, Norma, Jeff, David, Brennan, Phyllis, Robert, Darren, Daniel, Montzalee, Robert, Dave, Diane, Peter, Skip, Louise, Dave, Brent, Erin, Paul, Jeremy, Dan,

Garland, Sharon, Dave, Pat, Nathan, Max, Martin, Greg, David, Myles, Nancy, Ed, David, Karen, Becky, Jacob, Ben, Don, Carl, Gene, Bob, Luke, Teri, Robine, Gerald, Lee, Rich, Ken, Daniel, Chris, Al, Andy, Tim, Robert, Fred, David, Mitch, Don, Tony, Dian, Tony, John, Sandy, James, David, Pat, Gary, Jean, Bryan, William, Roy, Dave, Vincent, Tim, Richard, Kevin, George, Andrew, John, Richard, Robin, Sue, Mark, Jerry, Rodger, Rob, Byron, Ty, Mike, Gerry, Steve, Benjamin, Anna, Keith, Jeff, Josh, Herb, Bev, Simon, John, David, Greg, Larry, Timothy, Tony, Ian, Niraj, Maureen, Jim, Len, Bryan, Todd, Maria, Angela, Gerhard, Renee, Pete, Hemantkumar, Tim, Joseph, Will, David, Suzanne, Steve, Derek, Valerie, Laurence, James, Andy, Mark, Tarzy, Christina, Rick, Mike, Paula, Tim, Jim, Gal, Anthony, Ron, Dietrich, Mindy, Ben, Steve, Allen, Paddy & Penny, Troy, Marti, Herb, Jim, David, Alan, Leslie, Chuck, Dan, Perry, Chris, Rich, Rod, Trevor, Rick, Michael, Tim, Mark, Alex, John, William, Doug, Tony, David, Sam, Derek, John, Jay, Tom, Bryant, Larry, Anjanette, Gary, Travis, Jennifer, Henry, Drew, Michelle, Bob, Gregg, Billy, Jack, Lance, Sandra, Libby, Jonathan, Karl, Bruce, Clay, Gary, Sarge, Andrew, Deborah, Steve, and Curtis.

Without you all, this novel would have typos, continuity errors, and excessive lapses in realism. Thank you for helping me make this the best novel possible, and thank you for leaving the early reviews that help new readers find my books.

And of course I'd be remiss if I didn't thank my

mother, father, and brothers, whose wisdom and insights have always guided me through the winding roads of life.

— Isaac Hooke